LETTER FROM THE TOWER

Kay Stephens

severn House

This first world edition published in Great Britain 2005 by
SEVERN HOUSE PUBLISHERS LTD of
9–15 High Street, Sutton, Surrey SM1 1DF.
This first world edition published in the USA 2006 by
SEVERN HOUSE PUBLISHERS INC of
595 Madison Avenue, New York, N.Y. 10022.

British Library Cataloguing in Publication Data

Stephens, Kay
    Letter from the tower
    1.   World War, 1939-1945 England - Yorkshire - Fiction
    2.   Dwellings - Remodelling - England - Yorkshire - Fiction
    3.   Yorkshire (England) - Fiction
    4.   Love stories
    I.   Title
    823.9'14 [F]

    ISBN-10 : 0-7278-6297-9

In memory of my grandmother, Maud Eleanor Ellis,
who was born in the Tower of London,
the daughter of a Grenadier Guardsman

Typeset by Palimpsest Book Production Ltd.,
Polmont, Stirlingshire, Scotland.
Printed and bound in Great Britain by
MPG Books Ltd., Bodmin, Cornwall.

One

'I can't believe anything will make me want to live in Laneside House. You see where it is . . .' Isobel hadn't visited the place recently, but she had never forgotten this bleak hillside near the border with Lancashire. Sighing, she turned to her solicitor. 'I'm sorry you've had this wasted journey, but I did tell you.'

James Samuel smiled as he glanced towards her. 'I know. I'm not complaining, Miss Johnson, we've had a lovely drive out here. The sun's even shining.'

'It's blowing a gale, though. Just wait till we get out of your beautiful car – I know these Yorkshire moors . . .'

'And you've worked on farms among these hills; you did say. So, your Women's Land Army years aren't bestowing a love of rural life?'

Isobel laughed. 'Not exactly. I'm only hoping everyone's right when they predict 1944's going to see the worst of the fighting over. I can't wait to be back among old friends, but most of all into the only career I've ever wanted.'

'You have a position waiting for you?'

'I hope I'll find one. Can't be sure, yet. I'm still only a trainee designer, you see.'

'Designing what?'

'Fashions, dresses and stuff.'

'Very different from your war-work then.'

'Quite. Oh, it hasn't all been grim, some of it's good. I've rather taken to the animals – once I got to know which end of a cow you milked. And, this time of year, there's plenty of work with the lambing.'

'Your father would have been proud to see the way you've coped.' James was a contemporary of Alfred Johnson, and

1

regretted that his friend hadn't survived to see his only child maturing. He himself would have loved a daughter like Isobel.

'Well, Dad did tend to turn his hand to anything.' Even if she'd always been profoundly sorry that he had left the relative safety of his factory job to enlist in the army.

'How long is it now since . . . ?'

'Since we lost him? It was at Dunkirk, one of the ones who didn't get away.'

'Thought so. And your mother – how is she? Must confess I know her less well.'

'She's fine – married again, an American bloke, in their air-force. Stationed over here, of course.'

'If I'd heard that, I must have forgotten. She's still living in Halifax, I take it?'

'Just – on the point of moving to somewhere in East Anglia, where he's based. Thought you might have known.' This could be tricky. Isobel had expected her mother and Marvin to approach James Samuel or one of the partners about selling the Johnson's terraced house.

'You'll be in need of a new home then,' James observed with a wry smile.

'But not this one,' she assured him, nodding towards the old stone house only just below the crest of the hill, and a hundred yards ahead of them.

'You could always improve the approach road,' James suggested, while his grin confirmed that he didn't think much of finding that the "lane" once giving her house its name had ceased to exist.

'Even Aunt Hannah had moved out to that cottage nearer to the village, hadn't she? Do you know why?'

'I've got an inkling. Let's see, shall we?'

They had left the car and were trudging through tall grass, wet grass that was drenching Isobel's legs and the hem of her skirt. That house looked so *sad*. The stone porch was tumbling down, slates had fallen from its roof, and some-body had nailed boarding across the doorframe to replace the door rotting on the ground amid a scattering of glass from its window.

2

'From memory, the kitchen's to the side, if we can reach it through those brambles,' Isobel told him.

'Careful, mind your stockings – I know you ladies find locating replacements difficult.'

'Should have worn my Land Army gear, shouldn't I? No excuse really: even long before the war, we always had quite a job reaching this place.'

'Did a road run right up to the house in those days?'

'Don't believe so. Mind you, this is the first time I've come by car. Dad never owned one, we had to walk from the nearest bus stop.'

The kitchen door, when they reached it, was at least intact although the key James Samuel inserted in the lock required considerable persuasion before it would turn.

'Hang on, wait there, Miss Johnson,' he exclaimed as he began to push the door open.

'Oh, heavens!' Isobel cried when she saw why her companion was slow to enter.

What appeared to be the majority of the kitchen ceiling had collapsed, and was scattered over the floor. Stepping gingerly inside, she gazed upwards into the room above them. Immediately, it was evident that the floor in the upstairs room had suffered when several of the roofing slates had fallen through. Looking again at the rubble around their feet, Isobel spotted unmistakable signs of water damage. This was confirmed only too readily by the overall smell of long-neglected damp.

'Now we know why Aunt Hannah preferred to rent a little cottage! I'm afraid Laneside House is never going to be a viable home again. I certainly don't want it.'

'But it is yours already, Miss Johnson. Like it or not, you're the legal owner.'

Isobel refused even to explore the house more thoroughly, the dank smell was more than enough. She'd known all along how outmoded the place was, to say nothing of inconveniently sited. Scarcely bearing to look more closely about her, Isobel waited alone while her solicitor tramped through every room. She had watched when he opened the inner door of the entrance hall, and she'd been alarmed by the glimpse

3

of crumbling plaster that looked as though it hung from walls no more stable.

'I haven't been into the attic,' James said when he returned to her. 'I really felt compelled to balk at clambering up those rotting stairs while wearing a decent suit.'

'Don't blame you. It doesn't matter, anyway, I'm never going to take this on.'

During the drive back to Halifax James Samuel abandoned hopes of persuading Isobel to like Laneside House, and began to discuss arrangements for Hannah Johnson's funeral.

'As you requested, I contacted her local vicar on your behalf, and provisionally booked this coming Friday. You did say you could get the day off, whenever . . . ?'

'That's right. The farm will keep going for a few hours without me, and my boss said it makes no difference which day I'm absent. The other girls will cover.'

'Good, good. I shall attend, naturally. I'm not sure about other members of your family, perhaps you have more of an idea?'

'Not really. I suppose my mother will come and Marvellous Marv– sorry, that's Marvin, her husband. Don't know that there's anyone else. Dad's sister died years ago, there's some sort of distant cousin. Daniel Something, don't recall his surname.'

'I've already contacted him, or begun trying to. It seems he's a prisoner of war, somewhere in Europe. I'm trying to get the message through that he's inherited a sum of money in your great-aunt's will.'

'Pity she didn't leave him the house instead, he might appreciate it. I'm afraid I certainly don't.'

They had arrived back in the town and were approaching the row of terraced houses where Isobel had grown up. Thanking her solicitor for driving her to Laneside House, she promised to telephone him next day to finalise the funeral arrangements.

Entering her old home, Isobel called to her mother who, judging by the clattering and series of thuds overhead, was very busy in the front bedroom.

'It's only me, Mum. I've got details now about Great-aunt

4

Hannah's funeral. I hope you got the letter I posted the other day to say that she'd died.'

Amy Conquest appeared at the top of the dark staircase, thrusting one hand through her brown curly hair in a vain attempt to tidy it.

'You might have come a bit sooner. I could have used some help clearing stuff out, a lot of this clutter is yours, you know.'

'Sorry,' said Isobel automatically, until registering that she'd already explained that she would pack up her own belongings. 'But I did promise you that I'd be round to sort everything when I've another day off.'

'I dare say, love. It's only that Marvin and me have got quarters all of a sudden, like. We're off at the end of the week.'

'Not on Friday, I hope?'

'It doesn't make any difference to you, does it? Your stuff can stop where it is until this place is sold,'

'I'm not bothered about that, Mum. It's Auntie's funeral. I did tell you we were thinking of it being Friday.'

'Did you? Afraid I don't remember, what with having so much on my mind. With our move being brought forward, and that.'

'You couldn't perhaps . . . ?'

'What – put it all off? I'll not risk losing this chance of getting a place of our own on Marvin's base. Happen you could alter the funeral day – make it Thursday? Hannah Johnson's hardly going to care, is she? Though how I'll find time and set everything else aside to go, I don't know. Especially when it's so far out yonder.'

'Don't worry, Mum. We'll cope.'

'Without me and Marvin, you mean? Looks like it's best if you try to. I won't be a hypocrite and pretend I'll be sorry to miss paying my respects. Your Dad's Aunt Hannah and me never had much time for one another.'

In that case, she won't be surprised now, if she *can* know, thought Isobel.

She sympathised with her mother's evident struggle with preparations for moving out of the little house, though. It had been home more than long enough for Isobel to have been born there twenty-five years previously. Staying on for a few hours to help sort the chaos was the least she could do.

Three days later, arriving by bus about half a mile short of the remote hillside church, Isobel was resigned to being the sole representative of the family. She was finding less acceptable the March gale that was thrusting heavy rain into her face and blowing her raincoat open to either side of her legs.

She had toyed with the notion of wearing her Land Army trousers which laced snugly below the knee, but one of the other girls had persuaded her that they were not exactly suitable funeral attire.

Just as Isobel was wishing fervently that she had followed her own inclination a large car drew in beside her.

James Samuel wound down his window. 'Hop in, Miss Johnson. My father and I couldn't believe you were actually walking in this deluge.'

Getting into the back of the car, Isobel grinned after greeting them. 'I certainly am grateful for this! I always used to think the bus stops up here were too far apart.'

'James should have had the foresight to offer you a lift,' his father said. 'I'm afraid he is becoming so accustomed to the convenience of a car that he doesn't always consider those less fortunate.'

'He was very good the other day, though, bringing me up here. And there's been a lot of arranging to do regarding today.'

'That was nothing,' said James. 'Less than I'd have preferred, since we were unable to locate any further relatives.'

'I'm grateful that both of you will be there. Especially, as I don't even know my great-aunt's vicar.'

'You'll find Reginald Fieldhouse is very nice, I feel sure he will try to compensate for there being so few of us to dignify the old lady's farewell.'

James was smiling at his father's choice of words. 'More

practically, he assured me that his wife will be playing the organ for us while we're in church. They have a verger also, Jack Ramsden's his name.'

With the undertaker and his men, this swelled the group to all of a dozen persons. Still a small band of mourners, as Isobel later reflected when the time came to follow the coffin outdoors and assemble at the graveside.

There had been all-too-many funerals in her life since her own father's, way back during those early years of the war. One cousin had been lost in the RAF and another relative due to a motorcycle accident on the way back to duty with the Royal Navy. One other death, the most recent, had been of her very close friend. She and Jennifer had been school-pals and had attended St Paul's church together. Both had believed that they would always rely on their friendship, until Jennifer had married and subsequently died during a complicated labour.

Considered alongside such tragically early deaths, Great-aunt Hannah's might have seemed less traumatic, if only there had been more family members to witness her passing.

There's nobody of my own who cares, thought Isobel dismally, and willed herself not to permit such bleak emotions to outweigh the thoughtfulness of those who were attending beside her.

Was there really no one, though, she wondered? No one from among neighbours of that cottage to which Hannah Johnson had moved?

Forcing back tears caused by the old lady's isolation, Isobel blinked hard and glanced away as soon as she had scattered earth on to the coffin. Raising her eyes to the ridge of the moor which was concealing Laneside House from the church-yard, she noticed a group of skeletal trees, rare amongst the rocky outcrops and tangles of gorse, heather, and bilberries.

Those trees stood firm, and might perhaps prove guardians of Hannah Johnson's resting place. Staring towards them, still struggling to contain her tears, she seemed to see a movement, a dark shape that could have been a man. A man whose golden hair was so pale that it gleamed, even through the drenching rain.

'Daniel Armstrong couldn't attend today, that was what you said?' Isobel murmured to James Samuel.

The look he gave her was curious, but then he paused. Isobel sensed he could be reminding himself that bereavement was stressful, not everyone saw as much of that as he himself, and might be allowed strange reactions.

'Don't you remember?' James said gently. 'Your cousin is in some wretched POW camp. I'm sure he would have joined us today if that were humanly possible.'

'Of course, of course. Take no notice of me,' said Isobel hastily, feeling foolish. She hadn't needed confirmation that her distant relative could not join them, but she had wanted some explanation of the identity of the person she had spotted. *Or a word to reassure her that she hadn't imagined that she saw someone!* she thought ruefully when a further glance revealed no one standing near those trees.

Isobel dismissed the incident as soon as she followed James Samuel and his father to their car. At her request, they were driving down the hill as far as Ripponden where she insisted on providing lunch. The vicar, his wife and the verger had been pressed to join them, but had declined due to the demands of work.

Sitting with the two family solicitors, Isobel began to wish the other three might have come along. Affable though both James Samuel and the old man were, she found conversing with them difficult, particularly as her reluctance to take on Laneside House was creating some awkwardness.

Before leaving them to return to her work at the farm, Isobel tried to listen patiently while James Samuel reiterated that the house was already hers, and she should not simply discard it.

His father then continued: 'James tells me that you're influenced by your war-work, which has placed you miles out in the countryside. On a day like this, we can understand your being somewhat unwilling to continue to live any distance from a town. But it isn't always bleak, you know, and not always wet either!'

Isobel was compelled to smile. 'It isn't only the weather,

Mr Samuel, it's more the factor of being kept away from the career I want to return to – and that really can only be carried out successfully somewhere more – civilised.'

James seemed to comprehend that nothing, at that stage, would alter their client's thinking. 'Whatever the final outcome, Miss Johnson, there are certain things which will require your attention. You saw that there is a house-full of furniture in your great-aunt's home.'

'Is there?' Isobel had been so dismayed by the mustiness and dilapidation of Laneside House that she had taken scarcely any notice of its furnishings.

The elder Mr Samuel beamed at her. 'Even should you decide to sell the lot, you must not undervalue the useful-ness of such contents. If nothing more, you might utilise any amount realised to enhance the home where you ultimately settle.'

Looking so far into the future, and so seriously, disturbed Isobel all the more. Only the camaraderie of her Land Army colleagues eventually relieved a little of the weight of what she was beginning to visualise as her great responsibility.

Arriving back at the farm in time to do her share of the evening milking, she assured her friends that Great-aunt Hannah had had a good life, therefore she hadn't found the funeral unduly upsetting. Thankful that she didn't expect them to treat her more carefully than usual, they soon were chatting while they completed their tasks in the milking shed, then set out to check on other animals before night set in.

Isobel was sorry the following morning that she was assigned the job of delivering milk, work which took her away from the other young women and provided more time than she liked for thinking.

In addition to her concerns about the property she had inherited, she was perturbed by her mother's sudden depar-ture for East Anglia. It wasn't that Isobel had any doubts that Amy Conquest's second marriage would prove happy; on the contrary, she herself had dubbed the American *Marvellous* Marvin simply because, to Amy, this was so evidently what he'd become. Isobel's unease was created by this abrupt ending to considering she always would have a home in the terraced house where she had grown up.

Evidently, that house was on the market already: if it were to sell swiftly she would be obliged to find herself a home. The fact that joining the Women's Land Army had kept her away from Halifax during most of the war was of no consequence. The place had always been *there* – somewhere to which she might return, no matter how long she had been absent.

Isobel's feelings about her former home were confirmed later that day when, following her early start with the milk round, she finished work and caught a succession of buses to take her away from open countryside and into Halifax.

The house did, indeed, feel very empty and cold too, for the fire had died to ashes in the grate soon after Amy and her husband had departed. There was a note, however, written by Marvin and beginning with the hope that her great-aunt's funeral had not left her too deeply distressed. He went on to detail certain items of food which should be removed from the house if Isobel didn't consume them, and he listed all he had done to ensure that the place was left secure. His few closing words sent love from both of them and said that, as Isobel would guess, her mother was extremely busy.

The note, at least, made her smile. Picturing Amy as she would have appeared while preparing to depart, she reflected that there might be justification in comparing her mother to headless chickens (of which Isobel now had some experience!).

The smile did not remain with her for long. This place did not feel like home any longer. For the first time since its sale originally was mentioned, Isobel began wishing simply to be rid of the little house. Going through all the rooms confirmed that her mother and Marvin had removed much of the furniture. This was as the three of them agreed, but finding only her own small bedroom equipped was a reminder as stark as the whole interior of how drastically everything was changing.

Isobel would find somewhere of her own, naturally. She had planned to do just that ages ago, at the time when she'd discovered the freedom generated by living away from the family home. A couple of rooms should suffice, especially during the early months after this wretched war finally came to an end. She would be occupied with re-establishing her career, far too busy for becoming domesticated.

Being in one family house seemed to set her thinking about the other one, though. Surprising herself, Isobel began reflecting that their solicitors had been right to emphasise that she must look through everything that Hannah Johnson had left in Laneside House. There might be heirlooms, as well as furniture, some of which she would store until the end of the war brought the opportunity to establish a home of her own. Certainly, she would secure possession of that large picture of her great-grandfather, Edward Johnson. Isobel had always loved that painting. He made such a fine figure, splendid in the uniform of one of the Guards regiments. Wherever she settled, she would ensure him a place on her wall.

Of the furniture itself within Laneside House, her memories were less clear. There was a large sideboard, made of walnut, she thought, and a set of dining chairs which looked Victorian. Isobel couldn't believe that she would want those, but old Mr Samuel could be right and they would realise a sum.

Recognising this, Isobel decided she ought to use her next day off to trudge over to Laneside House rather than come back to her old home. This bedroom here in Halifax contained very little furniture, and many of her personal belongings had always travelled with her from farm to farm throughout the war.

Her decision to visit the place she'd inherited was shelved within days, though, when Isobel was asked to move to a different farm; the only good thing was its being rather closer to Halifax. Learning all the jobs required of her by Walter Robinson, her new boss, and getting to know a fresh set of Land Army colleagues became more than enough to occupy her.

*   *   *

Isobel had thrust Laneside House to the back of her mind by the June of 1944 when everyone began to look forward more optimistically. The mood was generated by the success of D-Day, which had ended speculation about the forces gathering at various parts of England in preparation. The landings along the French coast soon inspired feelings that the Allies could eventually bring the war to a close.

Her last move had brought her to a smaller farm than a lot of those augmented by girls from the Land Army. While missing the company of many colleagues who had become real pals, Isobel quickly made a close friend of one young woman, Flora Bright, who came originally from London. They had hit it off from the start as soon as Isobel discovered that Flora too had a peacetime job in fashion design. Although it sounded as though the Londoner's position was rather more grand than her own, Isobel relished the common interest giving them plenty to discuss.

'I haven't got a firm offer of a job when this lot's over,' Isobel admitted ruefully as they swapped ideas of how their future plans would be shaped. 'But I shall be free to choose where I need to live. I've got a share coming to me when my mother sells our old house, and I've been thinking Leeds might be a good spot to settle, there's so much clothing trade going on there.'

'Or you could come to London . . .' suggested Flora.

Isobel smiled, but shook her head. 'Don't think I'm cut out for that. And, to be honest, I'm not sure I can settle anywhere outside the West Riding.'

All their planning for the future was superseded within days of the Normandy landings, however, when London and the south-east of England began to be attacked by Hitler's latest weapon, the 'flying bomb'.

Flora was distraught, she had relatives in the East End of London still, people who had suffered repeated damage to their homes already. Windows had been blasted out and replaced more times than they could count. The fact that her family had escaped any loss of life seemed now to be a miracle too fortunate to continue.

'I shan't bear it if any of them get killed now, not after all they've had to endure so far,' Flora confided.

Isobel could sympathise while remaining thankful that none of these ghastly rockets were targeting her own part of the country. All too soon, though, she was suffering similar anxiety when accounts came through of flying bombs landing in East Anglia. She heard only rarely from her mother and Marvin, still busy settling in there, and would need to school herself not to worry perpetually regarding their safety.

Being fully occupied helped to quell their concerns as harvesting gave way to fruit-gathering along with the perennial cropping of vegetables. As people adapted to living with the new threat from these German V1s, everyone around the local farms began talking of what they might do to celebrate yet another wartime Christmas.

Isobel had been invited by Marvin to join him and her mother at his USAAF base for the holiday, whereas Flora was making a short trip to her old home in London.

When it became apparent that other workers on their farm also wanted to get right away to family, Isobel suddenly offered to stay on and help keep the place running.

She and her mother hadn't always seen eye-to-eye and, over the past few years, appeared to have less and less in common. During her one visit to them since their move to Marvin's base, Amy appeared preoccupied with her own life. There had even been times when Isobel had wondered what to talk about. And at the farm Walter Robinson and his wife, who were very agreeable Yorkshire folk, could use assistance arranging celebrations for those who were staying on over Christmas.

Isobel would miss Flora during the brief holiday. She wondered if she might have an opportunity to dash into Halifax and look up old friends. Only one other Land Army girl was staying on at the farm and, being a lot younger, often gave the impression that she thought Isobel altogether too serious.

And perhaps that is justified, Isobel reflected ruefully when she caught herself planning to spend Christmas deciding where her future home was to be. She was inclined to believe

13

Leeds might be a good location. After all, she had lost the majority of the war years, and needed to live somewhere where she might integrate into the heart of the fashion business.

There were her friends in Halifax still, of course. Longing to see them now, she was looking forward to the promised peace. For her, that would mean returning to the social life that she'd enjoyed since leaving school. If she did choose to live in Leeds, it needn't be too far away for becoming involved again.

Isobel had finished in the fields on that cold December night when she was startled by the loud droning of an unfamiliar engine. Increasing from a distant roar, the sound alerted her to glance beyond the drystone wall, towards the road where she expected to see the dimmed headlight of a badly tuned motorcycle. Only when none appeared and the noise became more of a rattling, and from overhead, did Isobel's gaze turn to the sky.

There the object was, made visible by the fire flaring from its tail. She turned slowly, following its course, instantly perturbed because it was heading straight for the moors to the north-west where Laneside House stood. *Her* house.

God, but that thing must not destroy it!

No one at the farm could find out anything about where that flying bomb had landed. It was Christmas Eve and Isobel was obliged to shelve her anxiety, and assist the efforts of the farmer and his wife to make the occasion festive.

She was thankful, nevertheless, when news reached them eventually that the V1 had landed a distance from her home, somewhere over Hubberton way on the Sowerby hillside. So far as she could learn, there had been no loss of life.

Strangely, though, following that incident Isobel grew more concerned about Laneside House, and resolved that she must go there again, if only to rescue family heirlooms and arrange to have furniture removed for safe storage.

The place looked no better than it had on her last visit, and by contrast with the surrounding snow its sandstone walls appeared black and forbidding. The only lighter stone was on chunks that had been dislodged and now revealed sides previously protected from the elements. Isobel caught herself wishing that she might find some means of making all the exterior look clean again.

She had obtained a key from James Samuel and, while declining his offer of driving her out to the house, had smiled to herself.

James was delighted that she was revisiting the place, so delighted that Isobel quickly had realised he believed she'd experienced a change of heart regarding taking possession. She hadn't disappointed him by explaining that she favoured the notion of selling any of the furniture that she did not require.

Her chief intention on this occasion, however, was to investigate the attic. Still wearing her sensible Land Army trousers, she shouldn't be daunted by tackling the stairs, no matter how dilapidated.

Isobel had noticed previously how dusty the lower rooms were, nothing within them prepared her for the state of the attic. Cobwebs that would have graced a Gothic film veiled all the beams while her boots created prints in the dusty floor to vie with any formed outdoors as she'd crunched through today's snow covering.

A capacious tin trunk stood in one corner of the room, beside it an old dressing-table on which lay a small folding desk.

'That should prove interesting,' murmured Isobel aloud, and wished that she possessed the key to its lock.

Disappointed, she turned aside to the trunk, which, minus its padlock, was more accessible. Her disappointment increased when raising the lid revealed little beyond a lot of old clothing, several worn blankets, folded bed linen, and a flight of moths.

Glancing all around her, Isobel found only a few bits of mostly broken furniture, several chamber pots and a slop-bucket. That desk remained the only item that could reveal something of interest.

It wasn't until she began to handle the desk again that she

laughed out loud. The desk was *hers,* why ever was she hesitating to break into it?

The lock yielded to attack from a gadget in the pocket-knife without which any farm-worker would be lost. Isobel gasped excitedly when she found it contained, not only several dreary-looking documents, but at least one letter.

Careful not to tear the fragile envelope, Isobel withdrew the sheet of notepaper and began to read.

Her surprise was greater still when the letter was headed **The Tower of London**. That was an address she would never anticipate might be connected with any member of her family. Whoever could it be from?

Two

Isobel suspected the letter might prove to be more mundane than the address at its head. Actually, it soon became very interesting to her. She checked the signature, discovered it was her great-grandfather's, then read through swiftly. She couldn't believe how fortunate she was; in the first paragraph he mentioned Laneside House.

Edward Johnson clearly had seen the property during a recent leave from his regiment which evidently was the Grenadier Guards. He was asking Eleanor, his wife, to ensure that she engage with their solicitor regarding its purchase.

'It would be unusual, I know, for any woman to act on her husband's behalf in such a matter. Even so, I judge your abilities more than adequate.

You are a fine woman, do not forget that, Eleanor. Few men of my acquaintance would better your common sense, or your foresight.'

The letter went on to assure her that he had already instructed their solicitor, Isaac Samuel, who would supply every assistance.

Isobel was pleased to learn that one of her female antecedents had been recognised for her capability, felt glad that Eleanor seemed to have been ahead of her time.

Towards the end of the letter, he turned to more personal matters, speaking of his joy concerning their marriage which seemed relatively recent, and looking forward to their creating a family home together. Edward compared this with his life guarding the Tower of London, which, however interesting, was keeping him from his wife.

'I remain proud, naturally, to be a part of the garrison here at the Tower, and still relish the ceremonial here. Who

would not be stirred by the nightly challenge of "Who comes there?" and the responses "The keys." "What keys?" "Queen Victoria's keys." And seeing the guard present arms followed by the cry "God preserve Queen Victoria!"

'While I love all this, I do so yearn for the moors of our beloved Yorkshire, and naturally for you,' he concluded.

Isobel smiled wryly to herself. That love of the moors clearly was one emotion which she had not inherited!

There were no further letters, but there were those legal-looking documents. A swift glance confirmed that they all related to Laneside House. She stuffed the lot into her bag and, giving the attic a final cursory inspection, headed for the stairs.

Neither of the bedrooms yielded anything interesting when Isobel hurried about opening drawers and looking into wardrobes. She assumed that Hannah Johnson had taken all personal belongings with her when she moved to the rented cottage.

She herself had only visited Hannah in that little place the once: although she'd intended going there again her war-work had kept her busy. She would need to discover who the landlord was, and to find out what had become of the old lady's possessions. No doubt James Samuel would help to provide the answer.

Isobel learned from the solicitor that most of her great-aunt's belongings had been put into storage. The landlord of her rented cottage had been inundated with enquiries from families desperate for accommodation after being bombed out of their own homes in other parts of England.

'I'll go with you to the store, then we can sift through Hannah Johnson's things together,' James offered.

Before that could be arranged, however, Isobel was moved again, and this time miles away to the Midlands between Birmingham and Stratford-upon-Avon.

The work was in fields and fields of vegetables. She missed the farm animals which had featured in her original Land Army job, and she missed her Yorkshire valleys and hills.

Everything around these fields was so flat, Isobel reflected whenever she stood upright to put a hand to her aching back. She could begin to understand Edward Johnson's yearning for their West Riding moors.

Even the fact that the weather was milder further south didn't compensate for being so far from home. Isobel saved up her leave and when Easter came set off for Halifax, to look up lots of her friends, and renew acquaintance with her home county.

She arrived in the early evening of Good Friday and went along to St Paul's, her usual church at King Cross. The building was relatively modern and, some might consider, a little stark, but Isobel felt she was home. After the service, her welcome was warm and enthusiastic, so pleasing that she felt a surge of elation; this was where she truly belonged.

She had contacted Diana, who'd always been so close that, with similar curly brown hair to her own, she'd often been taken for Isobel's twin. Diana was insisting she must stay with her, and had spread word of her visit to Polly, Betty and Louise, more of the young women who were delighted to see Isobel at home.

On the Saturday the group set out by bus up into the Dales. They had all taken picnic meals and found a spot in the lee of a drystone wall, where they laughed and talked while sharing out their food. Diana invited them all back to her house that evening, and they sat up until the early hours exchanging wartime experiences.

Returning to the church on Easter Sunday morning, Isobel was beginning to wonder how ever she would tear herself away from Halifax. The only good thing was the general opinion that this war soon would be over.

'I'll be back, don't worry!' she assured Diana and Louise when they waved her off reluctantly as she hurried to catch a train. This glimpse of the life she once had loved so greatly was making her long even more for the freedom to take it up again.

Isobel had intended to speak with James Samuel during her brief stay in the town, but she'd overlooked the factor of Easter being a holiday. She would need to telephone him

19

later from the farm. Her mother's old home had sold months previously, and Isobel's share of the proceeds was sitting around, waiting for her to decide where she would live after release from the Land Army.

The truth was that she was feeling torn. Leeds still seemed the most sensible place for getting back into designing fashions, and if she secured a good position there she would be able to afford to travel back and forth, visiting Halifax. On the other hand, she loved her home town, nothing could beat the welcome she'd received there during Easter, especially from Diana and Betty. But that visit had also proved tantalising, and for a reason that surprised her.

After years of working mainly with women, Isobel was really looking forward to being reacquainted with some of the men from her church. That hope had proved vain, this time, as she might have anticipated. Most young men were still either in the forces or employed elsewhere on essential war-work. Although there wasn't one man among their pre-war crowd whom she recalled as being special to her, Isobel had enjoyed easy-going friendships with lads from the choir or the dramatic society.

Leaving the West Riding behind now, she felt she'd been deprived by their continuing absence, and rather unnerved. How many of them would be coming back? Was her home life altered for ever? She needed to know that their original group of friends would be brought together again.

Isobel was still undecided about where exactly she must settle when the war came to an end amid intense celebrations. The Midlands farm where she worked became a fun place. They swept and hosed down the farmyard, and set out tables there for all the village children. If still feeling a long distance from her true home, Isobel threw herself into joining the other women to provide a feast that belied the rationing which threatened to continue interminably.

She came in for considerable teasing that day on account of being a 'townie', but Isobel took it all with a laugh, content in the knowledge that it shouldn't be all that long before she was able to return to her home territory.

It did seem an age, nevertheless, before she finally was packing up her farming clothes, but Isobel relished folding each item for the last time to be stowed in her case. Despite having them dry cleaned or washing them thoroughly, she suspected every garment would always carry the smell of dung, dank vegetation, or worse.

There had been so much during these past years which initially had felt offensive to someone unaccustomed to country life, but she had endured it all, could laugh now about unpleasant tasks like mucking-out. She certainly had grown to love assisting with lambing or calving, no matter how messy such events might prove.

Whatever her emotions regarding the work that she had done, Isobel was bubbling inside with scarcely contained excitement when she set off by train on her final journey back to Yorkshire. No amount of reminding herself that she was too old at twenty-six for becoming so exhilarated could calm her elation.

The purple-tinged moors were among the first sights as she neared the familiar valleys and hills, and her spirits soared while she thought of her great-grandfather's love for such inspiring scenery. Today, she empathised completely with his emotions. She was surprised that the feeling she was almost home was not being delayed until her initial glimpse of the buildings of the town where she belonged. Hadn't she longed throughout this war to get away from the cold countryside, which all too often was wet as well as bleak!

Her friends lived in Halifax, didn't they? She always pictured herself remaining among them. This was why, still unsure of where her permanent home must be, Isobel had decided to start by renting a couple of rooms in the town. Going over to Leeds a few times to discover what sort of work was available wouldn't be a problem.

Diana met her at the station, and helped immediately by telling Isobel about somewhere to let which was only two streets away from her own home.

It was quite a shock for Isobel, though, when they passed the terraced house where she'd grown up, and she found that upset her far more than she'd expected. She had thought when packing up her furniture for storing that she could happily relinquish her old home. Today, different curtains made the windows look totally strange, and the new owners didn't take the care that Amy Johnson always had. There was no sign that they kept the window sills and doorstep clean and freshly yellow-stoned.

'I don't like seeing it like that,' Isobel admitted to Diana.

'Wouldn't your mother have agreed to you keeping it on, if seeing somebody else in the house distresses you so much?'

'Nay, love, it's bigger than I want to be bothered with. Mum knew, as much as I did, that I shall need all my time to work at getting back into designing.'

'Well, the rooms we're going to see are just along here. And you'll not have much work to do, keeping them clean. I'm rather afraid they could be too titchy for you.'

The place was small, a tiny bedroom and a living room/kitchen at the top of the house. The bathroom was shared with the owner, a Mrs Hardaker, who was a widow.

Isobel liked the landlady, and said at once that she wished to take the rooms on. She was glad to move in immediately, and resolved to fill the place with enough of her possessions to make her forget her original home. Her reaction to that house being changed was quite unreasonable – it was years since she had lived there permanently, and home had never felt the same after her father had joined the army.

When Isobel still caught herself going out of her way to avoid seeing the old place, she became worried. And friends like Diana and Betty were sufficiently concerned to try to laugh her out of such feelings, but Isobel was unable to shrug off negative emotions. This wasn't the life she had visualised. Since the end of the war she seemed to experience too many disappointments.

Isobel was having difficulty in getting back into the career she had chosen. Time seemed to go racing by. Despite approaching three clothing firms and attending interviews at two of them, she was no closer to securing a position than on the day she'd taken the train back to Yorkshire.

The trouble lay in her not being able to show them designs

to confirm her ability. Years ago, before the war, Isobel had possessed a portfolio of her work, but glancing through it recently she'd soon realised that every pattern was terribly outmoded.

She had tried, instead, to create more up-to-date sketches, but her old flair seemed slow to return and everything Isobel drew felt laborious. That evidently showed in the end result. She couldn't be surprised that nothing she was offering caught on with any company she visited, but she was sorely disappointed.

The break came two months after her return to the West Riding. By this time Isobel was back into the routine of going out with friends, attending church, and taking part in the amateur drama which she always had loved. The play they were rehearsing was one of Noel Coward's, and although Isobel had only a small role she also helped to design the women's costumes.

This proved to be the challenge that released her old talent, even if some dresses were re-made from others found in the property box. It was her friend Polly, a glamorous blonde full of ideas, who pointed out that she ought to take along some of these dresses to her next interview. Isobel did better than that, despite clothes rationing. She had located some lengths of material which she'd been storing since 1939. Among them she discovered a fine wool cloth in navy blue. She still had the sewing-machine treasured after her old home went on the market. Making up the dress in a classical style with white piping to enhance the collar and cuffs, Isobel concentrated on ensuring that it fitted immaculately. Her own satisfaction confirmed that she hadn't lost her ability, and she wore it to her interview.

The woman behind the imposing desk was impressed that the style showed flair yet should not date. She also appeared equally impressed by Isobel's war-work which had prevented her from pursuing her career. They laughed together over accounts of some of the less-elegant jobs which farm work entailed.

Over all, Isobel pleased her with everything she presented

that day, including herself. She rode home in the bus from Leeds immensely relieved. She had, at last, been given a position with a company eager to use her designing skill.

The following few weeks were hard, but very enjoyable. Fortunately, rehearsals for the play were spread over virtually two months, and having a little part allowed Isobel to miss the odd practice, or to arrive late. Her work was demanding and had to be meticulous, the firm that had taken her on expected everyone to put in additional hours when required. As a means of returning to her original career this was providing plenty of satisfaction. It also quickly proved tiring.

From time to time, Isobel had to remind herself that she was doing the only work she really wanted. Away from the job, too, she was among the people who had been here for her when she returned from the war. With them, she was going to the Picture House, the Regal, or one of the theatres. And she was acting again, and attending the church where she had belonged ever since first joining St Paul's Sunday School.

Following her success with the dress she had worn for the play, Isobel had searched out other materials, she needed clothes for going out with the rest of the cast. After the final performance they were determined not to allow an anti-climax to set in. Some of the men she'd wanted to see again were demobbed in time to act in the play, and Isobel meant to show everyone that she had discarded her farm-worker image!

No matter what she intended, no one else ever seemed as tired as Isobel quite often felt, but *they* all worked in and around Halifax, and didn't have to travel back from Leeds. Several among them were school teachers and arrived home earlier in an evening, even if they complained of having books to mark and lessons to prepare.

Happy though she supposed herself to be, Isobel reflected occasionally that nothing really felt as good as she'd hoped it would. All her war-time dreams of returning to her old life were being fulfilled, but still something was lacking.

Her mother's invitation to visit Marvin's base in East Anglia was the occasion that began to provide the first clues to

Isobel's unspecified dissatisfaction. Amy Conquest had blossomed under Marvin's constant concern for her with the result that she appeared years younger when she opened the door to her daughter. In fact, Isobel wondered briefly if she herself might even be looking like the elder of the pair.

Marvin was on duty, but had left messages to welcome his step-daughter, making Isobel feel like a little girl again. A girl who had acquired a much-needed father-figure.

'You're looking great, Mum,' she enthused. 'I can see that Marvin is good for you.'

Amy laughed. 'He's certainly the lively one. Around the base, he's the one who always gets things going. You wouldn't believe the parties we have!'

If only Dad could see you! thought Isobel, and was glad that he couldn't do so. A very quiet man who shouldered responsibilities seriously, Alfred Johnson might not have appreciated this new Amy. And Isobel, always sensitive to his feelings, would have hated her mother's new happiness to hurt him.

'You're looking a bit peaky,' Amy observed. 'Though your frock's lovely. Is that one you made when you were after that job?'

Beginning to fill her in on all that she'd been doing, Isobel was reminded of the old days. Even if she hadn't always appreciated her mother's interest. Once, Amy had been keen to know every detail of everything that Isobel had done while away from home. Following each holiday, she was expected to describe every meal she'd eaten, all the places visited, the kind of houses in which she had stayed. Today was different, but Amy's interest no less keen. And now Isobel felt thankful to be with someone who was so eager for her to confide. Glad though she'd been to return to her Halifax friends, none of them had remained quite as they used to be. The war had changed everyone, to one degree or another, that had been inevitable.

The good thing was that it seemed Amy Conquest had changed for the better. Isobel soon began to understand that Marvin's effect had, indeed, proved 'marvellous'. Amy's confidence had grown, and with it her ability to relate to others and chat with them.

25

While Isobel described the company where she was working, and the smart dress designs she was engaged with, her mother listened avidly. She also made several comments which revealed how much she comprehended.

'I was thinking just the other day about your work,' said Amy when Isobel paused for breath. 'Your sort of job must be quite thrilling when something new happens. Like the ending of the war, for instance, bringing hope that there's going to be fewer restrictions. There'll soon be so much scope for them like you that's able to visualise how women will want to be dressing.'

'There is talk in the trade that there's going to be quite a revolution in fashion, with longer skirts to all the frocks and so on. Stuff that will cling to the figure in all the right places, then swirl out round the ankles . . .'

'As long as that, eh? I can't see that being very practical. Whenever would I get to wear something that fancy?'

Marvin came in on his wife's final sentence. 'Whenever we hold a dance here on base, sweetheart,' he told her, then crossed swiftly to kiss his step-daughter.

'You had a good journey, I hope?'

'Fine, thank you, Marvin.' He had sent her advice about the most reliable trains.

'Great. Well, I'll just take a quick shower, then the evening's yours. We want to hear how you wish to spend the next few hours – and the rest of the time you're able to stay with us.'

During Marvin's brief absence, Amy returned to pursuing the prospects she and Isobel had been discussing.

'You'll be wanting to get involved with such exciting new styles then. Let's hope you're soon selling your ideas to the best fashion companies.'

'I'm not certain that's entirely realistic, Mum. Although I'm with a good firm, they're not quite top notch. And I'm beginning to be afraid I'm not likely to be either. It'll be the leading houses in Paris which will bring out all the new trends once a greater variety of materials becomes readily available.' Shortages of fine cloth seemed a near-permanent limitation within the business.

26

'What's to stop you from being taken on over there?'

Isobel laughed. 'Experience, for one thing, or lack of it. I'd need to have had a fantastic amount more training, plus more actual flair.'

'What's to prevent you from training again, happen in Paris . . . ?'

'The expense, for one thing.'

'I thought you'd have a good bit put by now.'

'The Land Army didn't pay us so much. Glad though I was to have that share of the money our old home raised, I've got to hang on to that till I'm ready to buy somewhere to live.'

'Granted. But there was Hannah Johnson's property too, the one that was your great-grandfather's. You'll have sold that.'

'Not yet, as a matter of fact.'

'Why ever not? Get rid of it, and make what you can. I'm surprised at you, Isobel. What do you want with a place out yonder? You couldn't wait to get back to living in the town, could you, as soon as the war ended?'

'And I've been busy ever since.' Isobel reflected briefly, and added: 'With one thing and another.' She was glossing over the weeks when she might have tackled the matter of Laneside House, didn't have an answer (even for herself) on her reasons for hesitating.

Marvin had rejoined them, and offered immediately to provide any assistance she might require when she finally went ahead with selling the old property.

'Back home, my folks are in real estate, I had a grounding in that before I enlisted.'

'Thank you very much, Marvin. You're very good to both of us.'

Although the subject was discussed no further during what proved to be a pleasant stay with Marvin and her mother, Isobel left East Anglia resolved to do something about Laneside House.

When Isobel contacted James Samuel as soon as she returned to Halifax she was surprised by how reserved with her he sounded over the phone. When she mentioned her purpose in calling him she began to understand his reaction.

'You're telling me you haven't sold the property yet, or done a thing regarding taking it on? To be frank, Miss Johnson, I had assumed that you'd disposed of the house, and had engaged someone other than ourselves to act on your behalf. I really had not entertained the notion that you might be permitting the matter simply to drift.'

'I – I'm sorry. I can see now I should have been in touch. It's just that I've been so busy, trying to get back to my career . . .' And considering where to live, she thought, and forbade herself to mention that. James Samuel knew too much about the property she already possessed.

'We must see what we can do about arranging a meeting. You are agreeable to coming in to see me, I trust?'

'Yes, of course. We can arrange a date now. And I'm sorry if I left you in the air over this. I hope that hasn't created a problem.'

'I shall check with the file, naturally. But I do recall that I've been contacted regarding that property. Your cousin Daniel Armstrong was in touch when he arrived back in England after release from internment overseas. Believing the house already sold, I told him there was nothing I could do on his behalf. I shall now be obliged to acquaint him with the true circumstances.'

'If Daniel wants to buy the property, I might be only too thankful to have it taken off my hands.'

'You misunderstand, Miss Johnson, your cousin was under the impression that Laneside House should rightfully be his.'

'But why on earth—?' Isobel was so shaken that she hardly knew how to continue. 'I thought he inherited a sum of money in Great-aunt Hannah's will, why should he expect the house as well to go to him?'

She heard James Samuel sigh. 'I'll explain when I see you. It is some weeks since I saw Daniel Armstrong, if I rely on memory of all that was said, I could misinform you. We need an early meeting, Miss Johnson, to discuss all implications.'

Isobel replaced the receiver feeling thoroughly disturbed. James Samuel sounded irritated by her inaction. She might have dismissed that, and believed him a stuffy solicitor, but she knew enough about him to feel he was more paternalistic than that.

Her unease was increased by recalling how surprised her mother had been when Isobel had done nothing about Laneside House. Amy Conquest had no more interest in the place than she'd had in the old lady who once lived there. If Amy could be concerned now, that only seemed to prove how negligent her daughter had been!

Isobel was feeling no better on the day that she kept her appointment with James Samuel. He had implied that she owed him an apology for procrastinating, yet she couldn't see her inaction had caused him work.

He appeared cooler than she'd once thought him, but he did offer her tea. Isobel declined, she had been trouble enough.

As soon as she was seated and without any preamble, James indicated an open file.

'As I said, Miss Johnson, your cousin came to see us, intent upon securing ownership of Laneside House. That place is worth more than is apparent, it was improved during the late thirties. Your great-aunt invested in having the gas supply connected when cottages by the main road were doing so. She also intended having electricity installed, unless the outbreak of war prevented that. It's sad that as the fabric of the building deteriorated, increasing age meant she could not cope with living there. As I indicated to you, I informed Mr Armstrong that I believed that property had been sold.'

'But you'd have known, surely, if I'd have sold the place,' Isobel insisted.

'*If* you had engaged us to act for you in such a sale,' he reminded her. 'You were free to engage a different solicitor to act on your behalf.'

'But I'd never have done that.'

James shrugged neatly tailored shoulders. 'I might enquire how I was to have been sure of that? We've encountered you only rarely, don't forget.'

'OK. I've said I'm sorry, and I am. But I don't know what else I can do to put this right.'

At last, James smiled. 'You could make a start by reaching a firm decision now regarding Laneside House. I have delayed contacting Daniel Armstrong again, but if you are meaning to sell, it is only right that he should be informed. He must be given opportunity to put in an offer, and I feel obliged to say that I consider he deserves to be quoted a low price.'

'Wait a minute, though – you said he held the opinion that he'd a *right* to the house. However did he justify that?'

'There was some confusion on his part. To be frank, I had to inform him that he had no such right. Hannah Johnson's will was quite plain – he inherited a substantial sum, you got the house and contents.'

'He does know I still exist then!' Isobel exclaimed, thinking already that she meant Daniel Armstrong to be in no doubt of that reality.

'You could find *selling* Laneside House to him fortuitous, though. You would be relieved of responsibility for its renovation, and for future repairs to ,its fabric. You must not forget that, situated on the moors as it is, the property will always remain vulnerable to the worst of our West Riding weather.'

'Never!' said Isobel, without even pausing to think. 'I won't let any cousin – distant or otherwise – get what he wants, just like that. If he wants Laneside House, he's got a fight on his hands. And he needn't think that because I'm a woman I shall be a push-over.'

James concealed his sudden amusement. He was warming to this evidence of her spirit. 'Do I take it that you're not about to put your property on the market?'

'Not in the foreseeable future. Most probably, I shall keep the place in my family. And certainly I mean to do so until I have thoroughly investigated the entire site.'

James Samuel concluded the meeting by noting her intention, and added that he was willing to accompany her when she next visited Laneside House.

Isobel smiled as she thanked him but turned down the offer. James had made her feel small, she hadn't needed that.

What she did need was to confirm her own ability by going out to the house alone.

One thing that had been overlooked, however, was locating items of her great-aunt's belongings which it seemed were in store somewhere. She asked James if he would still be willing to assist her in acquiring them. Discussing them reminded her that the treasured letter and other documents regarding Laneside were also in store, but along with her own possessions which hadn't fitted into her rented flat.

Isobel couldn't believe how inept she had been in handling those months since learning of her inheritance. From this day onwards, she would maintain a careful watch, and prove herself equal to accepting responsibility for the property.

Isobel had only herself to blame for the fact that failing to make an early decision had resulted in its being late autumn, and a wet and windy one on the day she set out for Laneside House. Her resolve that she would not be caught out again was working for her, however, and she left Halifax well-equipped.

Smiling wryly at the irony, Isobel had dug out the Land Army clothing she had loathed during the war, and actually was finding it more comfortable than she remembered. Best of all, though, she had bought herself an army-surplus Jeep which seemed quite eager to tackle the moorland terrain.

Chuckling slightly to herself, she noted how readily the vehicle surged up the gradient and still, where there was no semblance of a path, approached the house without hesitation.

The place didn't look quite so dilapidated as on her previous visit, although Isobel couldn't have identified any one improvement. When she stepped down from the Jeep, she stood for a few moments looking towards her property.

The first thoughts entering her head were of her great-grandfather's letter, his undoubted affection for Laneside House and the moors on which it sat. How could she have neglected to take possession here? How *ever* could she have thought to sell it off?

Isobel entered through the kitchen again, noted immediately that the interior smelled less musty than it had, although the ceiling and the roof way above that and the attic room bore witness to the damage suffered. Instinctively, she glanced down at the flagged floor, and was surprised it looked no worse than rain-washed and, well away from the overhead hole, rather dusty. She didn't recall that she'd swept up any debris. Perhaps her initial reaction to the place during that last visit had been warmer than she'd thought. Had that compelled her to tidy up as a gesture of ownership?

She was thankful now that ridding the kitchen of all that rubble seemed to have sweetened the atmosphere. It wouldn't take much to convince her that it could become habitable, that she could fancy she smelled latent evidence of home-baking.

Isobel laughed aloud. Amy Conquest would be amused if she learned of her daughter's affection for freshly baked treats. In the old, pre-war, days Isobel had bemoaned the plain fare that Amy provided for guests when the need for economy had precluded purchases from the baker's shop.

'Sorry, Mum,' she murmured aloud to the empty house, before heading to the rickety stairs and the dismal bedrooms.

The sound she heard could only have been her own good Land Army boot on the first of the steps, but it still made her start, and had her turning her head towards the kitchen. The wind was wailing down from the summit of the moors, Isobel realised, and could perhaps be causing the outer door to rattle.

The rain in which she'd driven out there had ceased. Was that perhaps the reason that she only now noticed that tap dripping into the old stone sink?

'Upstairs,' she said firmly to herself, and willed away any ludicrous misgivings. Laneside House was in far too remote a setting to encourage uninvited visitors.

The bedrooms were much as she remembered, and inspecting drawers and cupboards revealed them all as either empty or containing nothing of interest. The stairway to the attic looked more hazardous than it had, she could believe that more of the rotting timbers had given up on providing a sound structure.

Resorting to clambering aloft on hands and knees was undignified, but no one was there to see, and Isobel was conscious that she must not risk an accident while nobody was certain where she was.

The tin trunk was as she had left it, and its contents appeared undisturbed, yet why did she sense that the pillow cases and sheets might be folded more neatly? This time, no moths arose from among them, and certainly the dank smell seemed less evident.

It didn't rain *every* day and the hot summer months would have dried the whole place out, Isobel reasoned, yet her feeling that someone had been there still persisted while she went around from room to room, taking notes. She needed to start listing details of all damage or decay in order to approach a builder for estimates of repair costs. A great many of these jobs would be more than she could tackle herself.

In the kitchen Isobel's thoughts regarding renovation extended to include new cupboards and a fresh oven. The tiny Main stove was gas-fired, and she was accustomed to an electric one. Taking a final glance about the room, she noticed something else – even the lighting was produced by gas mantles.

Did that mean that the house had no electricity supply at all? Isobel returned to the stove intending to check the burners. The one she tried lit instantly, startling her. But the biggest surprise was discovering that the burner next to it seemed to be radiating a few degrees of heat.

Isobel didn't like this at all. She would have to speak to James Samuel, and at the earliest moment possible. Eerie or not, there were altogether too many things here at Laneside House which pointed to the probability that someone else was using the place.

Three

If James Samuel hadn't said 'I think you're being ridiculous,' Isobel might have been glad to have him go with her to Laneside House. When his tone implied that she was being alarmist, even neurotic, she resolved to tackle this problem on her own. She knew James was her father's age, but he didn't have to sound so patronising. In fact, she soon was promised company for her next drive out to the property. Diana was intrigued by her friend's account of sensing someone had been inside the place.

'We'll go together, if you like, I'm itching to see this house of yours, any road.'

Isobel laughed. 'You're in for a mighty big disappointment. It looks a bit of a ruin, you know, there's a lot needs fixing.'

'Somebody must have loved it some-time,' Diana observed, blue eyes glinting.

Isobel needed no reminder of her great-grandfather's devotion to Laneside House, which had seemed so evident even before he completed purchasing the property. Before she and Diana could set out to inspect, however, Amy Conquest contacted her urging that she visit them at Marvin's base.

'I've met someone who wants to get to know you, Isobel love, and with you only living in a rented place I thought it'd be best if you could meet over here.'

Isobel had never really taken to her rented rooms, and only invited close friends like Diana and others from church to visit there; she needed no persuading that taking a trip to East Anglia seemed a solution. She certainly needed to discover what it was all about: her mother was creating a mystery, refusing to reveal who this visitor was.

34

Marvin was the person who opened the door of his quarters to her and, after giving her a hug, led the way through from the tiny vestibule.

'*You* can tell me, may be, who this man is,' he began, indicating a tall, extremely thin, individual who was rising swiftly from a comfortable chair.

His words placed Isobel at a disadvantage. She hadn't the slightest clue to who this dark-haired, rather saturnine, person might be.

She glanced over her shoulder to Marvin. 'Sorry, you've got me beaten there.'

'Daniel Armstrong,' the man announced, extending a hand for hers.

The fingers she offered were crushed in a grasp that belied his emaciated appearance. If she'd been in a mood to judge him more positively, Isobel might have reflected that his evident strength must have seen him through his wartime captivity. But she couldn't forget she'd formed her own impressions of this distant cousin some while ago, and was not impressed.

Daniel was smiling, indicating that she should take the chair near to his own.

'Thanks, I will in a minute,' Isobel said, and checked with Marvin that her mother was in the kitchen.

Amy kissed her eagerly, and began excitedly: 'Isn't this a stroke of good luck! I knew you'd be pleased – we've met through one of the chaps here, Vince Somebody. And it turns out Daniel's been trying to reach you at our original home. You'll be able to tell him what you found when you went over to Edward Johnson's old place.'

Amy was interrupted from the kitchen doorway when Daniel came to lean on its frame. 'I can't wait for you to describe it all, Isobel.'

She frowned. Things were suddenly falling into place, even if he wasn't coming out with the truth! 'Are you sure? Aren't you already more familiar than I am with that house? Surely, you've been out yonder. Did James Samuel take you there in the first instance? Or did you just break your own way into my house?'

Daniel was gazing blankly at her before his brown eyes veiled. 'What on earth do you mean?'

Isobel couldn't believe anyone except family would even find Laneside House, he *had* to be the one. Didn't he . . . ? 'Someone's been making themselves at home there. Somebody who now knows the property better than I do myself. And nobody else has been showing any interest whatsoever in Laneside House.'

'I've never been near since Great-aunt Hannah was living there, before the war. Not even sure I could find my way out to the place any longer.'

'Come off it – you told James Samuel you believed you'd a right to the property. Deny that, if you can.'

'I've no reason to deny it, but I swear I haven't been near since I joined the forces.'

'Someone has,' Isobel repeated, lamely, she was beginning to be embarrassed as she recognised that she had no real grounds for believing that person was Daniel.

Amy was starting to apologise for her daughter's hasty conclusion. Isobel checked her with a hand.

'I'll do my own apologies, thanks.' She faced Daniel. 'Sorry. I'm not tackling this very well. The trouble is, I had the distinct impression that somebody had been in the house, making themselves at home there. Our solicitor pooh-poohed the idea, didn't really listen to me.'

'And because I've shown an interest in the place, you assumed I'd decided to assert something? Not my style, I'm afraid, not at all.'

'OK then. Sorry,' Isobel reiterated, and slid past him into the other room.

Marvin was standing there, gave her a searching look. 'That went well,' he observed ruefully, blue eyes sparkling.

Isobel shrugged. She felt bad enough without anyone harping on about her misjudgement. 'We can't all be Marvel—' she began and, again, was appalled.

'Marvellous Marvin?' he suggested calmly. 'Did you figure I don't know?' He laughed. 'I reckon not many days go by without I'm called much worse here.'

'So, now you've sorted stuff out, aren't you glad Daniel

might be interested in taking Laneside House off your hands?' Amy asked her from the kitchen doorway.

'You don't understand, do you?' Isobel said to her mother. 'I'm keeping Laneside House. Despite what anyone thinks I ought to do.'

'But you've hated living in the country, you were grumbling about it throughout the war, from the first day the WLA stuck you on a farm in the back of beyond.'

'People change, Mother. Even you have altered a lot since 1939.'

'Aye. I lost your dad. And then I met the second kind man who's only ever done his best for me,' Amy smiled at her husband, turned back to Isobel. 'But you've got nobody that's made you think twice about settling on your own.'

'Happen you're right, and happen the years away from home taught me independence.'

'And that's admirable,' Daniel said, giving Isobel a smile.

'Does that mean you're deciding not to contest ownership of Laneside House?' Isobel asked him. She needed to be certain where they stood.

'Decided long ago, after speaking with James Samuel. I'd been under a misapprehension, you see. He hadn't explained that the house had gone to you. All I heard while I was still a POW was that I'd inherited some cash. It was only after I landed back in England that I remembered the house. I was afraid its existence had been overlooked somehow. When I put in a claim James Samuel soon set me straight. Of course, if you should have a wish to sell . . .'

'Not likely,' snapped Isobel smartly.

'*Now?*' Daniel suggested.

Isobel was embarrassed again, but he merely laughed. 'You go ahead, Isobel Johnson. With my blessing, naturally.'

'I can manage without that,' she told him.

Her own words, more than anything, soured the day for her. Isobel was thankful to excuse herself in time to catch the last train back to the West Riding. All the way home she felt uneasy. She could imagine her mother and the other two picking over all that she had said, and implied, throughout her visit.

*   *   *

Too embarrased to mention to anyone her assumption about Daniel Armstrong and her own accusations, Isobel was determined to keep events of that miserable day to herself. She had reckoned without her friends' concern for her. Eventually, while they were driving off, at last, to Laneside House one Saturday afternoon, Diana tackled her.

'All of us from church have been worried about you, you know. Ever since you went off to see your mother and Marvin. You've been thoroughly grumpy, and that isn't you, not really.'

'It is, actually,' Isobel admitted dourly. 'Grumpy, I mean. I made a right fool of myself that day.'

Diana laughed at her friend's description of accusing Daniel of breaking into Laneside House. Anything but amused, Isobel was inclined to let the burden remain on her own shoulders.

'My mother thinks I was off my head, that day, happen she's right. Daniel would be forgiven if he was convinced I was obsessed, believing someone had been inside the place. And as for the way I talked *at* him – I shudder each time I remember it.'

'Will you have to see him again?'

'Not if I can avoid it.'

'There you are then – forget the chap. Everybody makes mistakes. No need to become a misery about it. Me and the other girls want you back to being the old Isobel, the one that's ready to enjoy herself. And the dramatic society is casting their next play . . .'

'I'm becoming afraid responsibility for a house doesn't suit me. Any road – as soon as I've an accurate list for having this place rebuilt, I'll be my old self again.'

But would she? Isobel wondered. The agitation Daniel Armstrong had caused seemed to prove how protective of the old house she was being. She admitted privately that obsessive was a term that might apply!

Perhaps because of not being alone there, that day's visit to Laneside House provided nothing to make Isobel suppose that someone other than herself had been a recent visitor. And its condition didn't evoke the feeling that it could be

38

so valuable it should be protected: Diana looked shaken by the state the property was in.

'Are you certain it's a good idea to try to renovate this place, Isobel? It's not much more than a ruin, is it?'

'But it is *my* ruin.'

'And you're determined to keep it in the family?'

'It was purchased originally to be made into a family home.'

'How long since, did you say?'

'Just over seventy years.'

'Not that long then – yet it's deteriorated a lot.'

Isobel's grin was rueful. 'Happen we would have if we'd stood out here in all weathers! But it wasn't new, you know, when Edward Johnson first saw it.'

'Laneside House must have a history then . . .'

Isobel nodded. 'Maybe discovering that will be part of my job. I've already got some papers about it, and there might be more. I'm going to go with James Samuel to collect Hannah Johnson's personal effects.'

Diana gradually overcame her unease about her friend's determination to take on such a property. She assisted by jotting down all the problems which Isobel said would need attention, any original notes needed greater detail.

By the time they were heading back to the Jeep to drive home the list had grown lengthy. Isobel had groaned when handed the information, but Diana refrained from voicing her misgivings again. There could be no doubting that the current owner of Laneside House felt she owed the place considerable loyalty.

In fact, between her job and the thought she was giving to the property, Isobel was beginning to feel that she was neglecting her friends. She didn't like that – hadn't she spent most of the war longing to spend her spare time with them?

Most of her pals, like Betty, Polly and Louise, were involved with her church, and Isobel had invited them, plus others belonging to the dramatic society, to the flat for supper. On the way back from the moors, she stopped to buy more milk and some lemonade, she'd already got in a few beers which the men would appreciate.

It was really as an afterthought that Isobel had asked the men to come. Although some who had acted in the play were friends from before the war, they had changed considerably. They still were fun at rehearsals, but no longer so free and easy. A couple of new chaps had been strangers until taking part in one of their monthly play-readings, they integrated well, but to her seemed very young, even a little silly.

Diana went to her own home to get ready while Isobel dashed around changing into something rather more elegant, and preparing most of the food. She was almost ready when the first arrivals knocked on her door.

The evening seemed to be going well, they all knew each other and were eager to chat about the next play they intended to put on, or the latest church gossip. Without warning, though, Diana changed the subject.

'I've been to see Isobel's house that she's been left,' she began. 'It's not somewhere that we're likely to visit, or not so often! Miles out on the moors, it is, but that's not the worst . . .'

Diana had paused, glancing from one to the other of their friends, evidently intent on ensuring greater impact. Isobel steeled herself to smile. She mustn't let her frown speak of her reluctance to have the house discussed.

'It's nobbut much better than a ruin!' Diana continued.

'A bit of a burden then, eh?' one of the men suggested.

'A challenge, more like,' said Isobel firmly. 'I don't believe restoring it's going to be beyond me – with help, admittedly. I shall be in touch with a good builder as soon as Monday comes.'

'That soon?' murmured Louise, hazel eyes widening in alarm.

Isobel smiled towards her. She'd always thought the lass too timid. 'If I find I've tackled more than I can manage, I'll come to you, shall I?'

'Oh. I didn't mean – well, of course, I'd always have a try. But I'm sure you're very capable, Isobel. Very.'

A few of those present – especially the men – wanted to know more: where exactly Laneside House was, and if she intended living there when it was renovated.

'Depends where I'm working by that time,' Isobel told them, and wondered why she hadn't questioned her ultimate intention along those lines. Was her ambition changing now? Could she really be less dedicated to dress designing?

All she knew for sure was that she must restore the property, make it good. It seemed to her that she would be doing all this for her great-grandfather, but did that appear rather ridiculous? A relative she had never met.

I can't stop now, she thought, and resolved that she must leave the distant future of the house to be settled after all repairs were completed.

The decision confirmed that evening spurred Isobel on after the weekend when she telephoned the builder who'd been recommended by one of the men in the drama group. Bert Bradshaw evidently was semi-retired, and lived approximately half-way out from Halifax on the road towards Laneside House, which could be convenient.

He agreed to meet her there during the following Saturday afternoon, and Isobel explained a few details of the work needing to be done. She had no intention of having Bradshaw back down as soon as he saw the state of the property.

Isobel allowed herself plenty of time for the drive out to Laneside House. She suspected the place was not about to make a good impression, and was determined that she herself would compensate by at least looking efficient.

The day was typical of November, wet, with mist swirling around the hills. Afraid the kitchen could smell as musty as it had originally, she sniffed carefully, trying to guess how Bert Bradshaw might react. Isobel was agreeably surprised that the place wasn't so dank as she had feared. Indeed, glancing upwards, she wondered if the rain was not dripping from above to the extent that she'd noticed previously.

The builder arrived before she had ventured further than the kitchen. When she heard his van she went to the door and called him. 'Can you come round this way?'

Bradshaw certainly appeared close to retiring age, but sprightly. As they shook hands, he laughed. 'Looks like nobody'd get in at yon' front porch very easily!'

41

'I'm afraid that's true.'

He came stomping into the kitchen, flashed the beam of his torch up towards the gap in the ceiling. 'Aye – well, I reckon you'll think this has to be our first priority. It's a poor light today for seeing from outside how bad that roof is. I'll come round one morning when it's drier. That way I can get a proper look at them slates.'

'You'd do the ceiling, as well, would you? Or do I need to see a plasterer?'

'You leave it all to me, lass. That's if you accept my estimates. I do most of t'work myself, but I employ the occasional tradesman if necessary.'

'That's good. I have to keep working at my own job, and that's over in Leeds. There won't be so many days when I can get out here mid-week.'

'Fine with me, that would be. You can trust me to get on, and to make a proper job of it. Between you and me, I work better without folk breathing down my neck.'

Isobel asked if he knew whether the house was connected to the electricity supply. If there was only gas, it would need wiring up before any plastering was done. Fortunately, they found there was electricity present, although it seemed Helen Johnson had neglected to use it. Isobel was greatly relieved, having it connected would have increased her costs enormously.

Going with Bradshaw through every room of the house took what seemed a long time, but Isobel liked his apparent thoroughness. If the estimates he submitted seemed reasonable, she would be pleased to employ him.

'And what about the decorating, and that?' he enquired. 'Do you want me to find somebody capable of doing up the inside of the place?'

'I'm not sure, as yet. Can we leave that aspect until the roof is sound again?' Isobel really wanted to do the decorating herself, her love of colour was already prompting her with ideas for how each room might look when finished. The overall effect would have to be extremely light, she wanted anyone arriving there to feel they were entering a place that glowed in contrast to the surrounding moors.

He nodded. 'Aye, that'd be fine with me. So long as we both understood how far you want me to go with making the house ship-shape, like. What I'll do is, when I let you have my estimate, I'll set out what I consider to be the most vital jobs, such as fixing that roof. That'll give you some idea what order I'd tackle the work in.'

Isobel agreed that would be helpful. 'And if I do give you the go-ahead, what about payment? If you itemise the proposed work in sections, as you suggest, I could settle with you as each stage was completed satisfactorily.'

Bert Bradshaw beamed. 'That'd be champion, Miss Johnson! Getting hold of materials has been difficult ever since the end of the war. Still is. Having a bit behind me could ease things with suppliers.'

'I was wondering how you'd manage to obtain materials, with all the shortages we keep hearing about.'

'For the external work, a lot of the stuff's on site, isn't? Roofing slates and some of the stone that's simply been dislodged. And I can lay my hands on quite a bit myself – one job I did before the war was demolishing a place this side of Ripponden. Still got the materials in my yard. He were thinking to rebuild, but the poor chap didn't last the year out. Cancer. Told me to make use of the stuff if I could and I gave his missus a bit of summat for it. I'll be glad it'll come in now.'

Before the builder left, Isobel asked help with placing her great-grandfather's picture in her vehicle. After he'd gone she wandered through the house again. Her previous visit with Diana had made her more conscious of all the problems that would need attention: today she had grown acutely aware of them. When first seeing the house she hadn't looked very carefully around the entrance hall behind that unusable front door, now she recognised how dilapidated that area was, with plaster crumbling off the walls and rotting woodwork demanding replacement. She hoped that Diana had been wrong to question the wisdom of trying to renovate Laneside House at all.

The only thing in Isobel's favour was the sum of money which had come her way after Amy sold their former terraced home. Without that, Isobel might have been obliged to abandon all thought of resurrecting this place. And she would regret that now, far more than ever she would have believed possible all those months ago when told about her inheritance.

Isobel had been given a huge part in the next dramatic society production. Although somewhat daunted by the lines she had to learn and the prospect of being involved in just about every rehearsal, she was delighted that she was still considered to have some talent. Once, years ago before the war, she had dreamed of turning professional. She always loved thinking herself into a role so completely that she began to feel different, a fresh person.

Unfortunately, that person she might become on stage bore little resemblance to the real Isobel Johnson, just as any life she might depict when acting could never relate to her ordinary existence.

Isobel might once have been besotted by the notion of taking to the stage, she had never fooled herself that she could make the grade, and stay there alongside top actors. She knew how uncertain such a career was, and had equally surely accepted the fact that neither of her parents could have supported her through unemployment.

And so now she was finding acting fulfilling again, and the rehearsals fun as well as hard work. The play also was providing an additional interest for the winter evenings, and prevented her from worrying too much about the weighty task of seeing through the renovation of Laneside House.

She and her solicitor had gone together to collect Hannah Johnson's personal belongings, an informative occasion, but one which had ended before James Samuel could go through every document that they acquired.

'I'm afraid I have another appointment,' he said as he dropped Isobel off outside her tiny flat. 'If you have questions about any of these papers, please don't hesitate to get in touch. We could then go through them in detail if necessary.'

Examining everything that evening, Isobel soon found

that only one of them appeared to have any legal standing, and that was the document naming her great-aunt as the last owner of Laneside House. What interested Isobel far more was further correspondence written by Edward Johnson during the period when he was serving at The Tower of London.

My dear Eleanor,

I was so happy to have the opportunity to show you all my favourite places, and then to share with you the joy of having our son baptised in St Peter ad Vincula here.

This has helped to compensate for the months that we were obliged to spend apart while your health prevented you from staying at the Tower with me.

The christening of our first child will always be so special because of its taking place where so much history of our land was enacted. We will tell him as he grows big enough to understand, and expect that he will be thankful that his father once served our Queen Victoria in one building originally used as a royal palace.

And as for ourselves, I am sure that we shall always count as a privilege the circumstance that led to William's baptism being held here. Should I never return to the Tower after this tour of duty that is ending now, I shall look at our son and remember this place.

And now, my dearest, we shall continue counting the days until my new posting brings us together in quarters. Most of all, I look forward to having more time for making a true home in our beloved Laneside House.

Isobel was smiling, nodding to herself. She was doing the right thing. Her house had meant such a great deal to her family, she had got to look after it properly. The whole project was beginning to feel really exciting.

Bert Bradshaw submitted estimates very promptly, but the total amount he would charge was so high that it came as something of a shock. Isobel considered inviting other builders to quote for the work, but when she discussed the matter with her friends several said they thought Bradshaw's figure was reasonable, and they pointed out that reconstruction after the war was keeping the trade busy on new properties. Most builders were overworked, and might be reluctant to take on the work. As it was, Bradshaw would need to complete another job before starting on her own.

In one way this suited Isobel, the play was likely to have been performed before work at Laneside House really got going. In the meantime, she herself would go over there a few times and do some tidying of the interior and around the site.

The Saturday when Isobel eventually set out over the moors was dry, but followed a long period of snow and such torrential rain that she had feared she never would get anything done out there.

Thankful yet again that she had kept her old Land Army clothes and invested in the Jeep, she was smiling wrily to herself as she set out on the uphill drive to the moors. Even given the weeks that had passed since her decision to put everything she had got into the house, she wasn't really accustomed to this side of her which might relish tackling such filthy work!

Laneside House wasn't even in sight further up the moor when Isobel hit trouble. Fine though that particular day might be, the preceding ones had provided so much rain that the ground was absolutely saturated. As soon as she left the section of road that possessed some kind of surface, however rough, even a vehicle as stout as her own became bogged down.

Eyeing the way ahead keenly, she sought out every bit of the track that offered a few stones or the odd clump of heather or bracken to provide purchase for her tyres. Even this wasn't nearly enough, all too swiftly, her wheels sank into the slimy earth, and began to spin fruitlessly each time she attempted to drive further.

'I'm not turning back,' Isobel insisted aloud. 'I've come this far, I'm going to do something while I'm out here.' If she had to walk the rest of the way to the house, she would make certain the entire trip wasn't wasted.

'Walking' soon became an over-optimistic description of her progress up the hill. The marshy terrain was no better for her booted feet than it was for the Jeep's wheels. With virtually every step the squelchy ground threatened to drag the boots off her. Along with the massive effort required, Isobel's frustration made her quite breathless. She glanced around for some solution to prevent her returning to Halifax.

To the left, beside what remained of the track, stood a low drystone wall which, although crumbling in places, seemed to suggest a possibility. She need only trudge through the wayside grass, she could then somehow clamber along the wall to avoid the wettest of this ground.

Lurching over uneven tussocks of grass and heather, Isobel stomped towards the wall, reached out a hand for one of its top stones. The stone was loose, and her feet already unsteady. As the stone toppled down she slithered with it, no distance at all, but far enough to plonk one hand in the muddy grass, while the twiggy stump of a shrub caught the lacing at the knee of her trousers.

The lace snapped, she felt mud dowsing her leg as trousers and woollen sock parted company. But a second attempt secured her some kind of a foothold on top of the wall. Leaning forward, she dragged herself along until it looked as though the track to her right was offering firmer terrain for walking.

Renewing her trudge on foot, Isobel glanced ahead again, seeking reassurance that Laneside House was in sight at last.

All at once, she was laughing aloud, unable to contain rueful amusement. She couldn't yet see the house, it was concealed by a swirl of the mist which seemed a regular feature of this moorland hillside. No one else, surely, could be taking on so unprepossessing a home in such an inhospitable landscape!

Knowing the house was *there* encouraged her to continue her faltering progress until Isobel finally staggered on weary legs towards the kitchen entrance.

Perhaps in contrast with the frosty air outdoors, the interior felt warmer than she'd expected. Gazing around her, she discovered she was feeling quite affectionate towards her own personal sanctuary from the moors. As on a previous visit, Isobel noticed the tap was dripping into the stone sink. At least she had somewhere for cleaning herself up. Even without soap, she might wash the mud from her hands. She could use her handkerchief to wipe the worst off her leg. First, though, her sweater felt heavy with moisture from the air outside. She drew her arms out of its sleeves, pulled the garment over her head.

No one was there to see, and in her bra she was better able to move in order to begin on the cleaning process.

There was no plug to seal the sink outlet, Isobel was obliged to let the tap run while she was busy. Obviously old, its mechanism was noisy, as was the splatter of the water hitting the stone sink.

She heard no other sound until the exclamation close behind her.

'*Mein Gott! Es tut mir leid . . .*'

Isobel swung round, and met the gaze of sea-green eyes in a face weather-bronzed to contrast sharply with pale golden hair. She crossed wet arms in front of her breasts, glanced about for her sweater, and saw it was out of reach.

The man was tall, very tall, with arms so long that he scarcely needed to move in order to pick up her sweater and hand it to Isobel.

Struggling to overcome the moisture clinging to hands and arms, she slowly dragged the garment on. Her head emerged at last from the sweater with a shrug of her tangled brown curls.

'I own this house. What are you doing here?' she demanded before turning sideways to turn off the tap.

When he evidently failed to understand, Isobel's voice hardened. 'Who the hell are you?'

'*Ich bin Gustav Kassel.*'

She had thought his original words were German, his name was no surprise, which was just as well. She'd received enough of a shock finding a man simply standing there. Isobel wondered, fleetingly, if she ought to be afraid because he was German, although he appeared no less nervous than she herself felt.

'You've escaped from a POW camp, that's it, isn't it?'
She knew there had been a few camps in Yorkshire, doubtless others beyond the nearby border in Lancashire.

Gustav shook his head. 'Please, to understand,' he began falteringly, searching for the English words. 'Your aunt was very kind . . . to me.'

'My great-aunt, you mean? Hannah Johnson?'

He smiled slightly, nodded.

Isobel was shaking her head. 'No. You can't mean – Great-aunt Hannah would never allow you to come here – to use this place. Her home. *Mine.*'

'I said to her – now I tell to you – I am not prisoner, ever. I am Luftwaffe pilot. In the—' He halted, struggling for phrases. 'The last months of the war, my plane—' This time when he paused, Gustav gestured with one hand the swift descent of an aircraft. 'There was no one to see.' His gesture now was over his shoulder, to indicate the distant summit of the moor.

'But that is ages and ages ago now,' Isobel protested, disbelief plain in her brown eyes. 'How have you existed?'

He seemed not to comprehend, but perhaps again he was seeking a means of telling his story in her language. Eventually, words began to emerge more steadily. Gustav gave the impression that he hadn't had contact with anyone for quite some time. Isobel supposed that long disuse could have caused any fragments of English he'd known to slide to the back of his memory.

'I came to this house when your aunt – your great-aunt was taking more things to the home that she rented. I was sick from the injury after my plane—' Gustav stopped speaking abruptly, slapped one hand on to the other, and startled her.

'Crashed, you mean?' said Isobel, and he nodded.

'My leg was bad, poison in the wound.'

'And Great-aunt Hannah let you stay here?'

'Not for many weeks. I would not impose on her. It was summer then, warm.'

'Even this far out on the moors?' Isobel murmured.

A slight smile curved Gustav's thin lips. 'In my country

I live in the mountains, always very fit. Here, I make for myself a sort of tent – from the heather and – how you call it—? The ferns, big ones.'

'But what did you live on – eat?' Isobel was finding the whole story incredible. Strangely, though, she *wanted* to believe him. Gustav Kassel fascinated her, generating this sense that the simplicity of his present situation disguised far greater depth and intelligence than people might suppose. She longed to know him better.

'In the valley, near her tiny home your aunt grew things in a patch of land. Vegetables, and herbs, all kinds of plants. She gave to me of them. The ones that were medicine she used to tend my wounds.'

This much, Isobel could believe. A true countrywoman, Great-aunt Hannah had always sworn by traditional remedies. Smiling to herself now, she remembered the old lady giving her dock leaves to alleviate the nettle stings of childhood outings.

'But did she really allow you to come into this house?'

'When winter came, *ja*. She said to me is not practical to have the house empty.'

'You came to see her buried, didn't you?' said Isobel, remembering.

Gustav sighed, his eyes filled with tears. Swallowing, he tried to recall the necessary English words. 'I said to her goodbye already. She knew that she was dying. But I watch when they take her from that tiny house in the valley. And she had told how she would rest in the churchyard. Each day, I went near to it, until I saw the coffin in that fine car, and you.'

'Thank you, for caring,' said Isobel awkwardly. 'But I am afraid that cannot affect the situation now. This house is mine, soon renovations will begin here. There is no way that I can permit you to keep coming here, much less staying—'

'I do understand that. Ever since that Hannah Johnson died, I have visited rarely, only when driven by terrible rain or snow to dry out a little.'

What will you do? wondered Isobel, and clamped her

lips together lest she voice her concern. 'You will go home, yes?'

He shook his head. 'I can not. But we must think of today. Your vehicle is – is stuck in the earth, *ja*? I help you to fix.'

'I can't let you,' Isobel began, then sighed. 'Thank you, but please understand this cannot alter my decision that you must never come here again.'

'I do comprehend, most fully,' said Gustav. But he yearned to please this young woman whose eyes so reminded him of the one English person who had made him thankful to be in her country. 'You shall believe I owe to you assistance in return for the kindnesses of you great-aunt.'

'For *her* kindnesses,' Isobel murmured. She felt glad that a relative of hers had been good to him *here*. Something about this man made her feel that he belonged with Laneside House. No matter who excluded him.

They trudged down the hill side by side, until reaching the drystone wall along which she had clambered instead of the track. Isobel saw Gustav glance to the wall, smiling to himself, and realised he had watched her earlier efforts.

'Not this time, I think!' she said ruefully, and was glad humour hadn't deserted her. She would hate him to think her totally miserable and mean. Though why that should matter, Isobel could not guess. She intended never to see the man again.

Moving downhill seemed to make it easier to negotiate the boggy ground by striding from one relatively sound patch to the next. Once or twice, Gustav shot out a hand as if he would aid her, but drew back before making contact.

Isobel was thankful there was no cause for telling him to keep his hands to himself. Yet why should avoiding a reproof count at all, when she would not see the man again?

Four

Isobel made an appointment to see James Samuel, and told him about discovering the German at Laneside House, she would have been a fool not to mention it. He revealed his swift assessment based on thirty years' experience.

'We must charge him with trespass.'

She was surprised by her own reaction. 'Actually, I'd rather we didn't have to do that. Gustav seems a very *genuine* bloke, and he understands that he can't continue to enter the property now.'

'You'd be most unwise to take his word for that, Miss Johnson. What do you know about him? Only as much as he's told you, how can you believe any of it? According to what you've just said, he's a pilot who crash-landed, but where's the proof? It's far more likely he's an escaped Prisoner of War . . .'

'That's what I thought at first, but I can't credit that he is.'

'Then why hasn't he gone home to Germany? In their eyes, he's done nothing wrong, should be hailed as a pilot who served his country.'

'I've no idea why he hasn't returned there,' said Isobel. And recognised instantly that she wanted to understand the reason.

'Well, I can only advise you. I can't emphasise too strongly that I fear your inaction could prove foolish. You don't know that he isn't a spy. I trust you've taken back any house-keys in his possession?' The solicitor sighed as she shook her head. 'Don't forget that I'm here if you should decide to make a case of this.'

Isobel left his office in the centre of Halifax feeling more perturbed than she had when first suspecting that somebody might have had access to Laneside House. Ridiculous though it was, since meeting Gustav Kassel her anxiety was switching to concern on his behalf. Her forbidding his use of the place was depriving him of any shelter from the weather now growing increasingly wintry.

Deep in thought, she didn't even see the man watching her from the other side of Commercial Street until he crossed the road to grasp her arm before she hurried off.

'Isobel? Is something wrong? You look miles away.'

It was Daniel Armstrong. She wondered why she felt so astonished to see him.

'Oh – hello. Are you living in Halifax now, Daniel?'

'Not so far away – out at Holywell Green. Didn't you know my parents used to live out that way, up Barkisland?'

'If I did know, I've forgotten.' She couldn't remember either his father or mother clearly, had no recollection of seeing them very often and, today, couldn't really recall how or when they had died.

Isobel was beginning to feel ashamed that she'd had so little interest in these relations, however distant, when Daniel smiled.

'I've set myself up in a very nice cottage – one that's in better condition than Laneside House, from the way James Samuel described your place! I've got snaps of my new home on me, let me show you.'

She was trying to think of an excuse for hurrying on, but she did feel guilty about her tendency to ignore this part of her family, to say nothing of the accusation she had flung at Daniel. And he was still holding on to her arm.

'What do you say to a nice cup of tea?' he suggested, 'My treat – we're only a few strides from Webster's Café?'

Refusing would be churlish, and Isobel felt already that she risked being off-hand. 'Thank you, that would be nice,' she said, and smiled before walking beside him to the café.

Daniel smiled back at her and Isobel noticed how his brown eyes gleamed, they seemed to fill his still-sharp features with light.

He was looking less gaunt than he had when she'd met him at Marvin's base. When the waitress brought their tea and a plate of cakes, she saw that he waited only until she had chosen a cake herself before he began to eat.

'Getting my strength back,' Daniel explained, and grinned. 'Doctor's orders. Or a good excuse for becoming greedy. Got a lot of leeway to make up, according to him I'm still underweight.'

'You are looking better though. Did you have a very bad time of it, during the war?' On that previous occasion, she hadn't been in any mood for enquiring.

Again, Daniel grinned. 'Let's just say I'd not want to go through it again. Still, it does make you appreciate normal life. Even stuff you'd once thought boring.'

'Did you ever marry, Daniel?' He didn't mention anyone sharing his new house.

He laughed. 'Too frightened of responsibility before I joined up. Must admit, though, I envied the chaps that had somebody to come home to when the war ended.'

'And since then, have you met anybody special?'

'Me? Afraid I don't lead the sort of life that brings you into contact with smashing girls. Too much of a home-body, me.'

'Not through your job then? What do you do in peace-time?'

'I'm a carpenter, didn't you know? Finished my apprenticeship before I went into the forces. It's a grand trade, and will be especially now there's so much new building scheduled. So long as we can get the materials coming through. And I've plenty of work planned on my own place, but acquiring timber for that's even more difficult. Non-essential, you see. Except to me, of course,' he added and laughed.

Isobel began thinking it was sad that a man as sure a home-maker as Daniel Armstrong appeared to be had no woman with whom to create a home.

'How's the work on Laneside House going?' he asked. He admired Isobel for tackling such an immense task, even if she wasn't intending to do the whole of the restoring herself.

'I've got the promise of a builder for the major repairs, only he can't start yet, he's got other jobs to complete.'

'Have you any thoughts on the interior, what you wish to do where, and how you'll decorate it?'

'Lots of ideas as to the shades I want, but no firm plans so far. There's so much structural work needs attention, it's not always easy to visualise much detail.'

'Well – if you ever need a second opinion on anything, get in touch.' Daniel took out his wallet, and from it a printed card. 'Had these done by a pal of mine who's set up a little printing works with the gratuity the army gave him. He's not doing bad, quite a few folk are starting up on their own and need to let everybody know what line they're in.'

'Thanks,' said Isobel for the card. 'But I'm afraid it's going to be some time before I get as far as planning that interior.'

'Even so. I'll still be around. And at this stage would be happy to offer bits of advice, don't forget I know the building trade.'

'You're not going to resent my inheriting Laneside House then?' She couldn't entirely forget that Daniel had wanted the place, but he now seemed so affable that she wished to ease the atmosphere between them.

Once again, he grinned. 'If you saw my new home you wouldn't need to ask that. But I am still interested in the family property, would love to see it.'

It was Isobel's turn to laugh. 'You're not missing much, truly. If you like, though, I'll let you know next time I'm going out there.'

'Excellent! And we can get there easily. I've just bought a motorbike.'

'I can go one better – my transport's a Jeep. And, believe me, you need something of the sort, to make sure of reaching the house.'

'That bad – eh?'

They parted shortly afterwards, Isobel said she'd enjoyed having tea with him, and found that she meant it. But thinking about her last visit to Laneside House and that rough, uphill track, it was thoughts of Gustav Kassel that she resurrected, and of the assistance he'd provided so willingly when she was defeated by the muddy gradient.

* * *

55

Isobel's concern for the German pilot intensified as the weather through December and into January grew colder. Over Christmas, she'd wondered if he would have returned at last to his homeland, the alternative of living rough on the edge of the Yorkshire moors must be barely endurable.

On the next occasion when Isobel drove out to the house, she *didn't* ask Daniel Armstrong to go with her. It was no surprise that she still was preoccupied with Gustav. During the previous weekend she had pictured him vividly. The dramatic society show had been produced, was well-received by a good audience for each performance, and earned a flattering review in the *Halifax Courier*. Isobel's elation had faded so swiftly at the last-night party that she'd felt unable to join the rest of the cast and backstage staff in letting down their hair. Even this bit of enjoyment could be as artificial as the play they had acted.

Isobel felt quite guilty for participating in something that might seem so frivolous when judged beside the existence of people without a home. Her Land Army life might have seemed tough, but that had been soft compared with being homeless.

She could explain this to none of her friends, instead, while Diana, Polly and the rest of them laughed and danced with the men from the group, she tended to sit and watch, troubled by her thoughts.

That night she left before the party was beginning to wind down, earning herself a reproof from Louise and Betty for being such a misery. In the cramped little flat, Isobel felt no better. She would have welcomed company now but her landlady evidently had gone to bed, no lights shone from Mrs Hardaker's rooms.

I shouldn't be like this, Isobel thought. I have a roof over my head, have just spent hours doing something I enjoy with a crowd of people I'm fond of. *I'm* not out there somewhere, in a strange land, with no one – not even Great-aunt Hannah to offer sympathy and a word of comfort.

That thought accelerated her into action. She needed to know more about Hannah Johnson's befriending of Gustav Kassel, needed to know more about him.

*　　*　　*

56

Isobel slept soundly that night, packed sandwiches more than sufficient for one person, and set out in the Jeep. The day was unlikely to be easy, rain was descending with a wearisome relentlessness, and she hadn't the tiniest clue where she might locate the German pilot. Even if he had remained in Yorkshire.

'God, help me, but I must be mad,' she murmured aloud.

Despite the rain, the terrain was less saturated than on her previous visit, Isobel managed to drive almost to the edge of what masqueraded as the garden of Laneside House. Stepping down from the vehicle, she saw at once that someone had tidied the garden considerably. Most of the slates that had fallen from the roof were piled neatly to one side. And work had begun on stacking the stone which at one time had formed the majority of the front porch.

Bert Bradshaw *could* have come here to make an early start, but somehow she felt sure that he was not the man responsible. But if Gustav was the person involved, where ever might she find him?

A brief, foolish, wish made Isobel long to discover him there when she opened the kitchen door. The place seemed extraordinarily silent, a quick glance to the sink confirmed that the tap was no longer dripping. She felt the absence of this small indication of some other person's presence isolate her more keenly. Dismally, she crossed to stare out from the kitchen window. Until she spoke with Bert Bradshaw she couldn't be certain that *he* hadn't spent some time tidying up in the erstwhile garden out there.

About to move away and do something constructive, she noticed beyond the wall that surrounded her property a distinct pathway where the long grass and weeds looked flattened. It meandered between boulders for a few yards then climbed steeply, heading the rest of the way towards the summit of the moor.

Isobel left the house, locked the door after her and, disregarding the rain, set off up the track. The ground was slippery, she was thankful for her sensible boots, but reaching the top did not take very long. From there, Isobel could see the church and continued in its direction. If nothing else, she could make enquiries at the verger's house, Jack Ramsden might have heard something about Gustav.

Isobel did not even need to ask. Walking up the path to the verger's door, she noticed the room to the left. The light was on, providing a view of the interior – and enabling Gustav Kassel to work on the wall he was painting.

Explaining was embarrassing when Jack Ramsden answered the ringing of his doorbell, her arrival made no more sense to Isobel herself than her reasons for coming. Somehow, she managed to blurt out her wish to see the German pilot.

'I didn't have any reason for supposing I could find Gustav here, I just hoped you might have heard what had become of him.'

No matter how incoherent she felt, her wanting to speak with Gustav was accepted unquestioningly, and she was led through to where painting was in progress.

Gustav was astonished to see her, quite naturally, but his smile lit the eloquent sea-green eyes, and he set aside his paintbrush immediately.

'You are come to speak with me?' he checked when Mr Ramsden announced her intention. 'Is there some – some *thing* wrong at Laneside House? I have not been inside the house. I promised to you . . .'

'Nothing wrong, not at all. I – I just wanted to know if you were still somewhere around here. It was you, wasn't it, who did some tidying up in that awful garden?'

Gustav nodded. 'A little, *ja.*'

'Thank you.'

He was looking down at his paint-spattered hands, gestured with them. 'I go to wash. Quickly.'

They were shown into a smaller room to the rear where a fire burned and a kettle boiled on the old-fashioned grate. The verger's wife came to give them tea while Gustav gazed repeatedly towards Isobel, clearly puzzled by her visit.

'You're working here, I gather,' she prompted.

He nodded, felt thankful his English was improving again,

he wanted to tell her everything. 'I am fortunate. The good Herr Ramsden found me one day when I brought flowers to Hannah Johnson's grave. It was raining hard, as it is so frequently. He ask me where I was staying, and I had no place to tell him. They are such good Christian people, and are giving me a bed. And so I work, I am *happy* to work for them, for the church here.'

'I'm very pleased.' Isobel paused. 'You're improving your English too.'

He was delighted that she had noticed. 'It returns to my head, now I use again. I do not wish to lose, because your great-aunt taught to me many English words.'

Isobel smiled, but she remained puzzled. 'But – forgive me, and tell me to mind my own business, if you must. Only why haven't you gone home to Germany?'

'My home is there no longer. And no persons of mine either. You have heard of the German people of Sudetenland, yes?'

'I have, just about. But I'm afraid that's without understanding its significance.'

'I tell to you. After the war is over, the Czech government there turn against my fellow Sudetens, driving them out. I knew already that my mother and father were dead in the war. My sister and her husband became homeless.'

'And your wife? You were married . . . ?'

Gustav shook his head. 'Not married, no. The girl I loved, my sister's friend, is married to a Czech since – a long time. 1939.'

'Will you stay here now?'

He smiled. 'Until they have no more work for me to do, in the church or in this house.'

'Or in the vicarage perhaps?' suggested Isobel wishing to believe that Gustav need not leave the area.

The pilot sighed. 'I do not expect that the vicar will require work of me there. I do understand: he is a pacifist, you see. He might tolerate a man who served on the side of the British Allies – accepting a Luftwaffe pilot could be to expect too much.'

Isobel was digesting that when Gustav noticed her frown.

'You must not expect too much either, on my behalf. There is no need. I have a bed, I have this work here. For tomorrow, I have my faith. The good Lord did not provide that I should survive the war in order to have me starve. Nor even that I might perish on your cold, wet, hills!' he concluded with a laugh.

'Right then,' said Isobel, yet wondered how Gustav could feel so certain that his future should not trouble him.

She couldn't imagine anything more terrible than having no family, and no home anywhere either. Conflict between nations caused grief by more than death or injury.

'It was your great-aunt, you know,' Gustav continued earnestly. 'Hannah Johnson restored to me my faith. Her kindness was God-given, at that time when I was most in need. It only requires for that to happen the once. Afterwards there can be no forgetting.'

Moved by his words, Isobel felt tears rushing to her eyes. She wished she had really known the kind of person Great-aunt Hannah had been, wished she were more like her.

Noticing, Gustav grinned. 'We had fun also, Hannah Johnson and I. Our times together were not always serious. She told to me that I must learn to cook, that I had no wife, and I must not starve. I was not good at it, not good at all. But she show how that I bake a sort of cake in a pan, on the *Ofen*—' Gustav faltered, raised a quizzical eyebrow, then demonstrated lighting a gas burner.

'On the stove,' Isobel confirmed, and recalled the time when she had felt heat from the hob in the Laneside House kitchen.

She felt quite deflated, distressed by the fact that her taking over the house had removed all opportunities for Gustav to do anything there.

'Laneside House is yours,' he reminded her gently. 'I am not unhappy. I am pleased to know that you will make the house good again, that you care for it.'

'And in the meantime you have work here. Which I am preventing you from continuing.' Isobel stood up, smiled. 'I hope that we shall meet again, but whatever happens I wish you well.'

'And I to you. May God walk with you.' Gustav strolled with her to the door. And then he grinned. 'And ride with you also, in that big Jeep!' he added.

Isobel laughed with him, but was not laughing as she trudged over the hill back to Laneside house. Gustav was making her think very seriously. His evident faith challenged her. What had become of her own faith? How had it come about – when she attended church quite regularly – that she sensed her own belief was so feeble?

She might perhaps be cushioned by the very services that she loved – cushioned so comfortably that she no longer tested or really trusted her convictions. Throughout the war she had been directed in what she must do, removing decision-making from her. But surely that didn't excuse her recent lack of the spirit to make the right choices regarding her future? She wasn't absolutely certain what she ought to do about anything.

She should have learned from Great-aunt Hannah, whose generous heart had aided Gustav. And now it was too late. Too late for getting to know what made Hannah Johnson the person she had been, and too late for treating Gustav more kindly.

What could she do? She had barred Gustav from Laneside House, even before it began to resemble a true home. The fact that he now was staying somewhere where he was happy didn't console Isobel. The entire episode since meeting him had provided opportunities. She had wasted every one.

Arriving back at the house, Isobel felt too disheartened to do anything that she had intended. She ate a few of the sandwiches that she'd brought with her, but remembering how she had hoped she might share them with Gustav turned every mouthful sour. He hadn't needed her food, he did not need her, and she could blame no one but herself.

Leaving behind Laneside House and getting into the Jeep provided no respite from the self-recriminations. Gustav had wished her well for this short journey. She didn't deserve that, any more than her initial attitude towards him warranted anything but contempt.

*   *   *

Bert Bradshaw began reconstruction work on Laneside House in early February 1946. Isobel was thankful, but she also felt deflated. She had no one with whom to share her satisfaction that a start was being made. The concensus among her friends seemed to be that she was crazy, anyway, to be restoring such a remote home. Her mother and Marvin appeared so transparently *not* interested throughout her Christmas spent with them that she mentioned only briefly over the phone that work had begun.

More seriously, she worried about obtaining the paints and distemper she would need.

Finding Daniel Armstrong's card in a little-used handbag, Isobel telephoned him. After a brief chat he enquired how the restoration of the house was going.

'Just starting at last. I thought you might be interested to see what the builder is doing. I'm afraid I can only go there one day at the weekend.' Weekdays were exhausting. Isobel still found travelling to Leeds tiring and, despite loving the beautiful fabrics she used, with each bit of progress her work-load increased.

'Saturday would be great with me,' Daniel enthused. 'Especially if I can persuade you to come back here afterwards. You haven't seen my little place yet, remember.'

Setting out with this relative of hers, Isobel quickly realised that, however 'distantly' related, they were far more at ease with each other than she expected. They were laughing already as they clambered into the Jeep when Daniel had parked his motorcycle off the road in the tiny yard outside her flat.

'Or are you one of these men who don't enjoy being driven?' Isobel enquired as she took the wheel.

'I'll reserve judgement on that, until we reach Laneside House,' Daniel declared with a grin.

'Big of you! Trouble is, that could make me so nervous I create a proper hash of this.'

Resolving to do nothing of the kind, she started up the engine and set off very carefully, as smoothly as anyone might. All the way along the road which became progressively more remote, Isobel continued to be cautious, while still attempting to keep up enough speed to convince that she knew what she was doing.

Perhaps she had succeeded. Daniel certainly chatted away cheerfully, paying little heed to the road ahead, and apparently none to how she was performing behind the wheel.

'Have I passed then?' she asked as she slowed on the track leading up to Laneside House.

'Passed?' He sounded genuinely puzzled.

'That wasn't some sort of test then?' asked Isobel with mock innocence.

'If you're hoping I'll admit you're a better driver than I am, you've a long wait coming! Seriously, Isobel, you're OK.'

He helped her down from the vehicle, and kept a hand on her elbow as they negotiated the rough track to the perimeter of her garden.

'As you can see, the porch needs re-building,' she told him. 'But that's nothing to the state the roof was in. I'm hoping Bert Bradshaw's made that sound now. This way . . .'

Daniel was gazing all about him as they walked around to the kitchen door. They both looked up at the roof before Isobel inserted the key in the lock. From where they were standing it appeared that all the loose slates had been replaced.

As soon as they stood inside the kitchen, she smiled at Daniel. 'Welcome to Laneside House. Not very prepossessing, as yet,' she began, then checked herself. She recalled suddenly that Daniel had wanted the place when she inherited it.

'You'll make something of this, I'm sure. Especially when the actual reconstruction's completed and the rest is up to you. Your mother told me how artistic you are.'

'There's a big difference between designing frocks and decorating a house.'

'Even so. I'll wager you'll have a place to be proud of one day.'

'Given time – and I'll need a lot of that. It's bad enough trying to fit in a few hours here, never mind staying long enough to do any actual work.'

'Don't forget I've told you where to apply for a bit of help.'

'You did say that, I know. You might live to regret the offer!'

They laughed again, but Isobel grew serious, staring up at the gap which still remained in the ceiling above them. Beyond the upstairs room was a further ceiling which now looked to be intact again, if not yet plastered.

'I must go up there, and take a look,' said Isobel. 'I hope you haven't put your best clothes on, the stairs here aren't so good, and the next flight's even worse.'

'Just lead on, I'm ready for anything.'

When they reached the bedroom Isobel hurried to the middle of it, and smiled as she inspected the new ceiling.

'He's made a grand job of that, don't you think?' she remarked.

Daniel came to stand beside her. She felt his hand on her shoulder. 'I'd say nobody could have done better. When that's been plastered, no one would guess there'd been any damage. Are we going up to the attic then?'

'You bet! I can't wait to see how the inside of the roof's finished off. There was so much rotten timber, and years of cobwebs, you couldn't make out much of the original roof timbers.'

The first thing Daniel said after clambering up the worn stairs delighted her. 'By, but that's a champion job! You've picked a good builder there, Isobel. See how he's shaped that timber to line up with the old stuff. When the fresh wood ages a bit, you won't be able to distinguish one from the other.' He turned to smile at her. 'Pity this is only the attic, eh? You'll have to find a use for this room.'

'I'm just – *thrilled* with it, so far,' she told him. And couldn't say any more. She felt quite emotional. The house had looked so awful, and now she was beginning to believe that she might one day love it.

Noting the tears welling to her eyes, Daniel put an arm about her shoulders, squeezed them. 'I know. There's something special about putting your own home to rights. The first promise that it's going to be OK has nothing to beat it.'

They remained in the attic for a few more minutes before going down to the bedrooms. Isobel showed him the room that they hadn't inspected previously, then followed as Daniel insisted on preceding her down the rickety stairs.

'What's beyond the kitchen?' he asked, then groaned when she led on to the hall behind the front door.

'I do know that's going to take a lot of putting right,' Isobel remarked. 'Even once the porch and the outer door are made good. It's obviously been damp for a very long time.'

'That happens. Even when you don't live high on the moors. You'll be surprised, though. The walls themselves aren't that bad, a good plasterer will soon transform this hallway. What other rooms have you got?'

Realising that she had hardly examined the remaining ground floor room, Isobel crossed to open its door. She had been discouraged by too much about Laneside House during her first few visits.

She was pleasantly surprised by the good size of the room, plus the fact that it had two windows.

'That'll burn some fuel,' said Daniel, looking towards the hearth with its big old range. 'And this room's so large it'll swallow most of the heat before it can permeate the rest of the house.'

'I suppose so. There'll have to be electric fires upstairs or those bedrooms will be freezing in winter.'

'There's no bathroom, is there?' he said pensively.

'Just a lavatory out at the back. One that needs replacing.'

'Know what I'd do? Have the far end of this room divided off to make a proper bathroom. The plumbing must be there already for the outside lavatory, they could soon bring it through. Made smaller, this living room wouldn't require so much heating. It might not be ideal having a downstairs bathroom, but there didn't seem to be much available space up above.'

'No, there isn't. Having the stairs going up between the bedrooms makes them a bit small. I quite like your idea, I'll discuss it with Bert Bradshaw.'

Daniel was being very helpful, Isobel was glad that she'd

taken up his offer to accompany her to Laneside House. She certainly loved having someone to share her interest in the place, was feeling quite sorry when there seemed nothing more to do there that day.

On the way out to the Jeep, she thanked him warmly, then asked if James Samuel had told him about their great-grandfather's letters.

'No, never. Don't believe we got as near as that to discussing family history. Was there something special about the old man then?'

'Well, he was stationed at the Tower of London. With the Grenadier Guards. I only know because I found a letter that he wrote to his wife about buying the house. How much he wanted to start a family there, and so on.'

'That's interesting. When was the letter dated?'

'1874, if I've remembered it right.'

'I'd have judged Laneside House a lot older than that,' said Daniel as they drove down the hillside.

'And you'd probably be correct. I'm pretty sure the house wasn't newly built when Edward Johnson took it on.'

'I see. It'd be interesting to discover more of the history of the place.'

'That's what I thought. Don't know when I'd get the time, though.' She also wanted to learn more about the guards' battalions serving in the Tower during Victoria's reign. She had tried to unearth books in the public library, without success.

'Perhaps that's best left until the restoration's completed. You mustn't take on too much and wear yourself out.'

Isobel laughed. 'I do that already. Sometimes when I come in from work I'm too tired to make anything to eat.'

'You want to watch that, easily becomes a habit. Believe me, those years as a POW demonstrated how missing out on proper food pares down your strength. Which brings me to today – you will come to my cottage for a meal, won't you?'

'Thanks, I'd like that. And to see your place. Do you mind if we call in at the flat first, though, I'd like to change? I never wear decent stuff for going out to the house.'

Entering her tiny room, the first thing Isobel saw was the portrait of Edward Johnson. She had forgotten bringing it across for safety before work began on Laneside House.

'There's our great-grandfather,' she told Daniel. 'This belongs in the house, of course, but I couldn't risk anything happening to it while work's going on there.'

'He's handsome, don't you think?' he said with a smile.

Isobel agreed, but she was looking hard at the man beside her. He bore a strong resemblance to their ancestor. And, yes, he was handsome.

How had she failed to notice that previously?

Feeling strangely excited by the prospect of seeing Daniel's home, Isobel offered him a drink, then went to get ready swiftly.

Five

Daniel's cottage was well-cared-for, that was evident as soon as Isobel drew up outside its recently re-pointed walls.

'Doesn't that look clean with the pointing re-done!' she exclaimed. 'You don't notice that the stone itself is still quite soot-darkened.'

'Glad you spotted that. I'm pretty pleased with it myself. And the door's new – had to make one to fit, but I copied the style of the original Edwardian one. Enjoyed tackling that, as well.'

Isobel agreed that it looked totally in keeping with the age of his home. 'Can't wait to see the interior,' she added as they got out of the Jeep, and he went round to retrieve his motorcycle, which they'd carried in the back.

Daniel unlocked the front door and told her to go inside, but Isobel waited until he had secured his motorbike in a shed to the side of the cottage.

The moment he led the way indoors, she gasped delightedly. 'This is so beautiful, Daniel. It certainly does you credit.'

He had made the most of the fact that the door opened on to the living-room, using the absence of a hallway to enhance the impact. Walking straight in, she was drawn towards the warm peach tones of walls that, together with a terracotta shade of linoleum, complemented the golden tone of the wood fashioned into bookshelves and cupboards. To their left a brick fireplace and hearth stood well-equipped with logs.

'How welcoming this seems,' Isobel went on. 'You've got it just right.'

'Thank you,' Daniel said, his smile widening to include

his eyes. 'You're the first person I've brought here since it was really finished. And I'm glad you are,' he added huskily.

Isobel felt his arm about her shoulders, then he kissed her cheek. She willed herself not to relax against him, but resisting was requiring considerable effort.

'Let's see the rest of your home,' she suggested.

Daniel had surprised her today, but even more so had her own emotions. Always believing herself independent, she hadn't reckoned with this sharing becoming so enjoyable.

Visiting Daniel's cottage began to change a lot of things for Isobel, most of all because he had decorated the place so beautifully. He took her from room to room before they ate, and in every one she admired not only his taste but also his skill.

'You've done a grand job on this, you know,' Isobel complimented him after he had shown her all around.

'I'm pleased with the way it's turned out, I have to admit.'

'And it didn't take you all that long, did it? Doesn't seem that many weeks since you first mentioned the place.'

'Don't forget I've only myself to look after, so long as I eat regularly I can neglect some stuff. And I made sure I didn't work overtime on days when I was planning to get jobs done here. Not like you, by all accounts, you're putting in a lot of hours designing. How's that going, by the way? You don't say.'

'All right, I suppose. They keep giving me more work, they must be satisfied.'

'And *you* – are you satisfied, Isobel?'

'I ought to be. It's the job I always wanted.'

'That wasn't what I asked.'

She couldn't ignore the concern in his eyes. 'I've got to confess there are days when I get a bit fed up. Although the firm I work for is a good one, and I should be thankful – it doesn't feel exciting. Not the way I expected it to feel when I was looking ahead during all those years with the Land Army.'

'Oh, dear.'

'Happen it's just me, being proper daft. And growing up a bit more, perhaps. I used to relish handling beautiful materials, planning how they'd look when they were made up. Today, it's becoming –' She paused, shrugged. 'Just something I can do.'

'While lots of other people can not . . .'

'That applies to most work. It's the way I am, I'm afraid – threatening to become bored as soon as I master something.'

'There should be plenty of scope when Laneside House is ready for you to commence on the interior.'

'Don't remind me. I'm trying not to look ahead that far, in case it makes me more dissatisfied with my present work. Even before better fabrics become available again.'

'You wouldn't try to tackle the house while you were still designing fashions?'

'Nobody will pay me to do up the place.'

'So – you need that job, for now. But you might consider giving it a rest when the time comes for you to concentrate on your house.'

Daniel sounded so concerned for her that she was compelled to respond seriously.

'It isn't as though I'll be short of funds. You know my mother sold our old terraced place?'

'I gathered that when I saw her, yes.'

'Half of the proceeds came to me. Now you've seen my flat, you'll know the rent on that's not so high. I *could* manage for a while without earning.'

'And if you enjoyed decorating, and so on, you might take that up eventually. Use Laneside House as an advertisement. Renovation's the sort of thing I have in mind, one day. Become my own boss, drop stuff which doesn't challenge in favour of devoting my time to work that thrills me.'

'You've obviously got a lot more straightened out in your mind than I have.'

'Prison camp provided time for thinking. And finding this cottage afterwards gave me incentive to begin putting ambition into practice.'

'You'd better not say any more. Now I am itching to start making Laneside House look good. And there's a lot to sort out first, obtaining paint and so on. How did you get your stuff together?'

'A lot of that wood I'd stored through the war, I'd dreamed of having my own place. Getting things like paint and so on was easier with knowing folk in the trade. And I got in first, before so much stuff was restricted. Let me know if I can help you obtain supplies.'

Daniel had prepared a salad in advance and boiled a few potatoes which he offered along with tinned salmon when they sat down at the kichen table.

'I hope you like salmon,' he said. 'I can't get enough of it, now that supplies have improved since the war. My mother always said it was a good standby for when visitors drop in unexpectedly, I think it warrants more than that.'

They began talking about various foods which, once favourites, had been absent during the war, but now were returning to the shops. They also laughed when Isobel described some of the food they were obliged to eat, like whalemeat and dried eggs.

Daniel smiled wryly. 'Just don't ask what we were given in the camp, most of it was indescribable!'

'Stupid of me, I wasn't thinking. You must believe I'm terribly soft.'

'That isn't at all what I think of you,' said Daniel.

He reached across the table to cover her hand with his own, while brown eyes sought her gaze, their depths suddenly solemn.

I'm not ready for this, thought Isobel, but willed herself not to withdraw her hand too swiftly. Daniel had been a good companion that day, she'd no wish to spoil everything.

She came away from his cottage determined to do an equally good job on Laneside House. There would be differences, naturally, he had used his craftsmanship to create those bookshelves and cupboards perfectly integrated into the available spaces. She would be able to manage none of that, and she really did not intend to ever take up Daniel's offer of assistance. Unless it was over supplying paint.

His home had the benefit of being a newer, brighter, building too, constructed around the beginning of the twentieth century, and he had enlarged the windows in his living-room which introduced a great deal of light. She would need to bear in mind what was appropriate for her own place, and to resist making comparisons.

For weeks afterwards Isobel remained influenced by that day: she kept returning to the idea that she might in the future make a living designing and decorating house interiors. That would utilise her sewing skills, plus any talent she might discover for painting. It could only be a dream, as things were she hadn't yet had the chance to make a start on putting into practice her ideas for Laneside House. She caught herself wishing repeatedly that she had got more detail from Daniel about his intention of running his own business. There could be a few guidelines for setting up on her own.

Never in her life had Isobel suspected that she might do so. The war had caused such a gap in the progress of her career that she'd returned to it with the belief that she had missed out on opportunities. She still felt it was too late to make enough of her name as a designer to draw in sufficient clients to go into business.

If she should succeed in impressing with her renovation of Laneside House, however, that was a different field, one which might present its own opportunities. At least, the bit of cash behind her would enable her to make an attempt . . .

Isobel had no intention of discussing with anyone plans that lay so far ahead in the future. She had reckoned without the interest of her friends. Diana especially had been concerned that Isobel was working so hard in Leeds and also keeping an eye on the reconstruction out at Laneside House.

'How long can you keep this up?' Diana wanted to know, her blue eyes anxious.

She had called at the flat one evening, and found Isobel eating a sandwich while sitting at the table with her cheque book and a pile of invoices and other documents.

'Do you want a cup of tea?' Isobel offered. 'If you'll just wait until I've written this cheque, I can leave the rest for now.'

'No, thanks, *I've* just had a proper meal,' Diana responded. 'I can see you haven't! And that brings me to why I'm here.

We've been saying we don't see you at church all that often, these days, and you don't seem interested in the next play we're putting on. You haven't even asked when casting begins.'

Isobel sighed. 'That's because I shall have to give that one a miss, if not the production that follows. You saw the house – how much needs doing. The builder's getting on fine with it now, but there's still some plastering to do. And he's only just starting on the bathroom.'

'Haven't you thought that something's got to give, sooner or later? Aren't you frightened you might mess up your chances with your dress designing? You can't continue putting so much time into everything you've taken on.'

'Agreed. And happen it'll be the fashion business that will get along without me.'

'You can't mean that. Whatever would you do? For a job, I mean, after the house is finished?'

'There's an idea I have,' Isobel began, and went on to tell her.

'That won't offer much security, will it? Me and the others have been right worried about you, afraid you're risking your livelihood. And that was before this talk of ditching fashion for a scheme like this.'

'Maybe that's just what I should do, though. Security isn't necessarily all good, if it means we're not putting our trust in anything else . . .'

Isobel was remembering Gustav Kassel, and the way that he seemed to disregard all things that might make him secure, relying instead on trust.

'I'm going to try to have a bit more faith,' she confided to Diana. 'Be prepared to wait and see how things turn out.'

Her friend groaned. Their church-going might be about having 'faith', but not to the point of being reckless. Yorkshire folk were too sensible for that. 'I think you're mad, if you don't hang on to that good job of yours. If you kept that going, you could pay somebody else to do that house up.'

'To my designs for the interior, is that what you think? Or should I leave it all to an outsider?' That was the last thing Isobel would contemplate. Wasn't she longing to get started on making every room look lovely?

Diana shrugged, and persisted. 'Whatever suits you. And, naturally, as long as you had the last say over the final appearance.'

Isobel was quite touched that this was the second time Diana had revealed how concerned her friends were about how hard she was working. A part of her wished that she *could* revert to being the person who had emerged after the war determined to throw herself into just enjoying life with them. She hadn't chosen to be this busy. It seemed now almost as though Laneside House had chosen her to rescue it. There could be no turning back.

Neglecting the house certainly was not what Isobel wished, and as if to prove that she began going over there more frequently to check on Bert Bradshaw's progress, and to visualise more seriously how each room would look when she could express her own originality there.

Whilst the builder had declared that he didn't wish to have clients 'breathing down his neck', in Isobel's case, he appreciated her interest in everything he was doing. He had applauded her idea of having a bathroom created from the end section of the living-room, and was happy to inspect any leaflets that would help her to select a bath and other fittings.

For a time, deciding on how the bathroom would look was her most exciting task; she pored over illustrations, and visited the few showrooms that she could locate. Isobel supposed such enthusiasm was because that would be the only room where she could create everything from scratch. Throughout the rest of the house she was limited by the existing perameters.

Witnessing the reconstruction was interesting, nevertheless, and there were several days when she felt exhilarated by the completion of another stage. During the early weeks she had been delighted to see ceilings repaired and replastered. The next major work had been the rebuilding of the front porch. That took quite a time: Bradshaw had declared it entirely unsafe, insisting on pulling it down to the foundations and restoring stone upon stone.

Isobel was there one day while the builder was working,

and learned from him to appreciate the textures of the local sandstone. With him, she noticed its tiny crystals that glinted in sunlight, drawing the eye to shades that were far more than sandy, varying from dark blue to orange, from pale gold to black. She could almost feel glad about the necessary rebuilding of her porch now providing this opportunity to comprehend the nature of the stone from which her house was constructed.

Bradshaw had sub-contracted the making of a new front door, and Isobel had wondered if she should suggest that she'd a relative who might supply one. She had hesitated for days, pondering, then decided against: she wasn't yet sure how involved she wished Daniel to become. With the project of Laneside House, or with *her*.

To her relief, the new door when fitted looked fine, and well-matched to the windows that Bradshaw had built into either side of the porch. Once the original slates plus a few replacements were secured on its tiny roof, the whole front of Laneside House appeared infinitely better.

Internally, the porch still had bare stone walls. They were thick enough to need no additional layer of bricks, and her builder suggested Isobel might limewash the interior in white. While agreeing that was a thought, she favoured the idea of giving the walls a thorough clean, then leaving the natural stone so recently admired.

She was more troubled by what lay further into the house in the neglected hallway. Although Bradshaw assessed the walls as structurally sound, much of the plaster had disintegrated along with timber that had rotted. Isobel found it hard to accept his assurance that he would soon make everything look as good as ever.

'Once this is plastered, though, you'd best let it dry out thoroughly before you attempt any decorating, or you'll be storing up bother for yourself,' he'd added.

'That's fine with me, there will be plenty for me to tackle in the rest of the house.'

She could still see the scepticism that had shown in his eyes that day. 'You're not thinking of doing all the painting and that on your own, are you, Miss Johnson?'

She grinned. 'I fancy having a shot at it. Mind you, I shan't be surprised if I do have to call on somebody to help.'

'I hope you know what you're about!' Bradshaw exclaimed dourly. 'A bit of a lass like you. You might think this house isn't so big, just wait till you've been stuck at it for weeks, that's when the job will begin to pall.'

Isobel could believe he was right, but she resolved to push such negative thoughts to the back of her mind. Daniel Armstrong had renovated his cottage, and had done so beautifully, she wouldn't be satisfied until she could look around Laneside House and see that it was lovely. And her own work.

Her next visit there was on a Saturday when she planned to meet with Bert Bradshaw and inspect the newly delivered equipment for the bathroom, whose walls were now completed. Isobel was feeling elated, looking forward to seeing all the items she had chosen and selecting where precisely everything should be placed.

Approaching the site, she slowed the Jeep, sighing in bewilderment. The builder's van wasn't there, and the house appeared completely deserted. Leaving her own vehicle, Isobel ran through the garden towards her splendid front door. Only then did she notice that her gleaming new bath had been delivered and left to one side of the house where already it had acquired a shallow puddle of the previous night's rain.

'That won't do,' she said aloud. She would have to try to manoeuvre it inside the house somehow, lying out here wouldn't improve its good enamel. That was if nobody else came past and took a fancy to her lovely bath!

Entering the porch, Isobel found the scrap of paper, a note from Bert Bradshaw, apologising for having to leave without seeing her. He had developed a severe migraine, and had been obliged to return home too ill to do anything.

She was on the point of going through to try to work out how to bring the bath indoors when she saw that Bradshaw's was not the only note. Inside an envelope addressed to her at Laneside House in elegant handwriting, the second message made her smile.

Dear Isobel Johnson,

I walked this way today, and was happy for you when I saw how greatly Laneside House has improved. You should be congratulated on your planning of its restoration. Hannah Johnson would be proud of you.

I hope that you are well. If at some time you were to think I might be invited to see more of your house, I should be very happy. I stay at the home of the so kind verger.

Gustav Kassel

Isobel was delighted to receive word from him which, she discovered suddenly, helped to obliterate the disappointment of finding the builder absent. She hesitated only long enough to walk through the ground floor rooms to check that nothing was amiss following Bradshaw's abrupt departure. Leaving the house, she swiftly began climbing the hill, intent on finding Gustav.

Isobel didn't have far to search. Even before reaching the verger's house she saw the German pilot weeding between graves in the churchyard.

'You look busy,' she called. 'Perhaps I shouldn't interrupt you . . .'

'My friend!' Gustav exclaimed, rising swiftly and striding across to take both of her hands. He released his hold on them almost as quickly, and inspected his own fingers ruefully. 'I am sorry. I did not think how – how unclean . . .'

'Don't worry, it doesn't matter. But are you very busy? I came to see if you wish to go with me to Laneside House.'

Gustav was very pleased, and he did not have to finish tidying the churchyard that day. 'If you could wait for me, I go to wash very quickly.'

The speed with which he reappeared confirmed how glad he was to be invited to inspect her house. He continued to exclaim excitedly as they walked together to the crest of the moor before hurrying the short distance downhill towards

Isobel's property. Briefly, the sun appeared between heavy clouds, and she was glad to have Laneside House looking its best.

'You see from here how good the roof is now, I think,' he remarked. 'I saw it when the man was fixing. And so no more you have the rain inside the house.'

'Not one drop,' Isobel confirmed. 'And don't you think that porch looks fine now it's rebuilt? I have so much to show you,' she went on, so happy that she had to restrain her fingers lest she grasp his hand impulsively. She kept having to remind herself that they had met only rarely.

The sun disappeared again, and rain was beginning to fall, the thin kind which, if it persisted, could be just as wetting as a downpour. Isobel hurried to unlock her new front door, and motioned Gustav to go through into the hallway.

'I'll be with you in a minute,' she told him. 'Make yourself at home,' she added, then realised that he had known this house better than she herself did.

Isobel had remembered the bath, and was determined that she wouldn't leave it out in the garden to fill with rainwater.

Hurtling round from the porch to the side of the house, she was trying to fathom how best she might move the bath. Intent on working that out, she didn't notice the old paving stone half-concealed by weeds. Tripping on its edge, Isobel felt herself falling, tried to avert that and reached out a hand. She failed to grasp the bath, but her arm with the full force of her weight behind it scraped down its outside rim.

'That was sharp!'

The gash was deep and ran for several inches along the outer edge of her forearm. Blood was springing from the cut alarmingly swiftly. Hauling herself to her feet, Isobel sped to the nearest door, the one leading to the kitchen.

It was still locked and although she hammered on its panel with her good hand, so far as she knew, Gustav possessed no key.

Fortunately, he did hear her and emerged at the front to come running around the corner to find her.

'What have you done?' he asked, his eyes darkening anxiously.

'I only tripped. I feel a proper fool! It was wet, I was rushing and tripped. I suppose I'll have to leave it now.'

'Certainly until we have attended to that arm. But leave what, Isobel?'

'My beautiful new bath. It must have been delivered after Bert Bradshaw had left.'

His arm about her, Gustav was leading her around to the front. 'Bradshaw is your builder, *ja?*'

'Yes, he wasn't well and had to go home. He left a note.'

'You should sit here, I think,'

Beside the kitchen sink was a draining slab, also in stone. Using her sound arm and with Gustav's help, Isobel eased herself up to sit there, her arm held over the sink.

He turned on the tap with a rueful glance towards her. 'This will feel terribly cold,' he warned. 'But it should help to ensure the wound is clean.'

Isobel grimaced as the water stung. 'Happen its being so cold will limit the bleeding. It shouldn't be all that dirty, any road, it was the bath edge I caught it on. At least, I now have soap here, I brought some over when Bert Bradshaw started coming regular like.'

Gustav was rolling up his sleeves. 'Do you wish that I bathe the arm for you?'

'Not sure – I don't know I can bear anybody else to touch this.'

He nodded, gestured to her to continue. 'You must tell to me anything that you wish me to do.'

'I will, of course. You're very good.'

'Do you have bandages here in the house, perhaps?'

'Nothing like that, I'm afraid. I'll just have to hope this stops bleeding without a dressing.'

'You will still need to keep the wound clean. As I know only too well, the poison can develop swiftly.'

'There's some old bed linen in the attic somewhere. I'll tear a piece off that.'

'I have a better idea – ' Gustav felt in a pocket and brought out, not one but two, freshly laundered handkerchiefs. 'We use one soon to dry your arm, the second to form a pad which we shall fasten securely.'

Beginning to feel better, Isobel laughed. 'You come well-equipped!'

He nodded quite seriously. 'After that I had spent those many months living with no home, I vowed to myself that I would never again be so neglectful. I do not need many possessions, but I refuse to be uncivilised.'

'Good for you! That is certainly appreciated today. I can't thank you enough for looking after me.'

'But you yourself are tending the wound.'

The flow of blood was very evidently easing now, and the water running clear. Isobel turned off the tap and Gustav immediately began to dab gently at the gash with the first handkerchief.

'A moment and we wrap in the other one. Will you be well enough to search for some cloth to bandage it?'

'Sure. I'm okay now. Feel stupid more than anything.'

They went together up the stairs and into the room where she'd previously seen bed covers. Finding an old pillow-case, she asked Gustav to tear off sufficient to hold the makeshift dressing in place.

As she handed the pillow-case across, a folded sheet of notepaper slid on to the floor. Isobel picked it up and slipped it into her pocket.

Gustav insisted then on bandaging the arm for her, and surprised Isobel with his tenderness. She found it difficult to associate today's considerate German with the World War II pilot who had been sufficiently tough to exist out on this bleak Yorkshire moorland.

'Are you happy staying at the verger's house, Gustav?' she asked, suddenly needing to learn if he intended remaining in the area.

He smiled. 'Jack Ramsden is very kind, as I told to you before. I try not to let myself feel too comfortable in his home, but is difficult to think that I should perhaps go away.'

'Away? Where to?' Hadn't he said that he had no family left in his own part of the world?

'Much time has passed, and now I no longer know where

that should be. That my work for the verger is temporary is obvious, even to myself. But I cannot yet understand what it is that I must do tomorrow, and for the many tomorrows.'

'What other work interests you, Gustav? What did you do before you became a pilot?'

He sighed, shaking his head. 'I trained to fly, that is all I learned. It is all I wished to do for my life.'

And you'll never be permitted to do that in Britain, thought Isobel grimly.

Gustav raised his sea-green eyes to meet her gaze, gave a shrug, a happier one. 'With your great-aunt I discovered how plants grow. I think perhaps I spend my days tending them. But everything seems difficult, no English farmer will give work to a German of the Luftwaffe.'

'Or you paint. When I found you that other time you were decorating the walls for Mr Ramsden.'

You could work with me, on Laneside House, thought Isobel, but something cautioned against suggesting that. She knew so little about this man, could so readily be influenced by his gentle touch today, and by some force impelling her to like him.

'I haven't shown you around, have I?' she said. 'That silly mishap has knocked out my common sense. Anyway, the bedrooms here are looking better, aren't they, since the roof was mended, and the ceiling, the floorboards?'

They went into the second bedroom, and Isobel chanced to look out of the window. She noticed that the rain had ceased and the sun, emerging from clouds again, coloured a rainbow from one summit of the horizon to another. The landscape had adopted that special clarity which followed a downpour, sharpening the purple of distant moors, brightening the greens of trees and meadows descending steeply to hidden valleys. She thought how great it would be to awaken in this room to such glorious scenery.

Gustav cleared his throat. 'I think that you are fortunate to have this house. I could imagine nowhere finer to commence each morning.'

The similarity to her own feelings sent a shiver along Isobel's spine. She sensed that those beautiful eyes of his were willing her to meet his gaze. No matter how strongly she longed to do so, Isobel did not trust herself to submit to emotions which she was only beginning to comprehend.

'Do you want to see the attic?' she asked briskly. 'It's not particularly exciting.'

They returned instead to the ground floor where Gustav exclaimed in delight when he saw the new bathroom. 'And now we must bring its bath into the house, *ja*? I can do in a minute for you.'

He refused to let Isobel assist by more than holding the outer door open wide for him. Lifting the bath without much evident effort, he carried it through to leave it near to the doorway of the bathroom.

'I place here, I think. Your builder will have tasks to complete in there to make ready for the fitting.'

'Thank you ever so much, Gustav. You have been a great help to me today. I'd never have managed without you.'

Looking at him, Isobel recognised how swiftly Gustav was recovering from the exertion of carrying the bath through the house. But his cheeks still showed a flush of colour, and that made her increasingly aware of his pleasing features, the sheen of golden hair, most of all the gleam in those sea-green eyes.

Gustav Kassel, you brighten this place no end, she reflected, while a wild ungoverned thought tempted her to arrange that he visit repeatedly.

'When do you plan to commence your painting of this house?' he asked her.

'Can't say, as yet. There's plastering to be done, and I'm told I have to let that dry out before I can decorate the walls. Of course, once I make my mind up about colour schemes I should be able to start painting woodwork. Actually, most of that will remain the shade it is, anyway. The window frames and doors, for instance. I'll just re-stain if necessary and give them a good varnish.'

'And when you begin to colour the walls, what ideas do you have?'

'I still have to work that out. I shan't choose anything fancy, and nothing too bright either. Nothing like that would be right for this place. Nearer the time, I might bring a few samples over here – off-cuts of material that I have which will help me to see where certain shades might go.'

When she no longer had to go over regularly to Leeds for work, Isobel would love to draft colour schemes for every room.

'But first you have another priority – you must make sure that your arm heals well. I wish that I could help to care for you. Since I can not, you must promise me that you will not neglect that wound.'

Isobel grinned. 'I'm not as daft as I seem, falling over like that,' she assured him. 'I do have my sensible moments. If it doesn't start knitting together all right, I'll see what the chemist can recommend.'

'Or your doctor . . .'

'Aren't you the serious one! It's not going to be nearly so bad as that.'

'*Sehr gut.*'

Gustav was preparing to leave when Isobel remembered the paper that she had found among the linen upstairs. Taking it from her pocket, she smoothed it out and began to read.

'Don't go,' she said; 'not for the minute. Have a look at this.'

He came to stand behind her, placing a hand on her shoulder and leaning forward to read with her.

The document, small though it was, appeared to be a plan of the ground floor of Laneside House, from the condition of the paper and style of handwriting dating from at least the period when it was purchased by Edward Johnson.

'That is very interesting,' Gustav remarked.

'Yes,' Isobel agreed, but her voice was barely audible. She was completely distracted by the man who was standing so close behind her, by the touch of his hand which, however light, seemed to warm her entire body. Deep inside her, pulses awakened, their insistence asserting the urge to lean against him. Or that she should turn into the embrace of arms which she sensed would readily hold her.

Gustav moved, stepping backwards, withdrawing his hand. He cleared his throat.

'I must leave. I really must.'

He strode towards the tiny porch, hesitated only briefly before opening the outer door.

'Take care of yourself,' he called over his shoulder.

'And you take care,' Isobel murmured. But the door had closed after him. Why did she suspect that Gustav found this parting no less painful than she herself?

She had steeled herself against responding to the urge to keep him there, to indulge her own senses. Senses which were screaming that she must respond to the intense affinity created between them.

Six

Feeling shaken, Isobel remained in the house, unable to rid herself of the impression that Gustav had needed her as much as she herself, so unexpectedly, had discovered her multi-faceted need of him. She had seen earlier that he was attractive, of course, admiring his golden hair, his height, the pleasant features which so recently adopted a flush after he'd carried that great bath indoors. But she had seen attractive men before, several when working on farms, more still on stage with the dramatic society. A number of the members of that group were quite handsome.

She had flirted with them, indulged in snatched kisses backstage, experienced passion. Or so it had seemed – until today. Never in her life before had she known this degree of yearning. Isobel believed she was mature, yet she must be inexperienced: the attraction other men had created was an insignificant murmur beside this intensity deep within her. The fact that she had waited this long to be stirred so completely seemed strange. And strangely significant.

Isobel felt alarmed by the force in her feelings. She would have understood if this were the first occasion she'd resisted an impulse to come closer to someone, but it was only short weeks ago that Daniel had seemed charismatic. That attraction had waned, even perhaps before they had parted. This longing created by Gustav threatened to reiterate its message throughout her, until it could be sated.

She must get away, from this place, from the *essence* of him which lingered in Laneside House, an intangible force more powerful than physical contact. Her arm was smarting now, its pulsing an echo of her inner need, a pale echo. And his tenderness was there, in his dressing of the wound, his concern for her well-being. Gustav would love with tenderness to match his urgency. Would she ever have the opportunity to quiet this, her own, insistence and be tender with him?

Isobel forced raging emotions to submit to sense, and gathered her belongings, locked every door meticulously. Out in the darkening air, she drew in great breaths, and felt her heart, unchecked, pulse out her longing for him.

The Jeep felt cold, a chill Isobel required to stabilise her, for she must take care. Gustav had insisted. And she must preserve their future meetings.

Too disturbed to do more than tackle the journey ahead, she failed to gaze up the hill. There was no one to see that young German with golden hair who waited to see her one more time when she drove off towards civilisation.

.Near the end of her street in Halifax one of the woollen mills had worked an additional shift. The spinners and weavers had gone home, but its huge doors stood open. The smell of wool, moist from dyeing, surged across the pavement to hang in nostrils and throat, until she felt close to choking. Why does that seem more horrible today? wondered Isobel.

Mrs Hardaker, the landlady she hardly knew, was waiting near her own doorway. 'I never see much of you, do I, love? I keep meaning to put that right. If you haven't got anything planned for tonight, you might like to come in for a bit of supper. What do you say?'

Already too bemused to think, Isobel said yes, and thanked her. 'I'll have to change, of course, I hope you don't mind if I take a while?'

Washing and dressing slowly helped only as far as providing a tidy reflection before Isobel headed towards the other flat. Inwardly, turmoil persisted, refusing to ease as though assuring her that needing Gustav should remain constant.

The slight unfamiliarity between herself and Mrs Hardaker seemed to help, if only by neglecting to provide opportunities for questions. Isobel could believe anyone knowing her better would demand explanation of her distraction. She wondered, wildly, if she would ever dare to face her friends – they were concerned about her already – surely would recognise that she was seized by this overwhelming passion?

The evening felt surreal, listening to her landlady, who possessed a solitary's need for conversation. Fortunately for Isobel, little was required of her beyond a present ear, there seemed no end to the tales and opinions, too long suppressed in reluctant seclusion.

The supper provided was good, prepared with the care of a woman who yearned to have reason to cater for others. At any other time, Isobel's thanks would have been profuse. Today, she prayed silently that she was showing adequate appreciation.

It was late when Isobel gave her excuses and thanks, and left, but the late hour did not provide the relief wrought by exhaustion. Released from company, her emotions surged unchecked, now mingling affection for Gustav with attraction.

She could believe she'd never cared more for anyone, and that disturbed her greatly. Experiencing desire was troubling enough, but might be explained by chemistry which coincided – but *caring* . . . ? That, surely, was likely to emerge only during closer acquaintance?

Whatever she lacked, the absence of any kind of closeness made Isobel feel terribly alone as she went to her own flat.

She did sleep, finally, and dreamed. Unfulfilled desire proving so strong that it dominated her sleeping brain, to torture with what might have been . . .

The days that followed brought some respite. Her Sunday visit to church with its familiar liturgy influenced far more than she had feared that it might. Isobel could not, must not, permit private longings to obtrude entirely. By the time she was leaving with her friends, she felt confident that nothing in her manner would prompt them to seek explanation of her disturbance.

For once, Isobel was glad to fall in with plans suggested

by the others, and allow them to believe that working too long and too hard made her willing now to turn her back on jobs requiring attention. She stifled a laugh later that day when Betty supposed that Isobel had at last found visits to Laneside House boring.

'You need something to stimulate you,' Polly added with a grin, smoothing her blonde hair. 'And you'll not find that out yonder.'

'We've decided it's time we had a night out with some of the chaps,' Diana went on. 'Maybe you haven't time for acting in a play, you can't be busy every day. Betty's dad is opening up his café just for us after Evensong. Why don't you come along with us?'

Feeling rather alarmed by the prospect of an evening spent with the old crowd was what convinced Isobel that she did need a distraction. Getting together like that might result in her regaining a sense of proportion. It wasn't rational to become so obsessed about Gustav. After all, she could do no more than wish that she could guess what he was feeling.

While she dressed carefully for the evening and walked to the café to join the others, Isobel resolved to allow her friends the opportunity to haul her out of her preoccupation.

She couldn't afterwards identify any one thing that went wrong. Being among the drama group again provided plenty of conversation, and if it centred mainly on the current production that was only as she'd expected.

Most of the men who'd come along seemed interested in the renovating of Laneside House, and wanted to know how it was progressing. Even so, Isobel could not avoid feeling that she no longer belonged quite so surely with them all. She would have been blind to fail to see certain glances exchanged across the large table where everyone was seated. And she couldn't avoid wondering if such glances might express wordless comment on some way that she'd offended them.

Was she becoming neurotic, looking for signs that, by neglecting to participate in all their interests, she had turned herself into something of an outcast? Diana and Richard were laughing together a lot; Isobel couldn't help resenting the sensation that they might be excluding her. Diana had always been her special friend.

Quelling a sigh, she reminded herself privately that people did change, and she herself had changed more than anyone since taking on responsibility for Laneside House. She could never regret the interest that the place was bringing her, even while she remained so uncertain about the feelings of the young pilot she would always associate with her home.

Gustav had found some degree of peace seated in the back pew of this church on the edge of Yorkshire moorland. Leaving while his friend Jack Ramsden led out the choir and clergy, he avoided an encounter with the vicar. The embarrassment he wished to save was not his own; Gustav felt for the vicar's pacifist belief, could even condone it. The few occasions when they'd met had generated tension, though; he had no wish to worsen that for any man.

The priest was good, Gustav had witnessed that in his concern for people like Hannah Johnson, who always had spoken well of him. More than that, these past seven years had shown Gustav the evils of international conflict: truths now emerging from war-battered Europe demonstrated the savagery of much misguided killing.

Those truths had caused him to question his own motivation. But he had been so *young* all that time ago in 1939. Driven by his ambition to fly, the Nazi cause had offered such a ready route to success. Enthused, indoctrinated, he'd been an eager volunteer. He had relished piloting those planes, had *lived* for that life. Nothing now could tarnish memories of his Luftwaffe service. He would never entirely regret the experiences it had generated, especially towards the end when he had been privileged to participate in the development necessary for aircraft to improve.

His sole regrets now concerned the losses which that life had brought him, and Gustav supposed he deserved some reprisal for serving such ideals. The hardest lesson now would be to accept his own situation.

That brutal war had left him stateless, devoid of a home, with hope alone remaining to ensure that his existence continued. The war years had been bad, in the news of his parents' early deaths at a time when learning the cause of their demise proved impossible. Much later, when word from his homeland reached him here in England, it was of family members compelled on forced marches to quit the country they had called their own. The Sudetenland he had known existed no longer.

And now he was in love.

Gustav smiled, however rueful his thoughts. He should not feel surprise that the initial generosity found in this challenging countryside had sprouted affection, a love for an elderly woman whose concern healed all wounds, physical, and otherwise. Was it not reasonable, then, that the one closely resembling her great-aunt should become the subject of his secret devotion?

The irony cut sharply to his soul. Those many nights and days spent in solitude on these moors had so often been sustained by thoughts of Hannah Johnson's kindness. Yet now he must not even permit himself to *think* of the young woman to whom he had transferred all his deep affection. He was devoid of anything to give Isobel.

Seeing nothing, Gustav had walked instinctively, from the church to the crest of the hill. Gazing down, he saw the roof of her house: refurbished, a part of the place she was re-creating. He yearned to assist her, could visualise Laneside House, whole – light streaming from its windows, smoke from the chimney. He would give anything to have some part in it. To be a part of her.

Tomorrow, he should depart, leaving no word for her of his intended destination. That alone would be simple: he could form no idea of where he might be going! Only *away*, for otherwise he would be tempted by some means to convey his love for her.

The touch on his arm startled Gustav. He swung around half-believing that she stood at his side, half-hoping.

'I wondered where you'd got to.'

Jack Ramsden was breathless from the climb, but smiling. He looked quite excited, for a man who tended to be unemotional.

'I've heard of a job. For you, if you want it. Living-in, an' all. That'd solve a lot of problems for you, wouldn't it, lad?'

'Thank you,' Gustav responded, smiling back though he sounded grave. 'But I do not think that I should stay in England. I have decided only now that I must leave.'

'Whatever for? I thought you were comfortable stopping with us. In any case, like I say, this job would mean living-in.'

'Living-in?' Gustav repeated. His emotions were so confused already that he seemed unable to comprehend any English phrase that sounded unfamiliar.

Jack grinned. 'Stopping with the folk that were giving you work, that's all. Nothing for you to look so worried about.'

The pilot managed a smile. 'Even so, I fear that I must decline their offer. I really do feel it is time that I should leave here. Perhaps you would be willing to thank these people on my behalf, and explain my intentions . . . ?'

'This is all a bit sudden, like, isn't it? Has somebody upset you, or summat?'

'On the contrary. This is just something that I must do. Please do convey to your friends my – my regrets.'

'Well, you seem very sure. Only it's not quite so simple as that. This offer of work – it's really nowt to do with me. It was the vicar who'd told some friends of his about you.'

'The vicar?' Gustav was amazed. Hadn't he been certain the man had no time for him?

'Reginald Fieldhouse, aye. You must know he's been aware of your situation, and of how you've been so willing to turn your hand to anything around the parish. Any road, like I say, he's the one who's come up with this.'

Gustav sighed. 'And so – he is the person I should visit, to try to explain that I shall no longer be available to work here.'

'If I were you, I'd get that over and done with. He'll be in the vicarage now, he was locking up the church, left at the same time as me.'

The vicarage was a gaunt, Victorian house, adjacent to the church and sharing its aspect of the hillside graveyard. Gustav felt his steps slowing as he came nearer to the property, and tried to will away his reluctance. No one would blame him, would they, for resolving to return to his own country? The Revd Fieldhouse would be unlikely to know that Gustav no longer had a land to call his own.

The front door was opened by a middle-aged servant wearing a white apron over a navy-blue dress.

'Is it possible to speak with the vicar, please?' Gustav enquired, and told her who he was.

A door opened in the dimly lit hall behind the woman, and Reginald Fieldhouse came striding towards them, a hand outstretched to shake Gustav's.

'Come in, come in – I was expecting you. Gustav, isn't it? This way – we'll go into my den. Thank you, Mary, that will be all for the moment.'

The vicar's very personal room was smaller than Gustav expected, warmed by a fire in the grate, cosy. A large desk over by the rear wall was scattered with papers and books, its well-used leather chair set with its back to the room.

'I saw you were in church this evening,' the vicar began, indicating they should sit in worn armchairs to either side of his hearth. 'Unfortunately, before I could reach you to speak, you had left.'

Gustav simply looked at him. What could he say?

'Since you're here, I assume Jack Ramsden has told you, anyway, about the job?'

He nodded. 'Yes, he has. Unfortunately, I shall not be able to take that up.'

'Not?'

'I am sorry, Mr – er – Reverend . . .' Gustav faltered. His English, which had so improved, now was failing him. It was the awkwardness, naturally.

'You may call me Reginald. From Jack Ramsden, I think of you as Gustav. Now, what is this? Did he not tell you about the kind of work being offered?'

'I – I did not allow him opportunity.'

'A pity. From what I well-remember of old Miss Johnson's

account of you, I would have believed it eminently suitable. You enjoyed growing things, I understand?'

'Yes, but . . .'

'. . . You are returning to your home?' Even the tone of the vicar's question signalled his disbelief.

'I—' Gustav faltered again. He could not lie to the man, not when he was being so unexpectedly helpful.

Reginald helped him out now. 'You have no homeland, as such, if I understand rightly from Jack's explanation. He told me earlier of the extent of your plight following the Czech government's expulsion of your fellow Sudeten citizens.'

Gustav felt his face paling as the dismal truth hit him again. He swallowed. When he began to talk his voice was husky, barely audible.

'Between newspaper reports over here, and word that eventually came through from fellow-pilots returned to Germany, I learned that what little family remained to me had been compelled to leave Sudetenland. Were it otherwise, I should have found some means of reaching my home.'

'Returning to your wife . . . ?'

He shook his head. 'Perhaps fortunately, for *her*, we had not married before I joined the Luftwaffe.' He paused, felt his ungoverned feelings for Isobel rush colour to his cheeks. Thank God he had married no one else.

'You need not pretend, you know,' said Reginald gently. 'I may abhor fighting, that doesn't leave me incapable of comprehending a man's urge to defend his homeland. Whichever side that may represent.'

'No, certainly. You are right, of course. I should have – have anticipated that you would see how that I am feeling. How I have felt.'

'So – where will you go?'

Gustav's silence revealed his total bewilderment.

'There was a girl, you hinted at a girl. Do you need assistance perhaps in beginning to trace her? There are agencies who might perhaps—'

'No. Thank you, but no. She married before the war began, a Czech national.'

'So, it is you alone that we consider.' Reginald paused,

looked keenly at him. 'Do you truly not wish to learn anything about this potential job?'

'You are thinking that I am ungrateful.'

'Perplexed maybe, no worse than that. In order to weigh possible alternatives, let me just say that the work is not very far from here, near to Rochdale. An old friend owns a very large farm, and far more land than he can work at present. His ambition is to expand the market-gardening side – you know what market-gardening is?'

'I think perhaps to grow vegetables for the market, *ja*?'

'Quite. Whoever he takes on would live as family. They're a very easy-going lot, a couple of girls in their twenties now, and his wife, of course. The two girls are following their own careers, but help around the place at weekends. His wife is a good organiser, but misses the assistance they once had from Land girls. You understand that the Women's Land Army proved very useful during the war?'

'I know of it, indeed.' And could have wished to avoid reminders of Isobel Johnson. 'I still must move right away from here.'

'You're not in trouble.' It was not a question. Reginald found Gustav such a genuine chap, could not doubt his integrity.

'Only within me. In myself.'

'May I help? *Can* I?'

Gustav needed no more prompting. The words came gushing out. 'What was it all *for*? The war, all that fighting? And the events that preceded? We were promised so much – for all Sudetens, the protection by the great German nation, their strength to support our people as we retained our identity. I was young, I know, but I could not anticipate that our wills would be submerged.'

'Sadly, that is war. No matter how willingly folk offer their skills, themselves – all is surrendered, for good or otherwise.'

'You – you are against war, are you not?'

Reginald smiled. 'Jack Ramsden has been talking. I would not join any of the armed forces, and a priest does not, except in order to minister to his people. Without entering conflict.

I refused even to do that. I avoided imprisonment for my stand, by becoming a miner.' He smiled again, ruefully. 'My old bishop called coal miners the salt of the earth – I would like to believe that I warranted that. But never for one day! I loathed the work, loathed being underground, loathed every day of that wretched war.'

'But you paid your price. And would still preach peace?'

'A good question. I like to think that I would. But we mature, we see too much – through others' experiences, if not our own. We witness what war does, yes, but we grow aware also of what might become the situation, should we refuse to fight. Answers do not come more easily, do they, with increasing maturity?'

'I supposed that I was alone in thinking so. You make me sad that I did not really know you earlier.'

'There is still time. We have talked tonight, we could talk on further occasions. If you were to take that position, you would be living only a short distance from here—'

'*If* I should take that work.'

It would solve nothing, Gustav thought. As a farm-labourer, he would have nothing to offer to any woman. Least of all to Isobel, who owned Laneside House.

The night out with her friends resulted in no solution, as Isobel had feared. The fault could be her own: even when she wasn't feeling excluded, she hadn't been in any mood for the light-hearted banter so frequently engaging them. She suspected that Diana, Polly and the rest had conspired to 'jolly' her out of her recent seriousness. Isobel might have told them that superceding her inner turmoil would require a more dramatic remedy. One which, she was beginning to admit, Gustav Kassel alone might possess.

This was so unlike her. Had she let him take over her mind, along with her whole being, leaving her unable even to converse with anything resembling sense? Nothing any companions might do seemed likely to penetrate her preoccupation.

'Whatever's wrong with you now?' Diana enquired eventually. 'You're not like your usual self at all . . .'

And that, Isobel could only agree, was her own conclusion. Explaining the reasons was beyond her. And must remain so. Everyone present around that table seemed already to think her, if not crazy, distracted. She could never divulge the source of that distraction!

'Actually, I don't feel so good. Think I'd better get off home. There's one or two designs I need to take another look at before work tomorrow.'

Every bit of that was true, and as soon as she let herself into the flat, Isobel took out her sketches. Whether or not she was capable of creating anything worthwhile, she needed to surrender to an occupation.

The following morning at work brought additional relief. She had not realised in the past how welcome were the demands from colleagues, the input inciting her to concentrate on the only work which she once had wanted.

Working on the next season's designs was never easy. Concentration was required for creating something fresh to be worn in weather totally different from whatever was currently in force beyond their windows. Such intense concentration was precisely what Isobel needed at present and, no matter how inwardly disturbed, she still was capable of devoting herself to her job.

By the end of Monday the necessary effort had exhausted her, but she felt better adjusted for being obliged to shelve thoughts of Gustav Kassel along with her concern regarding Laneside House. Within a few days she was beginning to believe that she need only suspend her visits to the house for a while in order to decrease the alarming effect that he had upon her emotions.

Feeling so much more in control of herself, Isobel called one evening to see Diana, and was relieved that her friend endorsed her own belief that she seemed back to normal.

'Louise and I are going to the Picture House tomorrow night, how about coming with us? It's *Great Expectations* – wasn't that one film you said you were determined to see?'

Isobel agreed that it was, and arranged to meet them when she arrived back from Leeds next evening.

96

The three of them enjoyed the film, Isobel all the more so because its period setting increased its ability to remove her from her present situation. Emerging from the cinema, she found herself making arrangements to go out with Diana more frequently. She could believe that might prevent her from dwelling on the less satisfactory aspects of her life.

An invitation to visit her mother and Marvin for a long weekend arrived on the following day, and Isobel smiled to herself, thankful to be provided with yet another outing to prevent her from dwelling on the feelings Gustav Kassel generated.

It was bright with sunshine as she set out on the bus down to Halifax station to begin her journey. Isobel felt as though the pleasant weather was confirming her own sense of how good it was to be heading off to East Anglia. She would make the most of having this one weekend when she could not plan any designs; and if going there alone was less exciting than she might have chosen, she reminded herself not to even think about Gustav, who couldn't possibly have travelled with her!

Arriving at the American base assured her forcefully how lively everyone there always appeared. Laughter and music wafted across from the PX, the US equivalent of the NAAFI, while around the far side of the main buildings a routine drilling session added in its brisk beat of co-ordinated feet.

Marvin was on duty, but Amy seemed full of excitement when she welcomed Isobel with a hug. She waited only until her daughter had freshened up to explain the reason.

'You're not the only one coming here this weekend, love. Daniel telephoned to remind us that he has a pal with the USAAF, that chap who's been here since he was transferred from somewhere near High Wycombe.'

'And Daniel's visiting him while I'll be here?' This sounded too much of a coincidence for Isobel to feel comfortable.

Amy laughed. 'The day he phoned me he just said he'd see me sometime. That was until I told him when you would be staying with us.'

Isobel would be surprised if her presence had influenced

Daniel's timing. They might have got on well enough when they last had met, but he hadn't contacted her since then.

'You're not annoyed that he will be around?' Amy enquired when Isobel failed to enthuse about the prospect.

She shook her head. 'It doesn't bother me either way. We felt to have more in common when I saw him last, I think we're over any initial awkwardness.'

They were seated in the compact kitchen where her mother was making a pot of tea.

'It's good to be drinking tea, it's generally coffee that Marvin wants, I tend just to have the same. Yet another way in which I'm different from the folk here.'

Isobel's eyes darkened in concern. 'You are happy though, Mum – fitting in on the base?'

Amy laughed. 'I'll say I am! It's only really when Marvin's busy that I get to thinking how I've changed. I'm better for that, mind. Never had such a good time in all my life. Dancing several nights a week, then there's other kinds of entertainment.'

Dancing was scheduled for that evening and, although she felt rather too tired, Isobel agreed to go along.

It was there that they met up with Daniel Armstrong again, and from that moment there was no let-up in the tempo. Daniel's friend Vince seemed much older than he himself, and Isobel gathered he was quite high-ranking. Evidently the two had met during some period of their internment, and it eventually emerged that Vince had lost a leg and was still struggling to adapt to a prosthesis.

When he didn't dance, he immediately insisted that Daniel must not hang back on his account. 'We'll have time later for catching up on your news.'

Daniel turned to Isobel. 'Are you willing to take a chance on me?' he enquired, as the pianist began playing a Glenn Miller favourite.

Isobel couldn't refuse, and she wouldn't have, anyway. She had come away to fill her mind with something different. This weekend ought to displace her alarming reaction to Gustav Kassel.

They certainly were on the right base for just letting go.

Tunes followed on swiftly, many of them appropriate to the Yanks' love of jiving. Eventually, both she and Daniel were too breathless to continue, and began searching the crowd for her mother and Marvin.

'I've got to say hello properly to them, at least,' Daniel declared.

En route, they met up with Vince, and insisted he should come along. He knew Marvin already and, as soon as he was introduced to Amy, Vince began charming her while he teased about her Yorkshire accent.

The five settled around a table after ordering drinks, and Isobel was surprised how animated Daniel seemed. His dark eyes glittered whenever he sought her gaze, which happened quite frequently while he began questioning her regarding the progress on Laneside House.

'And have you discovered any more about what life at the Tower of London was like while Great-grandfather was stationed there?' he asked.

'Not so far. Must admit I haven't made time to look out any books that might help, but it is something I'd love to read up on.' These days, she rarely found a few spare minutes to go to the library, even for a bit of light fiction.

They danced again when a more leisurely beat crept into the numbers featured, and Isobel discovered that Daniel was a more than competent partner. He held her close, and led so effectively that fitting her steps to his felt effortless. Isobel was delighted, she'd always loved dancing.

'We're certainly well-matched,' he murmured into her hair. 'This makes me wonder why I see you so rarely.'

'I was brought up to believe it's the man who should make the running, as the saying goes,' she told him. Together like this, Daniel was making her regret the weeks when he had done nothing to ensure that he would see her.

'I'll put that right tonight,' he vowed, and drew her nearer still against him.

Although still lean, Daniel had put on a little weight since the ending of the war, she felt him powerful against her, while every movement of the dance seemed to compel her to witness his attraction.

Isobel was aware already that he was handsome, tonight she was beginning to accept that he possessed his full share of sex appeal. Dizzy with the emotions rushing through her, she began dreading the moment when she must lose him.

'You're staying with Vince, I suppose?' she asked softly.

'Only after seeing you safely back to your mother's place. And they look like they're preparing to leave. Let's have a word with them.'

It was all arranged – so speedily Isobel couldn't doubt Daniel's wish to prolong her company. Still bruised by suspecting some of her Halifax crowd were no longer quite so friendly, she needed someone to have no reservations about her.

'I can't think we'll be taking the shortest route to Marvin's quarters,' Daniel remarked, hugging her to his side as they went to tell Vince not to wait for him.

The base was hardly romantic, with its mass of obviously practical buildings and the distant well-lit airstrips, but the night felt balmy, and Isobel was in a mood to appreciate this new aspect of Daniel Armstrong. She couldn't help thinking of how she had compared his appearance to her great-grandfather's picture – it seemed suddenly that he was imbued with all the appeal she had felt for Edward Johnson.

They wandered up and down pathways, between the various types of accommodation, seeing scarcely anything, and sensing only awareness of each other.

Daniel kissed her at last, in the shadows of one of the hangars, their lips lingering, tongues venturing to explore, and then they strolled on, away from the workaday world of the airfield.

At her mother's home all was in darkness, they entered quietly through the door left unlocked for Isobel. Closing it behind them, Daniel turned her so that she leaned against its panels, and then he was kissing her again, his mouth eagerly exploring, while she felt him pressing ever nearer.

Isobel sighed close to ecstasy, moaned slightly when he made to move away, but Daniel was leading her to the sofa.

His arms were strong but gentle, pulling her down against him, his fingers traced the line of her spine, and then one breast. Elation raged from deep within her, willing him on, seeking further enhancement of all her feelings.

She could love him tonight, but knew that she would not, yet she understood more fully the compulsion that was her need of this suddenly attractive person.

'You've certainly got what it takes,' Daniel exclaimed between kisses. 'You may count on my getting in touch, just as soon as we are back in our home territory.'

I hope you mean that, thought Isobel. Thrilled though she was by all that Daniel was doing to her, she had no wish to believe it might mean very little to him. This might have begun with the need for reassurance that no particular man was the only one to attract her, she'd no wish to have these emotions disappear with the darkness.

Seven

Reginald Fieldhouse had helped more than he would ever comprehend. Gustav left the vicarage that night positive of what he must do. Fearing that his own intention might prove eventually to be stronger than his courage, he had not explained. But he had asked that the vicar should convey his thanks to those farming friends, and tell them there would be some delay before he could take up the position so generously offered.

There was something he was compelled to do.

Setting out the following morning, he wore the only decent clothes he possessed, his flight jacket and the uniform trousers which had not fitted after losing so much weight while living off the countryside.

Gustav caught the bus on its way over the moorland road between Lancashire and Halifax, stared out from the window en route, yet observed hardly anything of the unfamiliar scenery. Every nerve was wound to the limit, he'd not experienced such tension since the early days of hiding out on the moors, never perhaps to this degree since flying on operations.

He could not begin to guess how they would treat him. Had he possessed some prior knowledge of his intention, he could have enquired of *someone* what the attitude towards a German pilot might be.

Gustav could only imagine that he would be arrested, taken to one of the prison camps which remained after being created in England during the war. The one good thing about such a prospect was that he understood the British treated such prisoners more leniently than his own officers had led flight crews to expect.

The towns here were very different from the surrounding countryside, their dark, stone buildings crowding in upon each other, but the ugly smoke that misted their valleys looked familiar. He was reminded of some industrialised towns in Germany seen during his training with the Luftwaffe.

Gustav knew Halifax only by name, from Isobel's mention of the place. Before the bus even reached the centre of the town, though, he noticed one confluence of several roads, and wondered how ever he would guess which direction to take when they arrived at the terminus. And then he saw the illuminated sign on a building that dominated one corner. Rising swiftly, he prepared to get off when the bus stopped again.

He was in a busy street, had alighted beside one of the largest shops visible from where he was standing. It possessed a modest arcade, in which women were sheltering from another of the downpours that seemed regular in Yorkshire.

Gustav could not delay however wet the weather, if he hesitated now he might never again summon sufficient courage.

The entrance to the police station was hardly imposing, he guessed this might be a mere sub-office of the local force. It should serve, however, for beginning the procedures necessary to his facing the only solution to his problems.

'Good-day, I am here to surrender myself,' Gustav began, and withdrew from his pocket every item of identification which had survived that long-ago crash. 'Here, I have documents to prove my identity. I am pilot with the Luftwaffe, my number is, as you see . . .'

'Hang on a minute, sir,' the officer behind the desk interrupted him. A young man, who appeared not long out of training, his uniform fitted so poorly that it might have been supplied extra-large in order that he should grow into it. While still wary, Gustav could not feel quite so perturbed as on setting out.

'Have I got this right – you're saying you're a German?' the man continued.

He nodded. 'I served throughout the war, flying Messerschmitts and Heinkels, until the day that I crash-landed.'

'Not near here, was it?' The young man felt at a disadvantage. Surely he would have known if a Jerry plane had come down in Halifax?

'A few miles distant, in moorland to the west. I can show where it was.'

'You mean the wreckage is still there? After all these months?'

Gustav shook his head. 'Not visible, no. I shall tell how it was . . .'

'Hold it right there, if you please. Sir,' he added, struggling to remember courtesy amid his confusion. 'I'll get my boss to have a word. Would be surprised if this doesn't turn out to be one for the army.'

He'd no wish to detain a *German* here. That way, they could invite all kinds of resentment. There was trouble enough already when their own chaps returning from the war got into a bit of a fracas and spent a night locked up. If they were to find a Jerry in the cells alongside them . . . !

The constable's superior officer quickly confirmed that the military must be informed. Awaiting instructions from them, they were obliged to secure the pilot in one of their cells. Both policemen sounded quite apologetic about that. Gustav was slightly amused rather than perturbed. He had reported here to give himself up, it seemed to him unlikely that he would then abscond. He could not know that they were treading softly, afraid of sparking off trouble in an unknown situation.

There was a prolonged wait until army officers arrived, but Gustav could not complain regarding any aspect of his treatment. He was given tea to drink, and eventually a meal consisting of corned beef and mashed potato. Again, his sense of humour surfaced when he reflected that he might live better imprisoned than ever he had during those early months of 'freedom'.

The uncertainty about his ultimate punishment, however, was proving tiring, Gustav struggled as he attempted to marshal details that might explain his presence in Yorkshire. He needed to clear his head, to be ready for the inevitable interrogation.

Gustav was transferred to military premises before questioning could commence. Leaving the police station, he thanked his captors for their civilised treatment of him, and was rewarded by the astonishment in their eyes.

Gravity descended as soon as he was driven off in the military vehicle, and the sudden silence within the car told him that the interrogation would only begin in an appropriate setting. These people had no intention of sidestepping any regulations. That this was the way Gustav himself wanted the matter resolved was some consolation, while the quiet allowed him to continue mustering the facts concerning his arrival and subsequent stay in their country.

The room in which questioning would be conducted reminded him of Luftwaffe offices in Germany with its stark, utilitarian furniture and harsh lighting. At least, in no way did it resemble Gestapo premises. He had been given tea once more, and shown where to relieve himself; he could not criticise these people as uncivilised.

Two uniformed men were in the room already, one quite high-ranking, the other a sergeant who prepared to take notes. The senior officer faced him across a metal desk, glancing up from Gustav's documents which the police had passed on. Although sharp-featured and keen-eyed, the man spoke in calm, well-modulated tones that might be meant to reassure. *If* Gustav could trust him.

'You crashed, I believe you claim? That *is* your story?'

Gustav nodded. 'It is the truth. Towards the end of the war. I made a kind of log,' he added, indicating one of the papers. 'The date, and time of the crash, there are no further details. There was no navigator. I flew alone.'

The officer read back to him the date of the crash, received confirmation, and continued: 'And the airfield in Germany from which you flew out, it has a name . . . ?'

Gustav had been waiting for that question. 'It exists no longer,' he told them, and trusted that was the truth.

'Even so . . .' When no answer was forthcoming, the officer turned to a matter which was more relevant. 'Why was the aircraft never found? Our records have nothing on such an incident, there has been no report of an enemy aircraft being located anywhere in the area you indicate.'

'It was at night. The plane broke up on impact, the nose together with part of the fuselage buried itself in the moorland peat.'

'And the rest of the wreck . . . ?'

'Caught fire. Aviation fuel had spread everywhere. A few smaller pieces, chiefly of the interior, I buried.'

'The police tell me you claim you can take us to examine the site. Is that really so?'

'Indeed, yes. Why should I lie, I am not wishing to conceal anything.'

'But you *were*, were you not, originally? Your mission was to spy, wasn't it?'

'Spy?' Gustav echoed, incredulously. 'Why on earth would you suppose that?'

'The war in Europe was drawing towards its inevitable close. The German attack was being confined to V1s and V2s, the days of regular aerial bombardment were as good as over. I, therefore, find it hard to imagine what, other than espionage, your purpose in our skies might have been.'

Gustav said nothing. He did not mean to reveal anything about that final mission which had brought him over here. He had told them more than he need already and without any knowledge of how much the British understood of what had engaged the Luftwaffe at that particular time.

'Tomorrow, we shall visit the site. Without such an inspection, we cannot give any credence to your story.'

'That sounds just.'

The officer and his junior colleague stared at him, surprised.

Gustav slept more than he'd expected that night. He had found a sort of peace in giving himself up, and now felt reassured by knowing that he had done what was right. The morning held no fears, he had marked that spot on the moors and after months surviving in the vicinity was familiar with every contour of its terrain.

He was handcuffed in the vehicle, an unpleasant feature of the journey, but understandable on account of the area they were visiting. Gustav knew, didn't he, how readily one could avoid being seen out on the moors! Anyone choosing to make a break for freedom certainly would have an advantage. To him, however, such an escape would not be synonymous with freedom.

Reaching familiar ground made him emotional, gazing up to the left as they took the moorland road confronted him with Laneside House. Memories threatened to choke him – of the old lady who had taken him to her heart, most of all of Isobel.

Gustav swallowed, twice, quelled an enormous sigh while reminding himself that it was for love of her that he was trying to square things.

'Over to our left now, that track leading towards the summit of the moor,' he directed the driver. 'You will see an outcrop of rocks. Reaching it, you will notice a line of trees, absolutely due east of the rocks. Beyond the trees is a hollow where you will notice a small church, but we must go in the opposite direction.'

'Heading west?' he was asked when they reached the top.

He agreed. 'We must walk, I am sorry. It is not many yards from those rocks.'

Stumbling over tussocks and heathery roots, impeded by being linked to the officer, Gustav made slow progress. And somehow he did not wish to move any more swiftly. A great sadness was overtaking him, threatening all calm and resignation. He was ending an episode in his life, one in which he had been shown great kindness and where he'd discovered the quiet that is surrendering ambition to the acceptance of circumstances. He might have been happy, had he remained out here somewhere: had he not discovered the need to love a wonderful woman.

The place where fire had devoured a part of his aircraft could still be discerned. The earth was flattened, compacted, and scorching was visible still, with blackened twigs and undergrowth among a scattering of newly sprouting shoots.

'There's evidence of fire, sure enough,' declared one of the forensic experts who'd accompanied them in a second vehicle.

'And you claim you buried some parts of the aircraft?' the senior officer demanded.

'I show to you,' Gustav responded, leading them to a cluster of low rocks barely visible above the heather and bracken.

As soon as they applied spades to the earth where he demonstrated, the sound of metal grating on metal confirmed that he hadn't misled them. The peaty ground was soft and quickly yielded a portion of a pilot's seat, followed by scraps of a damaged instrument panel.

'I thought to take them with me, to substantiate my background,' said Gustav. 'But my leg was injured, infection overtook it, I could not travel anywhere.'

'I find it hard to believe that you survived out in the open like this, injured.'

'I had help, from a very kind woman who tended my wounds, fed me for a time.'

The uniformed men exchanged a disbelieving glance, sniffed.

Inwardly, Gustav shrugged. Whether or not they accepted the truth of his account seemed immaterial now. He had taken the first step to right the matter and ensure himself the quiet of mind which might, at some time in the future, allow him to contact Isobel on equal terms.

'I show to you now where it is that the plane hurled itself into the ground,' he announced, and led them a little way over the crest of the hill before pointing. 'On a good day, one may see how that the heather and gorse and other plants have formed a – a small hill.'

'A hillock?' the sergeant suggested.

'A hillock, yes. The plants grow very fast, I think, because of much rain here. And so it was that even I no longer saw very well where that my Heinkel impacted.'

The men with their spades began to investigate, and again struck metal with satisfying speed.

'Looks like we might have to believe this one. Or at least, some part of his tale.'

The senior man was again looking thoughtful. 'You will need to substantiate this, of course. Not difficult, I guess, since you mention having assistance from some woman.'

Gustav shook his head. 'Sadly, that very kind lady is dead.'

'There must have been someone else – one other person,

at least, who can testify to your having existed out here in the manner that you relate?'

'No one else, there was no one,' said Gustav. This was his problem, his alone. There was no one, nobody at all. He would not even contemplate the possibility of having Isobel contacted, expected by these people to speak on his behalf.

'You will be interned, you do understand? While our enquiries proceed, and until the veracity of your statements may be tested. I cannot promise that you will not face subsequent charges. In the meantime, you will find prisoners, even former enemies, naturally are treated less severely than they were during hostilities.'

The short stay with her mother and Marvin had produced quite an effect. Isobel couldn't have failed to enjoy dancing with Daniel and the excitement aroused by his kissess, but she'd quickly realised that the longing generated was altogether too disturbing. Even while experiencing this attraction, she had recognised it as almost entirely sensual. She had tried to ignore her misgivings, that evening with Daniel had provided the necessary distraction. But it also convinced her there was too little real love between them for the kind of relationship she needed.

By the following weekend Isobel knew that she had got to see Gustav again, if only to rid herself of this yearning which to her seemed based on little more than fantasy. In any one else, she would have ridiculed such near-obsession for being founded on no more than those few encounters during which she'd received sparse encouragement from Gustav to further their friendship.

She needed to test her intuition. Was there some reason perhaps why, somewhere within her, still persisted the feeling that Gustav experienced towards her much the same affection as she felt for him?

The verger smiled on finding Isobel at his door, yet he appeared slightly uncomfortable. When she asked if she might speak with Gustav, she learned the reason behind his awkwardness.

'Sorry, love. I'm afraid he's gone.'

'Gustav has?' She didn't wish to believe he would leave without speaking to her, without telling where he would be living.

'We're a bit taken aback, like, an' all. The vicar had told him about a job. Not here: over Rochdale way, with friends of his. Only Gustav hasn't taken that either. They were in touch to ask whether he wanted the work.'

Isobel was badly shaken. She had needed to test the impression Gustav had given, but hadn't wanted this. They had seemed to establish quite a rapport on that last occasion, how could he just go . . . ?

Fumbling for words because she was so distressed, she thanked Jack Ramsden, and walked wearily back up the hill.

From the summit, she stared dismally down at the rooftop of Laneside House, already afraid that everything she felt about her future home was marred by Gustav's disappearance. And then a thought occurred to her – he might have left word at the house, he had dropped off a note for her on another occasion.

Today, she had been so intent on enquiring at the verger's house that she hadn't even ventured inside her own place. Isobel ran down the hill towards her door.

There was no note.

Even the fact that Bert Bradshaw had completed fitting the bathroom did not cheer Isobel, all she could think of was the way in which Gustav had heaved that great bath into the house for her. And as for his tenderness while treating her wounded arm . . . She could live without that no more easily than she could imagine existing for ever without his loving.

Ridiculous though it would seem to anyone else, Isobel recognised that she always would associate this house with Gustav Kassel. He might have returned to his own country, and without saying goodbye to her, no matter what she did to the place she was afraid she might never cease to imagine him here.

Innate common sense took over before the day was ended. Isobel made herself work, washing out her lovely new bath, the handbasin, the lavatory. She cleaned the tiled floor next, removing every last footprint that the builder had left. The plastered walls were drying out nicely now, she must plan which colour would look best in here. The floor was of tiles salvaged from the outdoor lavatory, in a terracotta shade they should be flattered by a soft peach tone.

This reminded her of Daniel's colour scheme for his cottage, and further disturbed her. She had danced with him, had kissed him innocently enough, had responded to his kisses. Today, such actions felt close to a betrayal. *Of her feelings for Gustav.*

That seemed yet another ridiculous notion, especially in light of his off-hand dismissal of their friendship. Thinking about Gustav would have to cease. She had been a total fool to read so much into his kindness. If it required every last scrap of will-power, she would focus all her energy into making Laneside House look beautiful. The long-awaited time when she could begin decorating every room to her own taste was here. Somehow, she would rediscover her original inspiration.

Today, her kitchen with its memories of the time spent there with Gustav was too painful, but every room needed her attention. The bedroom that she intended using had a sound ceiling now, and any replastering was long-since dried out. She ought to take a look around up there, and decide finally on a colour scheme.

Gazing all around her from just inside the bedroom doorway, Isobel smiled to herself. In common with most of the house, the tendency was towards being too cool for comfort. Her innate knowledge of the effect produced by various shades would be very useful here. She would be able to select precisely the right tone for adding a little warmth without resulting in too much brightness.

Isobel thought she remembered that she had seen a bedspread stashed away somewhere. If that proved to be serviceable still, she could either wash it or take it to the cleaners, perhaps base her concept of that room upon it.

Although she had investigated the contents of that trunk more than once already, she'd never unpacked every item that it contained. She hadn't considered that she might discover something important there.

The object was wrapped in layers of newspaper, through which it felt hard, it seemed almost a foot wide and nine or ten inches high. When Isobel tried to lift the item out it was heavier than she expected, she had to use both hands.

Setting the thing carefully on the floor, she knelt down to tear off the paper wrapping. As soon as she discovered that she now possessed a marble clock, Isobel's eyes lit with delight. She had always considered that clocks seemed to be alive.

Turning the object around to examine the back, she saw its engraving, which told her this was a presentation made to Captain Edward Johnson to mark the ending of his service with the Grenadier Guards.

The body of the clock was black marble, with narrow, creamy-coloured inserts for decoration, but the whole thing looked quite grimy, she would need to learn how best to restore its condition. The face, though, seemed clean, and the hands were intact and appeared original. Opening the back, Isobel found no trace of any key, which was disappointing. Perhaps her best plan would be to take it somewhere for overhauling.

Isobel resolved to do that just as soon as her redecoration of this place provided a safe, suitable setting for the clock.

In the meantime, the find raised her spirits, issuing a much-needed reminder of her great-grandfather, and his love for Laneside House. This object reinforced the influence of those letters from the Tower and would spur her on, will her to re-create his family home.

Isobel's determination to concentrate her full attention and every free moment on the house was challenged less than a week later. She was busy as always at work in Leeds when she received a telephone call. Such private calls were permitted, but not encouraged, and she felt quite embarrassed when her boss handed the receiver across to her.

Daniel was on the other end of the line, surprising Isobel, until she realised that the mood of their last meeting would have led him to believe he should follow it up.

'I was wondering if you had anything planned for Saturday

afternoon,' he began. 'I thought we might go out somewhere, have high tea, or something.'

'Oh, Daniel, I'd love that,' she responded, not wishing to be unkind. 'But I've too much to do, at the house. The bathroom's finished, and I've got to make my mind up about the kitchen. Then I've got to start decorating one bedroom at least.'

'I could come with you. Might be able to offer a few ideas, could certainly put you wise on where to get paint supplies, they're still anything but readily obtained, you know.'

Isobel didn't need reminding about shortages, she experienced enough of those when her work demanded new fabrics. The war they'd all fought hadn't produced an easy life for anyone. Agreeing, she thanked him for the offer. But she did insist on their spending the whole Saturday at Laneside House, rather than the afternoon only.

'Fine with me,' said Daniel. 'And I'll bring a picnic meal, save you bothering if you have so much to do.'

When he arrived on his motorcycle, Daniel seemed to have so much food loaded on it that Isobel laughed.

'Who else have you arranged to meet there?' she exclaimed. 'I'm sure there's enough for four rather than two of us.'

'We'll be ravenous after all that work you're promising,' he retorted, kissing her cheek. 'We might even start on a bit of painting if you've decided on shades. There's a chap on our way out there. He's got quite a bit of distemper and stuff. Some of it's pre-war, but it seems to be all right still.'

Isobel hesitated. She could welcome Daniel's suggestions, perhaps, and she did need help obtaining materials. What she didn't intend was that he should do any of the actual work. Laneside House was *hers*, and keeping it that way entailed doing as much as possible of the renovation herself. She had been fortunate to employ Bert Bradshaw for the actual rebuilding, and that had been necessary, but she had felt at times that she might have loved to tackle more. She certainly didn't want anyone else to have a hand in the task.

Daniel seemed to understand when she explained, but she was happy to go with him to look at shades of paint and distemper, and to buy several cans while she could get them.

He was alarming her today with his account of future restrictions which would limit the use of materials to restoring war-damaged properties or in building their replacements.

The day was less of a success than Isobel had hoped. Although she did manage to acquire some distemper and paint, selecting them took quite a long time, and then she achieved very little once they arrived at Laneside House. Daniel was happy to go through from room to room with her while she told him which shades she was planning for each of them, but he couldn't continue to conceal his disappointment over Isobel's decision that *she* would do all the actual decorating.

She shouldn't have been surprised. She knew how swiftly and efficiently he'd done all the painting in his own cottage: standing around clearly was not something that he would find at all easy. Unfortunately, Isobel did not feel confident enough to begin tackling any of her walls while Daniel remained as an audience.

In the end they ate the food he'd brought along, and then set out for Halifax. He suggested an evening at the cinema where *Great Expectations* was showing, but Isobel had seen it already, and felt too on edge to be able to relax anywhere. She had intended making such a good start at the house, and wouldn't be happy until she was able to go there alone and make up for the time which she felt she had wasted.

'Sorry, I've been more of a hindrance than anything,' said Daniel as he went to pick up his motorbike after she drew up outside her flat. 'That wasn't my intention, you know.'

'I do know that. And I'm sorry too – it's just me being silly about wanting to do everything myself.'

Going indoors, Isobel felt utterly deflated. And also quite guilty. She'd been thankful enough to use Daniel's contact in order to obtain materials for the task, she needn't have blocked his efforts to give her a hand with the work.

Somewhere deep in her subconscious, she realised that she frequently felt to be on the defensive when Daniel was around. What on earth she might be dreading, Isobel could not imagine. He was the very last person she might suppose could persuade her to do anything against her wishes. He was so very nice, *too nice,* perhaps – too unexciting.

She would dismiss her unease about Daniel Armstrong tomorrow, by going out to Laneside House again, and spending the entire day slapping colour on to the walls of one bedroom.

This proved a good remedy for her mood, and by the time Sunday evening came Isobel headed back to the flat, feeling extremely tired but far happier about Laneside House. While packing up her tools she had gazed around the kitchen and was beginning to form ideas about the cupboards and shelving that she wished to install there. She had also decided to keep the original stone sink, and make a feature of it while improving the area for draining dishes to its right-hand side. At present, there was simply the slab of a similar stone, but she'd always liked the grooved wooden draining-board in her mother's old kitchen. She would have another word with Bert Bradshaw and learn if he could create something similar.

It occurred to her immediately that Daniel would be the obvious person to provide anything made out of wood, but she had no intention of contacting him. No matter what *he* might feel following their recent visit to Laneside House, she couldn't help sensing that she might be well-advised to avoid him for some little while.

Whatever else, she must not lead Daniel to believe that she was eager to deepen their relationship. She had decided to concentrate on renovating her future home, and there was little enough time for the task. Until that was finally completed to her own satisfaction, she would not be distracted by any man, especially while the physical attraction between them seemed to be the predominant feature.

Eight

Even surrounded by vast quantities of snow, Gustav could not dislike the camp. Indeed, he had adapted well to his surroundings. Living fifty or sixty to a hut produced its own benefits in these early months of 1947, providing enough heat through the sheer numbers of bodies sleeping each night there.

Once found innocent of any war-crimes, he had been treated better than he'd anticipated. The food was adequate, and from his arrival he'd relished regaining the company of his fellow Germans. Much about the circumstances of his stay resembled the life he had known during training as a pilot, and there were few restrictions so long as he, like the other inhabitants, kept to the rules.

Until this drifting snow stopped all outdoor tasks, the freedom he'd enjoyed was largely on a daily basis as he travelled back and forth to a nearby farm where the work he did caused Gustav a certain wry satisfaction. He was learning the sort of market gardening that would have been his job, had he taken up the position offered through the Rev Reginald Fieldhouse. In this instance, the scale of production was so massive that he suspected his potential experience could far exceed anything afforded elsewhere.

The farm manager and his immediate bosses all claimed to be happy with Gustav's methods of working, and he himself was grateful to be acquiring such a degree of skill. Always comprehending the futility of dwelling on the 'might-have-beens', he saw the sense in taking up opportunities, however much they should differ from past ambitions.

His future life was still in doubt, naturally. Many of his fellow-prisoners were being repatriated now, most weeks he lost a few among those who had become friends. He could no longer recall all of the occasions when he'd been told that he himself might expect to be freed. No one appeared fully to understand that his original problem of having no home to return to still applied.

With each account of the life he might discover in the region that he once called home, his desire to go there diminished. Since arriving at this camp, Gustav had been offered all possible assistance for tracing family members elsewhere in Europe. The news had not been good, confirming only what he had learned already.

As he had heard way back in 1945, any Germans still residing in the former Sudetenland were, indeed, driven out by the Czech authorities. During forced marches towards Bavaria and Austria, many had perished. Among those were listed his beloved sister and her husband.

Gustav had grieved afresh on receiving confirmation of the loss, but had been unsurprised by how few places in central Europe mattered to him. One or two around the Danube perhaps, in the Hinterbruhl where he had worked on that project resulting in his final mission. He had loved that area's scenery, its abbeys and monasteries.

His resolve to try his utmost to remain in Britain continued. He could not be the first to be disillusioned about the entire Nazi cause, hadn't he seen how the pre-war promises regarding his own people had failed to materialise? Likewise, he had been appalled when the truth about Belsen, Dachau and Auschwitz had emerged. Among his fellow-prisoners in this British camp existed the full spectrum of ideals, from staunch followers of the Nazi idiom to others, like himself, who were questioning the cause that they had felt obliged to support.

Perhaps because they were confined among such a range of theorists, few openly discussed their inner feelings, yet Gustav was heartened that it seemed he was not alone in seeking a future elsewhere than in Germany.

The expression 'displaced persons' had been much-used since the fighting across Europe had ended. *Displaced* felt to be an accurate term for himself, while he waited for at least some clue to where his future might place him.

Ideally, he hoped to be permitted to live out his dream of returning to Isobel once more, but only if by some means he acquired *something* worthy of offering. As a former enemy in a land foreign to him, that prospect seemed difficult, if not unlikely. And if, for himself, he was prepared to exist by labouring on some farm, he could not visualise inviting her to share that – unless his spirit underwent some massive feat of adjustment!

Isobel wasn't sorry that she had resigned from her designing job at the end of 1946. The terrible snows were rendering travelling anywhere difficult, and she could relish avoiding the daily journey into Leeds. The chief problem now was that she was virtually cut off from her home at Laneside House, therefore prevented from continuing any work there.

She had tried several times to get through, but even her Jeep baulked at the depth of snow. It had drifted from the top of one drystone wall to its partner where they normally marked the sides of every road beyond the towns.

Isobel was bored, and more than a little uneasy about the condition of her empty house. Although confident that Bert Bradshaw's work had left the property sound, fully water-tight, she was less happy about the plumbing and how it might succumb to the sharp frosts accompanying these heavy snowfalls. She would be extremely upset if burst pipes were to damage any newly decorated walls, or to ruin the carpet, stored after the sale of her former terraced home, and recently installed in her living-room.

On the day that she made her third fruitless attempt to get out on to the moors, she drove through a blizzard back to the flat feeling utterly dejected. Despite having this tiny place in the town, she felt just as cut off from everyone as she might have had she been able to reach the home that she'd inherited.

During her journey through the Halifax streets, she had called at Diana's house, and had found her friend already entertaining a group of people. She could see Betty and Louise, Richard, and two other men whom she knew from the dramatic society.

Diana was smiling when she explained. Those who taught were at home as most schools were closed, the rest had finished work early that afternoon, several businesses were ensuring employees were not stranded in yet another snowfall.

When Diana didn't invite her in for even a chat, much less to spend the evening there, Isobel couldn't help feeling upset. Admittedly, she hadn't seen her friends very regularly since beginning to decorate Laneside House, but they all knew how busy she was and might have understood why her time normally was so limited.

It wasn't until she had cooked herself a meal and was sitting down to eat, that Isobel realised that there could be some significance in the identity of those of her friends who were meeting at Diana's place. During her absence the three women could very easily have formed relationships with the men she'd seen that evening. Hadn't she thought Diana was becoming very friendly with Richard, for instance?

Isobel herself wasn't the only one who had missed out during the war years, which had provided an abnormal existence where courting and becoming engaged had not ensued along the usual routes. The others were of a similar age to herself, and could not be blamed if they were making up for the time they saw as lost.

Although this could explain the situation regarding that evening, Isobel's dissatisfaction intensified. She reflected on how her preoccupation with Laneside House, to say nothing of the actual physical work there, was preventing her from meeting anyone she might love. Except for Gustav Kassel, she thought grimly, and tried yet again to resign herself to the facts. If she had been right to believe he cared at all about her, he could not have gone out of her life without saying one word.

She shook her head over the irony. The letter written by her great-grandfather which had compelled her to take on the house had emphasised the need to make it a *family* home. Yet now she was afraid that restoring the place was likely to be the very task that would last so long that she never would be free to even think about having any kind of personal life.

Regarding the restoration, there seemed no end to the difficulties. Her supplies of paint and distemper were all but used up, and no traders she could find were offering anything to people not engaged in repairing war damage. Less than a month ago in January, George Tomlinson, the Minister of Works, had announced that no one would be allowed to spend more than ten pounds on private repairs without permission. Isobel would not dare to apply for consent. She'd always feared that the materials Daniel had helped her obtain might be forbidden, and she certainly didn't want anyone to begin looking into the rights or wrongs of having Bradshaw renovate all that structural damage for her. If there had been regulations against that at the time, she hadn't known of them, but she supposed that would never prove a valid excuse.

By the time that the worst of the deep snow cleared sufficiently for Isobel to be able to reach Laneside House again, she had completed sketches of the rooms still needing attention. On each page she had used watercolours to indicate her desired effect for the walls and had sketched in where her furniture should be placed. Although this wasn't much of a contribution, it made her feel that she had done something towards completing her renovation of the place.

She had brought a spade with her in the Jeep, and saw as soon as she headed uphill off the main road that she certainly would need to use it. The track that led towards the house from the road was hardly visible at all, so deep was the snow remaining on the moors. The property itself still had drifts reaching to halfway up the doors and ground-floor windows, but she couldn't be surprised to find that situation. Some photographs in the *Halifax Courier* had shown houses beyond the town with snow up to the bedroom windows, and gas-lamps buried almost to their tops.

The effort of digging out a route as far as the garden and up to the kitchen door kept her warm, and Isobel was relieved to find that the interior did not feel quite so cold as she'd expected. Perhaps the surrounding banks of snow had provided their own form of insulation. Certainly, her rapid

120

inspection of the building revealed no evidence that any of the pipes had frozen solid and subsequently burst.

She had brought with her enough wood and coal to light a fire in the living-room grate, and she intended using that to heat water in the old kettle that she kept at the house. There had been so many warnings against using unnecessary fuel, that she would avoid lighting the gas burners on the cooker.

While drinking the hot cocoa which she preferred to milk-less tea, Isobel studied the colour sketches that she had brought with her. This kitchen was the next room which she must finish off properly, and she really would have loved to have lots of new shelving and cupboards plus, ideally, a replacement for that ancient cooker. Most of such ideas would have to wait for a time when restrictions eased, but in the meantime she intended contacting Bert Bradshaw again to discuss the question of having that new draining-board she fancied beside the sink.

The sink itself, being stone, wasn't particularly attractive but she had scrubbed it from time to time, and had discovered that the tap responded well to being subjected to regular bursts of elbow-grease.

As for the storage-space she would require when living permanently there, she might have to make do with a few boxes instead of anything more elaborate.

Isobel was still considering the problem of storing possessions when she recalled the period of her mother's move to Marvin's air base. Had Amy, in fact, been obliged to place in store some of the smaller items of furniture from the old family home? She could telephone her mother and at least find out if there was anything suitable.

Back in Halifax, Isobel rang Amy from the telephone box on the corner of the street even before parking the Jeep in its usual spot outside her flat. Delighted to hear from her daughter, Amy chatted for a while enquiring how she had coped during the worst of the deep snow. When Isobel finally got around to asking about any furniture which might be available, she was rather disappointed.

'Eh, love – I can't rightly remember just what there was

that we didn't fit in here. Marvin might know, but he's on duty just now. Tell you what – why don't you come over? Now the snow's gradually disappearing, the journey wouldn't be so bad. And it's ages since we saw you.'

As there wasn't a great deal that Isobel could achieve at Laneside House before obtaining further materials, she agreed to visit her mother and Marvin. They arranged that should be during the following weekend, provided the journey wasn't made impossible by further snowfalls.

Leaving the telephone box and getting back into the Jeep, Isobel felt happier for speaking to her mother. When she drew up outside the flat, she was astonished to see Daniel waiting outside the door.

'How long have you been standing around here? You must be frozen through!'

'Only a minute or two, actually. I saw the Jeep was out, and your landlady was just off to the shop, she said I could wait inside with her when she came back. Anyway, here you are so everything's all right. I was beginning to wonder when I saw you drive straight past the end of the street.'

Isobel smiled. 'Only as far as the phone box. Wanted to speak to my mother. You'd better come in now, any road, warm yourself up again.'

She put the kettle on before removing her coat. The flat felt very cold, and the electric fire she used when she hadn't time to light a coal one gave off very little heat.

'How is your mother?' Daniel asked, taking the chair she offered. 'I trust she's all right?'

'Fine, she says, and I believe that. The US Air Force look after them, I should think. They won't have let lots of snow pile around their accommodation, I'll bet.'

'And I wouldn't be surprised if they had fewer restrictions than us about heating, and so on,' Daniel added, his friend Vince seemed to find life there congenial.

'I finally managed to get as far as Laneside House today,' Isobel announced, spooning tea into the pot. 'Fourth time lucky, I hadn't been able to reach it before.'

'Failing to make it there wouldn't please you. You like to get on with things, don't you?'

'When I've got the necessary stuff, but that's another story. Anyway, the house seems all right. No burst pipes, thank heaven! That had been my worst fear. At least, before another winter I shall be living there, I shan't be worrying over the place from a distance. That was why I spoke to Mum, actually. Wanted to know if they still have bits of furniture in store from the old place.'

'And has she?'

'You know Amy – can't remember for sure now. I'm going over there to find out, next weekend, I think.'

Daniel looked worried. 'Shouldn't you wait until you see what the weather's like? If there's any more snow, you could be in for a terrible journey. East Anglia can be as bleak and windswept as anywhere.'

'I'll be all right. So long as the main roads are open, that Jeep'll get me there.'

'Mind if I come with you? I'll not have an easy minute, otherwise.'

Isobel hesitated. Would agreeing to his offer encourage him to believe there might be more between them?

'For heaven's sake, Isobel – that wouldn't be committing you to anything!'

'Sorry, sorry. It's good of you to offer. Thanks. I'll be glad of your company. And Mum and Marvin will be pleased to see you again.'

'I'll ring them up, and square it with them. Pity you're not on the phone, we could have done that today.'

'I shall have to be – on the phone, I mean, when I'm living at Laneside House. Being somewhere that remote is going to take a bit of getting used to.'

When the day came for travelling to East Anglia, they used the train. Isobel suspected that was Daniel's idea, although he claimed that the suggestion was Marvin's. They were to be picked up from the nearest station, from where he and Amy would drive them to the furniture warehouse.

The train was running late, had been half an hour behind schedule for most of the way from Peterborough, and Isobel was becoming agitated.

'They'll be that glad to see you, they won't mind the wait,'

Daniel assured her. 'If I know those American cars, it'll be nice and warm for sitting around in. And you know Marvin – he'll not let your mother worry.'

'You mean she won't be like me,' said Isobel tetchily, embarrassed by showing her unease even though the snow covering that still remained explained delays.

Daniel laughed. 'When I didn't know you so well, I might have risked saying "like mother, like daughter" – not any more.'

Even Daniel looked perturbed, however, when they finally emerged from the station and found no American car awaiting them, no sign anywhere of either Marvin or his wife.

'Happen they've gone to find themselves a hot drink somewhere,' he suggested. 'The station staff would know how late our train would be.'

'They *did* say they'd come and pick us up?' Isobel asked. 'You did get that right?' Not all that accustomed herself to phoning people, she could believe mistakes easily made.

'Marvin even looked up the trains from his end, confirmed the time he would see us here.'

'No mistake then.' Isobel wished there had been room for error, anything was preferable to this increasing sense of panic.

When half an hour had passed and the car was still nowhere in sight, Daniel too was becoming anxious. The roads were treacherous in places, and the chilling winds in these eastern counties would create ice from any damp in hitherto clear spots.

A further fifteen minutes went by, and Daniel headed towards the telephone box. He had a note of Marvin's number. Of course there was no reply when he dialled. Another number he had was for the base itself, he had used that previously to contact his friend Vince.

The man on the other end could tell them nothing. Marvin's vehicle would have been booked out when it went through security on the gate, but checking on that would require time.

Daniel was replacing the receiver when a bus drew up. Enquiring about its destination, they learned it would pass quite close to the US base.

'We'd better get on that, hadn't we?' said Isobel. 'If we keep our eyes peeled we would notice any car that has broken down.'

They saw the car about a mile along the road. It had slewed off to the left and the whole front end was embedded in a concrete wall.

'Oh, God,' breathed Isobel.

Daniel swore, then called to the bus driver.

The man was stopping the bus anyway, leaping from his cab and running to reach the wreckage ahead of them. Isobel strained an ankle jumping off the bus platform and staggered, limping, across the road.

Daniel slithered to a halt and grabbed the car's passenger door, struggling to open it. He could see Amy's head was bleeding where it rested against the windscreen. Motionless, she looked to be unconscious. Beside her Marvin was crammed against the steering wheel, his head slumped on its upper rim. There was neither sound nor movement from him.

'They're dead, aren't they!' screeched Isobel at his side.

The bus driver was sprinting around the car to the driver's door. After wrestling for a few moments he succeeded in forcing it open. Marvin's shoulder shifted with the movement, his head lolled ominously to one side.

Suddenly so sick she was sure she would faint, Isobel felt Daniel's hand grasping her arm, and leaned her head against him.

'They could still be alive,' he insisted, though he doubted that Marvin had survived. 'We've got to get help, soon as we can.'

One of the bus passengers was running towards them. 'I'm a doctor, let's take a look,' he called.

With one swift glance in Marvin's direction, he concentrated on Amy. Her door was jammed and he was obliged to lean right across the American to reach her. His practised hand found the pulse in her neck and he nodded. 'A bit weak, but she's made it so far.'

'This is her daughter,' Daniel explained hurriedly. 'They were supposed to be meeting us and – well, you see the rest.'

The doctor looked searchingly at Isobel's pallid face and horrified eyes. 'Not going to pass out on us, are you? These people need all the attention we can muster.' He faced the bus driver. 'You must know this route. Where's the nearest house?'

The driver nodded to the road ahead. 'Round that next bend. Let's hope they have a phone.'

The doctor nodded. 'Fast as you can then. Get them to send an ambulance, and the police. I'll do what I can here.'

Shaking with shock, Isobel clung to Daniel, watching as the doctor tried to locate a pulse somewhere on Marvin, but she saw him shake his head. Her dread concerning her stepfather was confirmed when the doctor again turned from him to concentrate on her mother. Forcing open a rear door, the man flung himself into the back to reach over and check Amy's pulse.

'Mustn't move her, not even an inch,' he told them. 'There's no knowing what damage she's suffered – could cause more serious harm.'

Or kill her, thought Isobel, who'd learned some first aid during her war-work.

The ambulance arrived after what felt to be an interminable wait, by which time Isobel was shivering violently, steadied only by Daniel wrapping both arms around her. The doctor confirmed to the ambulance people that Amy was still alive, but shook his head regarding Marvin.

Isobel heard a moan, and realised it was her own. Daniel was explaining who she was, and how they had been in the bus when they discovered the accident. Its driver had long since returned from phoning to give what information he could before crossing to put his passengers in the picture.

Together with the wrecked car, their bus was almost blocking the road. As first on the scene, they should in any case wait for the arrival of the police.

The ambulance crew were tending Amy as she sat trapped in the car. Her head wound was bleeding heavily, and they were whispering between them concerning possible internal injuries.

Isobel shuddered, felt herself losing consciousness, and

heard Daniel say, 'Steady on, Isobel love, get a grip, eh? I'm hanging on to you.'

'Thank God you are, thank God,' she murmured, and sobbed.

She began taking control of herself as they were about to lead her towards the bus. 'You need to sit down,' its driver was saying.

'No, no,' she insisted. 'That's my mother in there. I'm stopping with her.'

The doctor who had tended Amy nodded. 'You can go in the ambulance with her,' he told Isobel gently. 'Just as soon as they get her out of the car.' He glanced to Daniel. 'There'll be another team on its way to take the car driver.'

The police were the next to arrive, coming with the necessary signs to erect in order to prevent other vehicles running into the crash scene. When they had spent some time by Marvin's car, acquiring details from everyone present, they took down all available information from the bus driver and allowed him to proceed on his way.

While the bus remained there Isobel had agreed to sit on the seat just inside its door, and somehow was managing to stay on her feet afterwards. Eventually, when Amy was being stretchered into the ambulance, Daniel helped Isobel to totter towards it and clamber inside.

'I'll deal with the police,' he told her. 'Then catch up with you at the hospital.'

'But I don't know where it is,' said Isobel feebly, desperate to keep him with her.

'The police will know. Most likely, will take me there very soon.'

All the way to hospital Isobel sat rigidly in the ambulance, keeping her gaze on her mother's face, willing her to live. The man who was tending Amy looked as perturbed as Isobel was feeling. She couldn't help fearing the worst.

Fortunately, the hospital didn't seem far away, and Amy's stretcher was soon on the move again as she was hastened through the doors and along a short corridor. The staff seemed to be expecting them, a woman doctor came running and at her side one of the sisters, while Amy was being transferred on to a bed.

The doctor's glance at her patient was swift, and frowning. Isobel heard her sigh. 'That head wound's bad, but I'm afraid we've got to be prepared for learning she has other, more serious, injuries. I've got a theatre on stand-by, we're going straight there. I'll give her a more thorough examination before we proceed, of course, but I'm afraid it sounds as though we should operate. Are you a relative?'

'Her daughter, yes. What – where is it you think she's hurt?'

'Internally somewhere, from what the ambulance chaps gave us. The spleen's often one organ to suffer. Can't tell until we begin exploring. Unconscious like this, she can't give her own consent to surgery, I hope you're not about to make that a difficulty?'

Isobel shook her head. 'Just – save her. Please. Do whatever you have to.'

'We shall do whatever is possible, you may be assured of that.'

A staff nurse appeared and grasped Isobel by the arm. 'I'll show you where you can wait. Miss Hardesty, the surgeon, will send word of what they intend just as soon as she's performed a thorough examination.'

'Thank you,' said Isobel dully. 'This is all my fault,' she added. 'They were coming to pick us up.'

'You have somebody with you then?' The nurse brightened.

'A friend. He stayed behind with the car, someone had to give the police details. My – my step-father's dead, you see. In the crash.'

'Oh, I'm so sorry. I didn't know there was more than one victim.'

'My mother's not dead, though, is she? You're not keeping something from me?'

'We don't do that. You heard Miss Hardesty – she wouldn't be speaking of surgery if there wasn't some hope. Now, you can sit here, and you'll be kept fully informed of what intervention might prove necessary. Can I get someone to find you a cup of tea?'

'Not for the minute, thanks. I feel so sick I couldn't keep anything down.'

Daniel came striding in as the staff nurse was turning away. Isobel sprang to her feet, but wobbled unsteadily and he hurried to ease her back on to the upholstered bench.

'Where've they taken your mother, love?' he asked, looking towards a nearby ward.

'Off to the theatre – upstairs, I think. They were heading towards the lift. The surgeon said she might have to operate.'

'On Amy's head?'

'Don't think so. She was saying Mum might have damaged her inside. They seem to suspect she's bleeding in other places. Oh, I don't know . . .'

Sitting at her side, Daniel placed an arm around her shoulders, hugged her to him. 'That's right, lean on me – in every sense. I'm just thankful you weren't on your own.'

'This might not have happened if I had been. I keep thinking everything would have been all right if I'd driven here in the Jeep.'

Or *you* could have been rammed into some wall somewhere, or a telegraph post, thought Daniel, but he didn't mention what that would have done to him. He had sensed for some while that Isobel had a problem with accepting how he felt about her; this was not the time for piling more difficulties on to her.

'Marvin was dead, wasn't he?' she asked him.

'I'm afraid so. Instantaneous, the police believe.'

'Poor Marvin, and he was only trying to help us, me as well as Mum. That's what he's always been like, you know. He really was marvellous.' She exhaled in a long-drawn-out sigh. 'However will we begin to tell my mother?'

'Don't start worrying about that today, Isobel love. She won't need to be told until she gets a lot stronger.' Daniel went on to ask if she had given any details about her mother at the reception desk.

Isobel shook her head. 'Nobody's asked me to, as yet. I was just told to sit here. Miss Hardesty – the surgeon – is going to let me know if they have to operate.'

As she was speaking the nurse who had accompanied the

surgeon came walking towards them. She sat beside Isobel, placed a hand on her arm.

'I'm afraid an operation is going to be necessary, my dear Miss Hardesty is convinced there is a quantity of internal bleeding which must be investigated. I'm sorry to say there are also further injuries, fractures, cracked ribs. This does mean that we shall be looking at an extended recovery period.'

'But she will recover?' Isobel persisted.

'We shall be doing all we can. In the meantime, if you could give your mother's personal details to the clerk at the desk. She will complete the necessary documentation and supply guidance.' The nurse turned to Daniel. 'I take it you are staying with – ' She looked towards Isobel. 'I'm afraid no-one's told me your name.'

'Isobel – Isobel Johnson. And my mother is Amy Conquest, it's her second marriage.'

The nurse showed them where to find the reception desk. Before rushing away, she warned that Amy might have to spend several hours in surgery.

'We'll find a waiting-room somewhere, make sure someone knows where to find us when there's any news,' said Daniel, taking charge.

'I don't think I can bear any of this,' Isobel confided as soon as they were left alone. 'It's all so gruelling. And I can't stop wondering how ever we'll break the news to her that Marvin has died.'

Nine

The hospital people were very good. They showed Isobel and Daniel to a tiny room where they could wait alone, and provided her with a blanket when she couldn't stop shivering due to the shock.

Eventually, in the early hours of the morning Miss Hardesty herself came to tell them about the operation. As she'd suspected, Amy's spleen was badly damaged and had had to be removed.

'She'll get along without it,' the surgeon assured them. 'But I'm afraid there were further injuries. A couple of ribs had fractured, penetrating a lung, we've done what we could to repair that.'

'When can I see her?' Isobel enquired. Until she did so, she wouldn't believe that her mother was alive.

'We'll let you know in the morning. For the present, she's still heavily sedated and that will take a long time to wear off.'

Shortly after the surgeon left them a member of staff appeared and asked if they wished to go home. 'Your mother won't be fit for receiving visitors for a while yet, anyway. It wouldn't hurt you both to get some sleep.'

'I couldn't,' said Isobel. 'In any case, we've nowhere to go locally. We live in Yorkshire.'

'I might be able to do something about that, once we have seen Amy,' said Daniel when they were alone again. 'I've got to speak to the base as soon as it's morning. Make sure the police have reported what's happened to Marvin. They might have spare rooms they'd give us for a night or two.'

When Isobel finally was taken into a ward to see her mother, she was even more shocked then earlier. No amount

131

of warning not to be alarmed by the array of obligatory tubes and wires could have prepared her for how altered Amy seemed. She was just about conscious, but totally unable to speak, and her eyelids kept drooping over eyes that looked glazed.

For a while Isobel sat beside the bed with her hand grasping Amy's arm. Every few moments she would say something, but her mother wasn't fit to respond. After a time Daniel suggested that they should have a word with the ward sister to obtain more information regarding Amy's condition. He could see that they weren't doing any good in the ward, and Isobel was making herself ill with anxiety.

As expected, they again were told that they must not hope for any rapid improvement. Amy's injuries were serious and the necessary surgery had placed its own degree of stress on the body.

'If you can rest somewhere and come back later, it would do you both good,' the sister advised. 'There truly isn't anything for you to do here.'

'What do you think's best?' Isobel asked Daniel. She could see well enough that they weren't achieving anything, but she hadn't the heart to decide to desert her mother.

'I think a few hours' break might mean we were then better able to cope,' Daniel suggested. 'The US base is no distance from here – if they can find us somewhere to hang around, we'll still be able to keep in contact with Amy's ward.'

The authorities at the airbase couldn't have been more helpful. As soon as Isobel and Daniel arrived in a taxi, they said how deeply saddened they were by Marvin's death, and they'd be only too willing to assist his step-daughter until Amy's condition improved. They gave no hint that they might doubt that her mother would recover, and that alone helped Isobel, who had been deflated by the hospital's cautious prognosis.

She and Daniel were allowed use of accommodation which temporarily was empty. Designed for a single person, it was extremely basic, consisting of a tiny kitchen, bathroom, and a bed-sitting room, but for them it provided what they needed.

Daniel insisted immediately that Isobel should rest on the

bed. 'I'll lie on the settee,' he added, after tucking a blanket around her. The room was cool but, as they had supposed earlier, the base had been cleared of much of the snow and ice affecting the rest of the country.

To her surprise, Isobel slept, but only for around four hours, and then she was wide awake, urging Daniel to help her find a telephone.

'I've got to discover if there's any change in my mother, can't rest any longer till we know.'

Together, they went to find the man who'd organised their stay, and he directed them to the public phone. As Daniel had feared, there was no improvement to report, but he persuaded Isobel to wait until evening visiting before returning to the hospital.

Re-entering the ward, Isobel was struck by how ill her mother looked, worse even than she recalled.

'Has she deteriorated?' she asked one of the nurses, but was assured that there had been no change in their patient's condition.

This situation was to continue for days. On the Sunday Isobel asked if Daniel wouldn't have to return to Yorkshire to get on with his job. She dreaded being on her own, but she would remain there for as long as her mother needed her. And she couldn't allow him to make too many sacrifices when he had his business to consider.

Daniel explained that he now had an apprentice who was very reliable, he would telephone him on the Monday morning, and the lad would get on with the work awaiting them.

Isobel was so relieved that she didn't even check that Daniel really believed the young man would cope without him. All her normal self-reliance had drained out of her under the strain of discovering that car accident. The whole future had altered. From being content that her mother would always be well-cared for, she had been plunged into wondering what on earth she herself would be expected to do.

Even if Amy were eventually to get over these injuries, she would need looking after. Isobel had nowhere suitable for tending someone who was convalescing: the flat was too small for one person, never name two, and Laneside House wasn't nearly restored sufficiently yet. An even more pressing anxiety concerned Marvin's funeral, she supposed that as his step-daughter she ought to take in hand the arrangements.

Noticing her preoccupation, Daniel asked if she was worrying about something in addition to her mother's condition.

'Yes, I am, actually. This may not be the time yet, but I can't stop wondering if I'm supposed to be doing something about Marvin. There'll have to be a funeral, and somebody's got to see to it.'

'We'll have a word with the people here about that. They'll have some idea of how to set about it. They also will have records of what relatives he has in America.'

The officer who invited them to talk over arrangements asked them to sit in a small but comfortable office where he quickly made them at ease.

'Whilst this, naturally, is a distressing time, we aim to assist in making everything progress as smoothly as we may. We already have contacted Marvin's mother in the States, after reaching her via his brother. Old Mrs Conquest, unfortunately, is not a well person and will be unlikely to attempt the journey across the Atlantic. For this reason, his brother leans towards a cremation rather than burial – provided, of course, that this does not conflict with your own wishes.'

'I haven't really thought that far ahead,' Isobel admitted.

'That's understandable – you have the deep anxiety regarding your mother also. Until such time as she shows more sign of improvement, your preoccupation must be with her. However, you may feel assured that we shall do however much you require of us when making arrangements for Marvin.'

'Thank you so much, that is a relief to me,' she told him. 'I imagine we shall be guided by you regarding the sort of funeral, but that will depend, of course, on what my mother wishes.'

When we tell her, thought Isobel, and again began to dread explaining to Amy that Marvin had been killed.

The officer was nodding sympathetically. 'May I take this opportunity to say that we have always been impressed by the way in which your mother has integrated into life here. Adapting to a US base can't have been that easy for her, but she has settled well. If there is any means by which we may assist her, I trust that you will let us know.'

The help and reassurances which they received at Marvin's base were the only good things during the following anxious days. Amy's strength appeared to increase only to then diminish with a regularity that became alarming. Once or twice during their visits to the ward Amy would rally slightly and manage to speak, but although she seemed to recognise Daniel as well as Isobel, few of her words made sense. Isobel felt that it was too soon to try to break the news about Marvin to her, a view with which the nurses agreed.

On the rare occasions when they secured a word with Miss Hardesty, the surgeon declared that she was confident that operating had been successful, and further surgery seemed unlikely. However, she reminded Isobel of the warning that recovery would be slow.

Isobel was unable to become at all optimistic. Visiting daily when her mother appeared no better was wearing her down. At the end of the first week when Daniel was compelled to rush home to catch up on business matters, she found it difficult to avoid sinking into depression.

Dependable as ever, Daniel had promised to telephone her at the base during his stay in Yorkshire. When she was summoned to the office to take a call early one morning, Isobel hurried there eager to hear his voice.

'Miss Johnson?' the woman at the other end of the line asked, and then continued when Isobel confirmed her identity. 'I am terribly sorry to have to inform you that Mrs Conquest died an hour ago. The cause will have to be confirmed, naturally, but we suspect she suffered a massive haemorrhage following those injuries.'

'Oh, God, no!' Although she had been fearing that her mother might not recover completely, Isobel hadn't until that moment anticipated that she might receive this news. And Daniel was miles away near Halifax.

The woman went on to add that Mrs Conquest's personal possessions would be retained for Isobel to collect, and when she was able to attend the hospital they would acquaint her with details of the procedure regarding registering the death and so on. Everyone would assist in any way they could.

A similar offer was made at the US base as soon as she told the person who had summoned her to the phone. She thanked him dully, and asked to have a call put through to Daniel's number.

There was no reply. Isobel had half expected that he would be out checking on a job somewhere, especially after he had spent so many days away from the business. So, it was all down to her, she though dismally, preparing to go back to their temporary quarters and get ready for facing everything at the hospital.

The few belongings which Amy had had with her when admitted looked pitiful in a hospital bag, making Isobel want to weep, as she hadn't as yet that morning. Only the fact of being alone and obliged to take in the necessary details prevented her from breaking down. The procedure was explained slowly and thoroughly, and sounded quite complex, perhaps more so due to Amy's marriage to an American serviceman.

The bits that she understood immediately, Isobel jotted down. Her memory was no longer to be trusted while this all felt totally unreal. She was able to grasp that the certificate of death would only be available once the cause was finally established. Ahead of that, however, she might wish to discuss provisional funeral arrangements, and a funeral director could be recommended.

Isobel heard herself mentioning that the USAAF already had in mind arrangements for Marvin Conquest's funeral, and that his family considered that should be a cremation. She herself only knew that she was shattered, totally unsure of her wishes regarding her mother. Just as she was unsure whether she wished to see Amy's body.

That might be something she should do, *if* Daniel were with her. Alone, she could probably give in and sob. And she'd decided there was too much needing attention now for her to go to pieces.

Somehow, Isobel got through the day. She saw a funeral director, discussed choice of a coffin, and explained that she needed a bit of time before confirming that a cremation would be appropriate. A part of her wanted to take Amy home, to lay her to rest in a family grave in their beloved Halifax. Common sense asserted that tending a grave in the town when she herself intended living miles away over the moors did appear to lack practicality. If she opted for a cremation, she might place the ashes alongside Alfred Johnson in his grave – or she could scatter them over moorland close to Laneside House.

It was late evening before Isobel succeeded in contacting Daniel, still at his desk, and sounding as though he had tackled two weeks' work in the one day.

She told him all in a rush that her mother had died, not at all in the manner that she had meant to convey the news. He sounded distressed when saying how sorry he was.

Isobel felt she must say something to make him feel better. 'I think it's going to be all right. We don't have to worry how ever we're going to tell her that Marvin didn't make it.'

Only it wasn't all right. Nothing would be the same ever again. She clattered the receiver down, sobbing too wildly to speak.

The news Gustav received was not something he could ever have anticipated. He was called into the camp office one morning, and felt surprised to be greeted with a wide smile by the British officer behind the desk.

'Excellent news,' the man began. 'Concerning your future.'

Gustav swallowed down an instant protest. He had no desire to be told yet again that he would be free to return to his homeland. He'd already explained too many times that he had no homeland awaiting him. No home, no family, nothing.

'You had not revealed to us the precise nature of the work engaging you prior to your crash-landing . . .' the officer continued.

Gustav raised an eyebrow, smiled back, ruefully. The secret

nature of his work had prevented such a mention, from the time of that crash, and throughout the repeated questioning after giving himself up.

'Your work, your *experience* have far greater value than any of us here could have guessed, Herr Kassel. Fortunately for you, your name is known – and respected as a test-pilot – far beyond your own country.'

Gustav allowed his own smile to widen, felt excitement stirring, exhilaration. He had never dared even to hope, yet . . .

'In the process of inspecting documents regarding repatriation, your name came before certain authorities who comprehended precisely who you are, and the quality of your previous work. To cut a very long story to the vital information, the Americans would be very interested in engaging your co-operation.'

'The Americans?' Gustav's earlier elation was deflated. He had no desire to live in the United States.

'It's no secret that their technology is way ahead of ours, surely? And I understand your role as test-pilot was advanced – especially on jet-powered aircraft.'

Gustav nodded. 'I could take you to the wreckage of one – unless your authorities removed what was left of it.'

'I believe that has been done; further investigation ensued when our people learned of the development work engaging you at – ' the man paused, glanced down at documents on the desk. ' – At the underground site in the Hinterbruhl.'

Gustav allowed himself a quiet laugh. 'So – our very secret work is secret no longer. Also, it would seem, our Heinkel 162 has won international interest.'

An entire new vista of possibilities was opening before him. Excitement renewed its surge. He might work again as a pilot, challenge his brain once more in development, prove he'd lost none of his skills. In *America* though . . . ?

'That particular aircraft, perhaps,' the officer went on. 'Although it could be that model is superceded already by something more advanced, technologically.'

'As is more likely, I suppose. No matter, looking to the next stage must always be the way if we are to advance.'

The man across the desk eased himself upright in his seat, faced Gustav squarely, but with a degree of embarrassment. 'I am obliged to ask this of you, and caution that this could be only the beginning of such an enquiry. But – where do your loyalties lie now? If you were to be accepted for any work of a development nature the authorities would need to be confident of your commitment to them.'

'Naturally. May I, in turn, ask something of you – why do you suppose I have not taken up any one of the opportunities to return to Germany? Had I retained any loyalty towards the Nazi cause, or any other, I should not have remained over here.'

'But you do not leap at the chance to find a new life in the USA?'

The man was observant. Gustav acknowledged that with another smile. 'It is something I had not contemplated. To be honest, I feel comfortable with the British way of life. Were there similar opportunities for employing my knowledge and any skills here, I would settle in England gladly.'

The officer glanced through the papers before him again, considered briefly, then met Gustav's gaze.

'To date, the US offer is the only one that's on the table. Yet I can't believe we ourselves are not active in such an advancing field. If you wish, we could make the necessary enquiries. That might, of course, occasion considerable delay. And I feel compelled to point out that the remuneration available is likely to be a lot lower that whatever you might be offered on the other side of the Atlantic.'

Gustav grinned. 'Since landing so unceremoniously in Yorkshire, I have learned to live on practically nothing. Your camp here is luxury to me. You may take it that I do not seek a massive salary. Wherever I go.'

Only, pray God, that should not render him unable to see Isobel again.

Daniel arrived during the following day, and found Isobel no longer in that temporary accommodation. She was beginning already on the huge task of sorting through everything in the home that Amy and Marvin had shared.

Opening the door to his knock, Isobel flung herself into Daniel's arms. 'Thank God you've come,' she exclaimed. 'I do need you here.'

He hugged her close, smoothed her hair affectionately, then kissed her cheek.

'I couldn't get back quickly enough. I am so sorry, my love, about your mother.'

Isobel nodded as they drew apart. 'It was a blow, even though we'd seen that she hadn't improved very much, if at all. Don't know yet why she just – died. There'll be a post-mortem, of course. That's going to delay funerals, and all that.'

Her voice had quivered, she swallowed hard. Isobel had never been more thankful to see anyone than when Daniel walked in. Suddenly, she knew she was going to cry. He knew that too, and drew her to him again.

For what felt like several minutes, he simply held her. She could feel his heartbeat against her breast, it felt so *sure* that Daniel might have been strengthening her with its steadying pulse. She could believe that without him she would no longer survive.

'Do you want a cup of tea, or something, or a meal?' Isobel asked eventually, releasing herself from his arms.

Daniel shook his head. 'Made sure of something en route.' He hadn't known what he might find here, had wanted to be ready to tackle taking over from her. 'Should you have begun sorting things here, though?' he enquired, alarmed by how haunted she looked.

Isobel shrugged. 'I suspect it might be the only way. Can't be more upset than I am, it's best to get this done while everything feels so unreal.' Once the truth really sank in she might not be able to function.

She had emptied both wardrobes and stacked their contents on the double bed, was starting to go through each item of clothing. 'The people from the base here will take over all Marvin's uniform things, and I've offered them any of his good casual gear that they think some of the other men might want. Or, I've only just thought – his brother might wish to take something.

'It's Mum's stuff that's going to be a problem. We're nowhere near the same size and, in any case, I've no room at the flat for anyone else's clothes. Yet I can't bring myself to chuck anything good in the dustbin.'

'Of course you can't.'

'If we were in Halifax I could see what the Salvation Army might use.'

'There'll be a branch somewhere round here. Or you might see if the hospital people can suggest something. That's if you are sure you want to get rid . . . ?'

'Certain. I shall never forget what's happened, but I can't take being surrounded by reminders. They were both so *young* to go.'

'I know. I do know that, Isobel love.'

Daniel helped, sorting all the clothing into piles, and then insisting that he would attend to disposing of the lot. He made a phone call to the hospital and the people there said they always were grateful for unwanted clothing.

'With everything still requiring coupons, few patients have enough spare garments to allow for delays over getting things washed. If you're sure, we'll take everything being offered.'

Daniel had driven his van over from Yorkshire, and used it now to take every item round to the hospital. He didn't want Isobel upsetting any further.

'If you think it's something I ought to do, I can come with you,' she volunteered. 'I'd be all right so long as you're there.'

'There's no need, and I'm sure there's plenty of other stuff for you to get on with.'

That was only too true. When glancing through the kitchen cupboards, Isobel had been surprised by the quantity of equipment that her mother and Marvin had acquired in such a relatively short time, especially bearing in mind the continued restrictions. She wondered if some of the utensils were USAAF issue. She would need to ask someone to come over and take a look through everything. But not quite yet. She couldn't face disposing of much more belonging to her mother's home.

They also would need to hold on to enough utensils and

141

provisions to be able to cater for themselves for as long as they were expected to remain at the base. Or until they were informed that these quarters were needed for personnel entitled to live there.

When Daniel returned from disposing of Amy's clothing, her first question was if he thought they might be asked to leave. 'I don't think I'm up to looking for somewhere else, couldn't cope with another set of unfamiliar rooms.'

'I'll have a word with them in the office tomorrow,' he promised. 'I shouldn't worry, though, they'd be expecting Marvin to remain here ad infinitum, wouldn't they? I can't believe they'd have someone lined up for this so swiftly.'

In the event, it was they themselves who decided to go back to Yorkshire for a few days before returning for the funeral. Even when the post-mortem had given Amy's cause of death as haemorrhage resulting from multiple injuries suffered, there was a further delay while Marvin's brother made arrangements to fly out from the United States.

The news of his family was bad. Their mother had been gravely shaken by her son's sudden death, and was so upset that letting her remaining son out of her sight felt altogether too much. Only when it was organised for a relative to stay in her home, had Marvin's brother felt able to plan his journey.

Isobel had looked forward to a brief respite from the atmosphere on Marvin's base, where everyone seemed distressed by his loss, and from all sides she received reminders of how greatly they had liked Amy. Touched though she was, Isobel felt overcome by the enveloping sadness.

Arriving among the familiar West Riding hills with the sun gleaming on fields and valleys emerging from snow, she was faced with a trauma that she hadn't anticipated. So many memories of childhood, adolescence, and her later years were embraced by these surroundings. Snatches from the past returned with every step: here it was that Amy had walked her to school, there had watched when Isobel paraded with the Girl Guide company, and along so many paths they had walked together with her father.

'Everything has changed,' she confided to Daniel. 'And changed forever.'

He had known how she would feel, and was prepared with a temporary solution.

'That's why I'm not giving you time to think. We're collecting a few things from your flat, then we're going to my little cottage. Before I left the other day, I made the bed up with fresh linen. And I got enough covers together for me to use the settee.'

Isobel wouldn't have argued against that arrangement, and Daniel wouldn't have permitted her to overrule him on it. She looked quite ill, and he meant to ensure that she didn't succumb to being overwhelmed with grief.

Entering his little home again acted as something of a tonic. She had forgotten just how beautifully he had renovated and decorated the place, simply gazing around at the colours and the skilful carpentry seemed to enliven her.

'By, but you did a grand job here!'

Daniel smiled as he took some of the belongings she was carrying. If he had his way, he would be sharing this home with Isobel permanently.

To earn that privilege, however, he must justify his position in her life, and before them lay the trauma of that joint funeral. He would need to recover some energy from somewhere to overcome his immense tiredness, and become the prop that Isobel needed. Nothing in the near future offered much comfort. Leaving Yorkshire behind would be a terrible wrench, and one that was worsened by the prospect awaiting them in East Anglia.

The unreality of living in Daniel's home while he spent each weekday working seemed to be helping Isobel begin to adjust to the differences that would be inherent in her future life. Glad though she was to spend this short time in the cottage, she wasn't entirely protected from the real situation.

Even her old friends appeared to have changed. She had insisted that she must go to her usual church, and Daniel had taken the precaution of ensuring that Diana was told of Amy's death. None of Isobel's friends could have been more sympathetic, but nor could they appear anything like the people she'd always known. After the service she received all the sincere condolences which she might have expected. But the reserve with which they treated her was quite unlike their normal, easy friendliness. By the time Daniel drove her off towards his home, Isobel was feeling that she had been among people who were no longer so familiar to her.

'Have I altered so much?' she asked him in the van. 'They seem as if they daren't talk to me properly any more.'

'That's how folk react, love, to somebody's bereavement. It was just the same when my mum and dad died. Nobody else knew how to handle it. Didn't you find that when your father was killed?'

Isobel couldn't recall that she had. But his funeral, in war-time, had seemed hasty, and she'd had to return swiftly to the farm where she was working.

She would have relished some haste in the time leading up to this cremation looming ahead of them. There was nothing for her to do in Halifax, and although she'd contemplated going out to Laneside House, she hadn't been able to face that. Would the place always threaten with its reminders that it was in the attempt to find additional storage for the house that she'd arranged that visit to East Anglia?

On the day of the funeral Isobel felt numbed by the feeling that she couldn't really be about to endure her mother's cremation. A part of her was thankful that so many people from the USAAF were surrounding her with arrangements which had sprung from their concern that the service should epitomise their regard for Marvin. Naturally, she had been consulted about the hymns and prayers and, together with Marvin's brother, had chosen favourites familiar on both sides of the Atlantic.

His brother was something of a surprise, no less helpful than Marvin, but of a quieter disposition. Appearance-wise, there was a resemblance, but nothing so marked that it caused anyone to give a double-take. It was in his voice that he seemed most like his brother, and Isobel felt reassured by this from beside her in the crematorium.

At her other side was Daniel, one hand grasping her arm,

an assurance of his constant concern for her. On the way over from Yorkshire he had spoken of his affection for Amy. Isobel felt warmed by knowing that this man, who'd seemed to appear from the ranks of distant relatives just a short while ago, had become a vital part of her family.

In this chapel filled by American servicemen Isobel sensed their support, a near-physical power that strengthened her to participate more fully. Her dread of having her voice waver during the hymns diminished as soon as she was carried on the music of their voices.

Marvin was their comrade, his wife had become their friend, they were contributing this, hoping it might help Amy's daughter, along with Marvin's brother.

This was the sentiment confirmed during the brief address, and Isobel revealed afterwards that they had eased the traumatic experience greatly, she always would be grateful.

Meeting Marvin's brother would have delighted her in more cheerful circumstances and pleased her, anyway, because it gave her opportunity to offer him a few of his brother's cherished belongings.

'Our mother will be pleased to see these,' he said, then sighed. He was depressed about taking Marvin's ashes home, longed for something to ease the family's pain.

Isobel had a similar dread regarding her mother's urn, and admitted to Daniel that she felt unable to face taking charge of it.

'I'll see to all that,' he promised. Silently, he vowed to delay until Isobel recovered from the worst of the shock before discussing the disposal of Amy's ashes.

'I don't know how ever I'd have got through all this without you,' she said, and saw his serious little smile.

'I'll always be around,' said Daniel.

Ten

Gustav would have found it difficult to explain in his own language the reason why he would hesitate to move to the United States; in English he did not rate his chances of convincing. And he must not ruin this opportunity to fly again, to be respected for his knowledge, his skills and – yes, even for a certain courage.

He might have learned, since crashing on the test-flight, that accepting his circumstances could bring a kind of peace; he understood only now that he had lived through those intervening months purely in order to be granted the life for which he had trained so assiduously.

Wherever it took him, he must resume the role in which his expertise might be utilised to the full. Every last thought of tending the land, of growing things, had been dismissed in a moment when a potential return to working with aircraft was proposed.

Those who had, justifiably, questioned his current allegiance would be rewarded with his whole-heartedness. All he required was being allowed to prove the extent to which Gustav Kassel would commit himself.

He had loved that experimental HE162, the *Volksjäger*, had forgiven its unforgiving challenge during each landing and take-off, would relish tackling its idiosyncrasies into submission. His final flight had prevented his complete mastery of that particular plane, but it seemed now that there could be a further chance, or with others. Just as he had loved the Heinkel, he would always cherish opportunities to learn and to progress, to test himself along with an aircraft.

At best, he would be a pilot once more, himself again. At worst, his technical knowledge would be of use at some stage in development of what could become world-class aeroplanes. Progress in jet-propulsion was the key – progress founded on expertise gleaned on both sides in the war that had spawned few advantages for either.

To this new life he would bring his spirit renewed by these people he once believed were enemies, would carry with him understanding and fresh values. He had acquired a degree of tolerance, but alongside that discernment. The flaws he'd identified already in the German nation might be offset by some of the good advances in technology which could benefit other countries.

Gustav felt inspired, no other word expressed the motivation compelling him to press onward, urging his demand to learn, *at once,* more details concerning the future proposed for him.

Reality intervened to remind him that a mere two days had elapsed since first mention of such work, persuading him that he must learn patience. Pestering any authorities could serve to convey the impression that he was too immature to handle the responsibilities on offer.

And *responsible* was how Gustav meant to be – a conscientious man who might still retain the courage to put his own mettle to the test, but while considering the hazards.

Flight needed to be safe and, even disregarding the numbers that were shot out of the skies, too many of his comrades had plunged earthwards. His own crash had occurred after too many near misses. The experience of war pilots must be utilised before commercial airlines developed further. No matter where such development was destined to take place.

Most importantly of all perhaps, this co-ordination of skills and ideas from across the world should be for the benefit of everyone. A sign that, once and for all time, people had recognised the evils in venturing to create a single master race.

Unhappy and exhausted, Isobel became disappointed as well when she and Daniel were denied access to the furniture placed in store by her mother. Even providing proof of her identity did not change a thing, she would be obliged to wait until probate was granted. Amy had made a will, Isobel could be grateful that Marvin had made sure of that. For the present, however, that fact felt to be of no significance.

She and Daniel stayed one night at the US base following the cremation, and had already emptied Marvin's quarters of all personal items belonging to Amy. Isobel was perturbed by planning to find space somewhere for them, although there were photographs and some jewellery which she would treasure.

Rather than keep anything in Laneside House while it remained empty, Daniel had offered her storage in his loft for as long as necessary. This was only one of countless ways in which he couldn't have done more for her. Whilst being thankful, however, Isobel was beginning to feel just a shade alarmed.

She had relied on Daniel so much throughout this dreadful time and sensed something within herself that could continue to depend upon him. He had tried to encourage her to stay one night with him when they again arrived back in Yorkshire, but Isobel felt compelled to decline, no matter how gratefully. From the moment of discovering the wreckage of that car, she had felt so unreal, totally unlike her usual self. Somehow, she needed to recover her normal identity.

'I'm going up to Laneside House tomorrow,' she told Daniel when he drove her to the flat. 'I'm more thankful than I can say for having you looking after me, and so on, in East Anglia. But I do need to get back to work and, as you know, getting that house right is the only job I've got now.'

Daniel wasn't at all happy that she would be spending time alone out there, and said so.

Isobel turned to him and smiled. 'Bless you, that's just what you would think. But you needn't worry – I'm not the first person to have to come to terms with loss. Folk do survive, but happen it's best in the long run if you have to begin getting on with that straight away.'

'I could spend Saturday at Laneside, if you'd let me.'

'I'll see how I feel when I've got a few days' work done there. I promise I'll phone you before the weekend.'

Even her tiny flat felt desolate when she went into it alone, though. Isobel began to dread going over to the house on the moors. Knowing herself, however, she silently vowed that she would not weaken and give in to negative feelings. She was accustomed to work, evidently had found it a solution years ago after her father's sudden death; she would utilise it again.

That resolve seemed to help next morning, and the brightness of the day raised her spirits slightly, as did having the Jeep start instantly. Isobel had meant to ask Daniel to check it over last evening, but had forgotten. She had been in a hurry to get out of his van: not to *escape* him, exactly, but to return to her old way of life.

Driving along the roads out of Halifax, Isobel started to feel that she might perhaps be on the threshold of rediscovering her original self. Before leaving the flat, she had gathered together the sketches that depicted the shades of paint and distemper that she wanted in rooms she hadn't decorated already.

One of them was the kitchen, and that needed her attention most urgently, she couldn't even quite remember if she *had* spoken to the builder about having a new draining-board fitted, and where various items of equipment might go. Once she arrived at Laneside House, she would remember. A decision about storage would have to be made, though; waiting to see what she inherited from Amy no longer seemed very practicable.

One pleasant surprise awaited her as soon as she entered the kitchen. Bert Bradshaw had installed a wooden draining-board, with grooves for water to run off, and fixed to provide the necessary slight slope. He also had used something stronger to clean the stone of the sink itself, the old tap as well. That small area was looking good.

Isobel smiled, this seemed like an omen that here, at least, things were beginning to work out as she wished. Great-grandfather would be proud of her so long as she continued to work hard on his home.

She was glad to think about her father's family. The recent funeral had brought home to her the fact that there were no close relatives remaining on her mother's side. Few relatives at all. Had Daniel's parents been still alive they would have been offering a bit of support, because her father and his mother had been cousins. So far as she knew, there was no one else related to them. She would always have to remember that she owed Daniel a great deal: he need not have come to her aid at all.

By the Friday evening when Isobel rang him from the phone box near her flat, she was preparing to assure Daniel that, much as she appreciated his offer of assistance, she really preferred to tackle decorating Laneside House on her own.

Somehow, their conversation didn't emerge at all like that. Isobel hadn't said more than 'Hello,' before Daniel came in with his idea.

'I've been thinking how you haven't yet acquired any of Amy's storage stuff, we could find that's not going to matter. I've got hold of some second-hand cupboards that came out of a house demolished by a flying-bomb. They're not perfect, but I know how I can smarten them up for you, if that's what you'd like. They're in the van now – nowhere else to keep them. I thought we could take them to Laneside tomorrow, measure up and see where they might fit in.'

'That's very kind of you, love, but—' Isabel stopped speaking. She'd been about to refuse, suddenly she couldn't.

'But what . . . ?' Daniel asked, sounding more patient than she deserved.

'Just – are you sure you can't make use of them yourself?' she improvised.

'You've seen my place – no room for anything more here. If I wanted to add anything, and I don't. Look – wait until you've seen this stuff before you decide. You don't have to take it, there's plenty of folk would be glad of cupboards, with all the shortages still going on.'

Isobel felt churlish about thinking twice before accepting, doubly churlish because she wasn't snapping up his offer of help with decorating. Daniel was so good to her, she ought to be ashamed of herself.

'Is there any more paint you need?' he enquired. 'I've

150

been looking through the stuff I had left over, it'll not be much use if it's left to dry out any longer.'

'It's distemper I need more than paint,' Isobel told him. 'Bert Bradshaw was very good, and where he'd replaced any woodwork he gave it a coat of paint. I daren't ask where he got it from, somebody might be going short.'

'Happen that was left over from some job he'd done.'

'Don't think so. Didn't I say he's retired really? I think he'd worked through the war when other chaps had joined up, then he didn't enjoy being idle afterwards.'

'Sound like you were lucky there.'

'Oh, I was.' And she was in so many ways, not least in having Daniel around. Isobel just wished that she could show him how she appreciated that.

When his van drew up outside the flat on the following day, Isobel reminded herself that it was high time she ceased rebutting Daniel's attempts to help her.

No matter how laudable her efforts to renovate that house on her own, there were certain jobs that she couldn't quite manage. Why should welcoming aid from him be any worse than employing a builder where necessary?

'You'll have to let me settle with you for any materials you use,' Isobel told him, just so that there were no misunderstandings. 'And did you have to give somebody something for those cupboards?'

'Not so much as a penny. But if you'll feel better, I will keep a tally of what the paint and so on cost, provided you do go ahead.'

A quick glance while the cupboards were in the van told Isobel that they appeared quite sound, if covered in layers of dark brown paint which had suffered masses of scratches.

'I'd take them down to the bare wood, then I thought of creating a light oak effect with graining before a final varnishing. You need something light in that kitchen, assuming that is where you could use them.'

'I imagine so. It's where I'm short of somewhere to store stuff. Up in the bedrooms there's still some of Great-aunt Hannah's furniture.'

'We could look in the attic as well, might find something I could do up for you.'

Isobel steeled herself against saying she didn't wish him to do so much for her.

'Or would that place you under an obligation?' Daniel demanded, brown eyes glinting with humour, as he drew to a halt outside Laneside House.

'You know me too well!'

Daniel quelled a sigh. This was not the time for stressing that he needed to know Isobel a lot better. He must try simply to be thankful that he was going into the house like this with her today.

'I could charge you for my time,' he suggested with a grin.

'I'll remember that. You do have a business to run. How is that going?' A further source of her guilt concerned the time he'd recently devoted to her.

'Well. Subject to shortages, and restrictions, of course. But starting up was timed just right for hitting the building trade when so much renovation and reconstruction is in hand. You might bear that in mind, should you decide you wish to continue as a decorator.'

'If I do ever finish this place, you mean.'

Daniel had been gazing all around the kitchen before bringing in the cupboards from his van.

'You've got some nice ideas. Keeping the old sink retains a bit of character, and you've got a grand piece of wood in that drainer beside it. The walls are coming on, and I like the shade, one more coat and that'll be fine.'

'I thought cream would be best, it can be so dark in here on a bad day. In fact, I was a bit tempted to use whitewash, as it was before. Only that made me think of Dad whitewashing their cellar, I felt it might not be good enough for in here.'

Despite herself, Isobel couldn't be other than delighted by Daniel's approval of her choices in the kitchen. She had seen and admired his own good taste.

When he had offloaded the cupboards and brought them indoors, she could see how awful their paintwork was, but they certainly were of a suitable size to fit the spaces available.

'Just ignore the finish on them,' Daniel said swiftly. 'As I say, I can make them good for you. What do you think to their being grained in light oak?'

'I believe that'd go very well here. If you're sure you wouldn't mind all that work?'

He laughed. 'I shall enjoy tackling it. Mind you, it won't be completed all that swiftly, I'll only be able to put in time at weekends.' And that would suit him, he would relish good reason for seeing Isobel regularly.

'I'm thinking of moving in before so long, any road. It's silly paying rent on the flat, and it'll do this place good to have a fire lit every day. Once I've got myself organised here, I'll be able to cook proper meals when you're busy on those cupboards.'

'I trust that you'll eat properly when you're on your own here too. I seem to recall telling you before that you need to look after yourself.'

'You sound just like my mother!' said Isobel. *And remembered.* The tears began slipping from her eyes before she could control them. Within a minute she was sobbing. She would so have loved to share her growing enthusiasm for this place with Amy.

'Hey, there – Isobel, don't.'

Daniel strode the few paces between them and hugged her to him. 'Don't, love. I know you've had a terrible shock, but it isn't the end of everything. I'll look after you, I'll always be around.'

Despite all her determination, Isobel clung to him. He was warm and unutterably kind, a part of her history even though there had been years when she had never seen him.

'Let me face this with you, Isobel love. You'll need time, but I understand that.'

Daniel's words made her sense how greatly she needed someone to anchor her life. Her awareness of often feeling surrounded by a massive emptiness surged. These wretched tears seemed ungoverned, she could feel her body beginning to shake with the force of them.

'Isn't there anywhere where we can at least sit down?' asked Daniel.

'Only upstairs.' Isobel sighed, and paused to blow her nose.

She felt too upset to protest when Daniel led her to the first few steps and, keeping hold of her hand, encouraged her upstairs. An arm about her again, he walked with her to the bed, then drew her down with him on top of the old counterpane.

'It's probably damp,' Isobel began.

'It certainly will be if you don't stop crying!'

Isobel tried to laugh, and hiccupped.

'That's better,' Daniel approved and hugged her to him. 'I know you'll have to get this out of your system, grieving's a necessary process. But you don't have to cope with it alone.'

He kissed her forehead, and then the eyelids which already felt hot and swollen. He was caressing her hair, seemed to be soothing her troubled spirit.

'I was there with you, remember,' he said. 'I shall always know and understand when you feel all emotional. Always,' he added under his breath.

The arms holding her felt good. Even through their outdoor clothing, she could feel the warmth of him. A warmth that had seemed synonymous with Daniel throughout these dreadful days of loss.

'You are so good to me,' Isobel murmured, and suddenly was weeping yet again. This was the reason that she'd refused to give in to emotion while alone.

Daniel kissed the tears away, from her lashes, her cheeks, the side of her face where they trickled into her hair. And then he was kissing her lips, fervently, willing her to accept the love that he ached to give her.

He held her so securely, his arms the assurance that she needed, his lips the promise that he would not disappear in a moment.

'I've been so – so *shattered*,' Isobel confided.

'I know, I do know. Together, we'll rebuild your life, you can depend on that.'

His words and kisses were so full of affection. Affection that she needed when all she'd felt was bereft. Isobel kissed him now, no longer able to resist her own desperation to *belong*, as she hadn't belonged to anyone since that dreadful accident.

His mouth welcomed her own, his lips moving over hers, savouring her, testing her teeth, parting them.

When Daniel stirred Isobel stirred with him. She felt the pressure of his chest, his stomach, recognisably taut even through their clothing, while his arms locked her to him, drawing her ever nearer. She needed to be closer still, to lose herself there and exclude her troubled world.

Their kisses went on and on, exploring and exciting, creating within her a tumult of delicious passion. He might have been awakening her from being semi-conscious. How had she lived without this, how existed with no means to express this intense emotion, this longing? Proof that she was not alone.

She slid on to her back, and felt Daniel on top of her, pressing close. His fingers slipped inside her coat, began to caress one breast. Her own response startled Isobel. It made her shake her head.

'No, Daniel, not now.'

'You know what I need, though,' he confessed; 'And I guess *you* do too. This may not be anything like the right time for us but, one day, that time will come. There'll be an end to solitude, don't you forget that.'

His next kiss seemed chaste, the final one, the one to seal his promise. Isobel followed him downstairs, slowly, pensively yet scarcely able to form coherent thoughts. Every pulse in her body appeared to be coming alive, for him.

'We'd better get on with some work,' she said ruefully at the foot of the staircase.

Daniel smiled. 'Quite. Before you render working impossible!'

He had brought paint-stripper with him, and sandpaper. After Isobel confirmed that she would love to have the cupboards, they discussed where they would best be placed, then Daniel began on the long task of renovating them.

Isobel got out the distemper that she'd reserved for the kitchen and began applying a second coat. The task proved anything but easy. Even by the time that she had removed her outdoor coat and put on the overall kept at the house, her hands were still shaking with emotion.

She hoped Daniel couldn't see how disturbed she was. Hearing him refer to her own need was enough of a shock. She couldn't recall meeting any young man who had been so outspoken, he might have been relishing the effect he had upon her.

And Isobel supposed that he *was*. Didn't every chap love to know he could have some power over a girl?

Steadying her hand in order to paint the wall, Isobel tried also to steady her rocketing senses. Whatever Daniel might have intended, she herself was the person whose emotions scared her. How had they reached this situation where she might even contemplate surrendering to this fierce attraction?

And how ever would she continue to work side by side with Daniel in this place (as she was committed to working) while struggling to suppress her feelings?

On the next occasion when Isobel and Daniel arrived at Laneside House together, she came equipped with her sturdiest self-discipline. In a way, the sudden loss of her mother helped, so long as she refused to give in to tears again. When she reflected on all that Amy meant to her masses of earlier resolutions resurrected.

The many hours spent alone since that accident had filled her mind with memories of the ways that she and her mother had talked through potential problems. During the days preceding her departure for the Women's Land Army especially, Isobel had listened while Amy revealed awareness that her daughter would face a whole spectrum of fresh opportunities. The words used remained now to echo in her ears.

'You'll meet lots of young men as well as the girls in your team, and you'll be in places where there's nobody to object if you give in to a bit of passion. You could find you're tempted more there than if it would entail sneaking some man up to your bedroom at home. That's when I hope you'll try to weigh what's right for you. Me and your dad tried to bring you up properly, giving you the ability to judge how you're to behave.'

Isobel hadn't needed to weigh what should occur between herself and Daniel. Whatever he might arouse in her, she never meant to give in to that attraction. Her natural caution forbade it. She knew very little about Daniel Armstrong apart from his being a distant relative, and other than his willingness to assist her.

He was a hard worker, which was laudable enough, ready to put in long hours to establish the business he'd set up after the war. He sounded prepared to be patient over her hesitation about deepening the relationship between them, but this was early days. Isobel couldn't be certain he would continue to be so understanding. Their passion had escalated so suddenly she wondered if Daniel was highly sexed.

Life away from home during the war years had taught her that lots of men and women were far more experienced than Isobel herself. She had soon become aware that more people than she supposed were driven to make love without first getting married. Daniel had jolted her into suspecting that she might be about to spend a great deal of time with one such person!

Isobel would be compelled to rely on the fact that she considered herself different, someone who did not allow desire to overwhelm her circumspection. Or her common sense. She had seen too often how chaps could disappear after they had got what they wanted from a girl.

Seeing Daniel working beside her in the kitchen, Isobel felt reassured. She could believe that he was no more than an ordinary young man whose affectionate nature had led to a few kisses and a bit of a cuddle. She was finding it difficult already to credit that they had clung together on that bed for all the world as though nothing must keep them apart.

Like this, working – working for *her* – he was a man she respected.

'I shall respect your wishes,' Daniel announced suddenly, out of the blue, and shook her with his echo of the word going through her mind. 'You may be assured that I shan't try to force kisses on you, if you're not in the mood.'

Isobel was initially too surprised by his sudden assertion to say anything. And she would have liked to state that she had never thought otherwise, but she was a stickler for the truth. 'Good,' she managed eventually. 'I like to know where I stand.'

'I saw all kinds in the forces, you know, before we were taken prisoner. Too many chaps were out for all they could get, had no notion of committing themselves beforehand either. That's not my way, never has been.' He paused, waiting for her to respond. 'Just thought I'd let you know,' he concluded when Isobel said nothing.

She felt quite awkward now. Daniel's words seemed to have emerged in answer to her own reservations regarding him. She didn't like the notion that he might have read her thoughts. And his serious tone generated a fresh anxiety – was he attaching too much significance to what had occurred between them?

Isobel's concern increased when she remembered that she had revealed her plans for moving into Laneside House as soon as it became really habitable. If she was living there, making meals as promised whenever Daniel came to work on the cupboards, might she be creating a more intimate atmosphere?

That would be tested as soon as the kitchen was ready, unless she gave an adequate excuse for delaying, and Isobel could find none. Daniel had completed one cupboard which looked beautiful, and that was sufficient for storing the essential items of equipment that she was bringing from the flat. Most importantly, she owed her own peace of mind to moving into Laneside House, and proving that she was up to taking such a positive step.

She would minimise risks, as she'd decided already, by keeping in check any affection between herself and Daniel. She could not fault his behaviour, and had no intention of letting her own emotions prove overwhelming.

The testing began on the Saturday when Isobel moved out of the flat. Daniel insisted on helping her, pointing out that she shouldn't waste good money on hiring a van when he had one available. During the previous few days she had packed most of her belongings, leaving until the last minute only items to keep her clean, dressed and fed until the actual move.

Having scarcely slept that night, Isobel had stripped the bed and eaten breakfast, and was stowing her final possessions into boxes when Daniel drew up outside. Between them, they carried everything out to the van, and paused only while she asked her landlady to check that everything remaining in the flat was in order. She was astonished, Mrs Hardaker seemed distressed to see her leaving, but Isobel reminded her that another tenant was due to arrive early the following month.

'I'm surprised she was sorry to see me go,' Isobel remarked as Daniel started up the van. She had seen the woman so rarely.

'I'm not – anyone would be glad to have you living near.'

Isobel swallowed, decided not to say anything. She didn't mean to encourage him to add any more. She was worrying ahead over how much he might make of his visits to work on the second cupboard once she was installed in Laneside House. And when that task was completed, she would be torn between her gratitude for all Daniel had done and the need to establish her independence.

This moving-in day wasn't a good one for analysing feelings. Isobel was plagued by an increasing sensation that her mother ought to have been around for her, and would have enjoyed this experience. Sharing it with Daniel was not the same.

They worked together very agreeably, nevertheless, and he enjoyed the meal that she rustled up for them in the evening. Both were tired and she was thankful that she had thought during the previous week to make up her bed in readiness. In Daniel's case, the tiredness led to his preparing to leave at nine o'clock, and Isobel naturally went to the door to wave him off.

He took Isobel by surprise, dashing back from the van, and astonishing her further with a bouquet of flowers.

'To welcome you to your home, and just to remind you that I'm never far away.'

He kissed her full on the lips. Instinctively, Isobel responded, touched by his thoughtfulness which made her eyes mist over. She tried to conceal the tears, recalling only too well where his concern for her weeping had ended previously.

On this occasion, Daniel caused her no alarm. He gave her a friendly hug before running off towards the van once more.

Finding a vase among the possessions she had brought over took several minutes, and arranging the daffodils and narcissi a further ten. Isobel was yawning when she filled a hot-water bottle and headed up to her bedroom.

She had finished distempering three of its walls in a pale, buttery yellow, the fourth required just one more coat and the room would be looking really good. Isobel wished that she'd found the time to complete the job. She felt so exhausted that any work daunted her, she longed to have someone offer to tackle the rest.

Quite unbidden, her memory resurrected the sight of Gustav Kassel painting that wall in the verger's house. Isobel recognised in a rush that *he* was the reason why she was so reluctant to strengthen her relationship with Daniel. None of this made sense. What on earth possessed her to raise numerous obstacles when Daniel was always so eager to do whatever she wished?

Getting into bed, and pushing her feet down to rest on the hot-water bottle, Isobel willed herself to cease allowing thoughts of Gustav to affect her. He had left without attempting to see her again, had gone out of her life. And that life remained *hers*. Tomorrow, when daylight came, she would gaze out on her view of these splendid moors, and everything would be all right.

And then she remembered. Gustav had spoken of how good it would be to awaken here. Was she to be haunted forever by such memories? She would need to muster all her will-power if she was to exclude him from her foolish thoughts.

Eleven

Isobel felt exhausted still when she awakened the following morning, and quickly began to discover that, although living in Laneside House facilitated completing the various tasks there, the actual work continued to be tiring.

She started putting in longer hours, of course, which soon went some way to explaining further tiredness. Isobel sensed, though, that now she was living in such an isolated spot she was being overtaken by all the grief of her sudden loss.

Certainly, all about her every day, she noticed reminders of how Amy would have enjoyed exploring the place. This seemed to reverse her original feeling that her mother wasn't particularly keen to share in the experience of restoring the house.

Isobel did share it all, naturally, with Daniel, who continued to visit in order to finish painting and varnishing the second cupboard for her. When that job was completed she felt awkward about dropping the habit of inviting him over for a few hours on at least one day of a weekend.

Awareness of how much she owed Daniel was a part of it, but Isobel suspected that her own loneliness contributed.

Eventually, when she'd completed all the decorating for which she had the necessary materials, she invited Diana, Louise and Betty to supper one Friday evening. They filled Laneside House with their chatter and laughter, and music also for Diana had insisted on bringing her latest acquisition, a portable gramophone.

In the living room they danced to tunes from *Oklahoma* and *Annie Get your Gun*, then eagerly began bringing Isobel up to date while they ate supper. She learned she was correct to assume the three of them were now 'going steady' with the young men she had seen in Diana's home. She was surprised at first to be told they all were planning to marry shortly. Only then she recognised that her friends were of an age to be wanting families. The war had kept apart so many young men and women during a time when normally they would have been meeting someone to settle down with.

Naturally, they were elated and, one by one, each was insisting that Isobel must make a note of the her wedding date and be sure to attend.

'Once I decided to take the plunge with Richard, the others followed on. We're none of us in favour of long engagements,' Diana said, straightforwardly. 'Not fair on the chaps, is it, expecting them to wait for ever when it puts such a strain on them.'

'Well, I'm pleased you've all found somebody you want to settle down with, and with the six of you getting on so well already, that's going to be nice.'

'It is that!' Louise agreed. 'And we're even looking out for houses that aren't going to be too distant from each others'. It's a pity you've gone for somewhere this far out, cutting yourself off like you have.'

'Oh, I shall be fine, don't you worry. Once I've done everything necessary on the house. And there's a church just over the top of the hill here. I expect I shall start attending there when I have more time.'

'And you'll be going back to work, I suppose,' said Betty.

'Or setting up a little business. I seem to have quite an eye for colour, and I'm wondering if I could make a go of decorating for other folk. Daniel's idea, actually.'

'Daniel, eh? And what sort of other ideas has Daniel got?' Diana asked, her wink knowing.

Isobel smiled, and decided to keep them guessing. She might wish to avoid giving Daniel too much encouragement, but she did rather enjoy having the other girls believe she had some man who was interested.

'He was very good when my mother and Marvin were killed in that accident, you know. And he comes here a lot, he's the one who made those kitchen cupboards look so lovely.'

'And does he sleep here, an' all?' Betty enquired.

'If he does, I shan't let on to you lot, shall I?' Isobel responded, and felt a glow ascending from her neck to the roots of her hair.

'Don't blame you, you're not answerable to anybody else, are you?' said Diana.

Isobel was perturbed, she hadn't meant to mislead them about such a personal matter, and she suddenly knew she had no wish to have Daniel stay the night with her.

Long after her friends had departed, Isobel remained disturbed. Their plans had unsettled her, while their reminder that she was living so far away from her old life in Halifax made her feel they were accusing her of deserting them.

As, in a way, she was, Isobel supposed. She had inherited this house, agreed, but it was her own choice that she now was living in it.

'I am going to be happy here,' she asserted aloud, and wondered why that sounded like a challenge she was making.

Isobel knew herself very well, and that she was only content when she was working. With so much of Laneside House redecorated to her ideas, it was time to seek advice from Daniel about setting up a business to use her flair with colour.

'Good idea,' he said after she broached the matter on the following Sunday when he came for lunch. 'The only difficulty is obtaining paints and wallpaper and so on, they're still in short supply, mostly available for use in buildings that have consent for going ahead.'

'I'd never get in on it, is that what you're saying?'

'Might be tricky – unless, well I could be able to arrange something. Especially, if you were agreeable to coming in with me.'

'In *your* business?' That prospect didn't appeal at all.

'I could introduce your work through my contacts in the building trade, couldn't I? Lots of firms take me on to do their carpentry. It shouldn't be that difficult to persuade folk that I've got someone who might follow on with a bit of decorating. You've got an eye for colour, so long as you improved your actual painting.'

163

Isobel didn't like the criticism, nor the idea of working under Daniel. 'I'm not sure that would be quite "me".' She had visualised being independent, creating her own list of clients, people whom *she* impressed with her ideas for enhancing their homes. She wanted to design entire rooms, co-ordinating carpets and curtaining with the shade of their walls.

'Forget it then. Just remember you've got to be realistic. Replacing and renovating war-damaged property is where the bulk of new materials will be going for many a long month. If not for years.'

'Happen I'll go back to fashion designing then. I've got to bring some money in somehow.'

She had enjoyed this freedom to work on her own place, though, and at her own pace. The experience had given her a taste for this fresh means of using her skills.

'You don't have to work, Isobel love,' said Daniel. He was toying with the Brussels sprouts and Yorkshire pudding on his plate, avoiding her gaze.

'Of course I do. Renovating Laneside House has taken most of the cash from my share of the old family home, plus any savings.'

'What is it you really want to make of your life now, how do you picture your future?'

Isobel hesitated to answer. Since her friends had announced their wedding arrangements she had been feeling particularly dejected because of lacking any such plans of her own. For as long as she could recall, she had dreamed of one day having children. Yet to date she hadn't even met a man she wished to spend her life with. Or not anyone who'd remained around long enough for her to really get to know him . . .

Daniel sought her gaze across the table. 'Isobel – what impressed you most about your great-grandfather's love of this place; what made you want it?'

She gazed towards Edward Johnson's picture, and couldn't lie to conceal her own longing. 'His determination to make it a family home.'

'Precisely what Laneside House deserves, don't you think?'

'Well – yes.'

'We could turn it into that – a real family home.'

'*We?*'

'Don't you know I love you, Isobel? Haven't you noticed?'

She sighed. 'Oh, Daniel – I'm not ready for this.'

'You've not long since had one massive upheaval, losing your mother, I do understand. I wouldn't pressure you into rushing into marriage, not unless that was what you wished. But I do love you and I do want you to be my wife. Please, please say you'll consider it.'

Isobel tried not to sigh again. She had been perplexed so many times during the past few weeks, this proposal increased every doubt that she'd ever entertained. About her life in general, about living here alone, about Daniel . . .

'I won't turn you down, or not immediately,' she promised. 'But I won't pretend I don't have a problem with the idea, Daniel. I've got to be honest, I'm afraid, and say I'm not at all sure that I'm in love with you.'

'I know that, but you are a loving person, affectionate, I've seen that already. And I could settle for the less romantic aspect of loving. After all, we're neither of us youngsters any longer, we've experienced too much of life to expect a future that's entirely rosy.'

But I wanted it to be romantic, thought Isobel, wanted the dream, falling in love.

'Think about it, love. We have a lot in common, and you can't pretend that we're not attracted to each other. I can't forget that time upstairs here . . .'

But I've been attracted before, you're not the only one who's had that effect upon me, thought Isobel, and could say nothing.

Gustav was saying nothing, hearing the interviewer out. It was the latest of several similar meetings, and with each his exhilaration was mounting.

The smartly dressed man with silvering hair smiled across the desk at him. 'We would count ourselves fortunate to take you on as part of our team, you know. It's no secret within the industry that the Heinkel which you tested was a good forerunner of the many jet-propelled aircraft which eventually will fill our skies.'

Gustav smiled back at him. Mention of that Heinkel had swung it today, sweeping away any lingering doubts. Their being impressed by his knowledge of the HE162 counted for so much.

'You have convinced me that I must accept. I thank you for your confidence in what ability I possess, please be assured that I shall employ it to the full on your behalf.'

The other man laughed. 'You will indeed! We shall work you to the limit, it is good that you are young. We mean to exploit every asset that you bring with you.'

'And when do you wish me to start?'

'You ask that without even inspecting our workshops, don't you require some reassurance regarding your future conditions?'

It was Gustav's turn to seem amused. 'Have you not seen any underground sites where the HE162 was produced? The assembly line I knew was in a former gypsum mine.'

'Cold and damp then. I had heard,' said the senior man dryly. There was no part of Gustav Kassel's working life which had not been scrutinised.

'I guess you would have.' From the day that he first learned that the plane he crashed had been disinterred, he had understood their examination would be thorough. And they wanted him.

There was a pause while documents on the desk were being checked. Again, the interviewer smiled.

'You are eager, and we require a degree of urgency now that we are satisfied. I shall arrange an immediate visit to our site. By that, I mean you will hear within days what arrangements are in hand. From there, we shall take it that you would begin working with us, just as soon as the necessary documentation is authenticated.'

'That sounds as though there could be some delay?'

'Not necessarily. You might be surprised by the amount of preliminary work that has gone into satisfying the mass of regulations. I think you may accept that as an indication of how seriously we regard the desire to have you with us.'

Gustav's elation soared further still. He had not felt like this since the early stages of becoming a test-pilot. And this would be better still: he was not plagued by all those old doubts regarding the integrity of the nation for whom he was working.

'You will receive detailed instructions on how to reach the site. Our people know to expect you, and understand that you are not at all familiar with the surrounding area.'

Gustav thanked him warmly. 'I have travelled far, as you well know, and am happy to travel wherever you wish. I needed only this confirmation that I shall once more be applying myself to tasks for which my training fits me.'

Diana was the first of the old crowd to marry. Isobel wasn't surprised as she always had seemed to stand out from the others, to lead the way. When her friend insisted that Isobel should bring Daniel with her to the wedding, she wasn't certain how to respond.

'He's not my boyfriend or anything, you know. In fact, I'm not entirely happy that a wedding is the best thing to bring him to.'

'You don't want him to get ideas?'

'He's got those already. It's me that's having too many doubts. I'm putting him off because of my mother dying earlier this year, but I know that's just an excuse I'm raking up.'

'Why be like that, Isobel? I thought he was smashing-looking that time you came to church after – after you'd been to East Anglia.'

'Oh, he's that all right, and *he* doesn't think he's handsome either, not like a lot of blokes. There is that in his favour . . .'

'But not much else? Don't you get on?'

'When he's not trying to tie me down, or persuading me I should join him in that business of his.' Isobel explained how her own longing to employ her flare for colour as a decorator seemed hampered by Daniel's suggestion of working together.

'Why are you that scared of becoming involved?' Diana

demanded. 'He's a good man, isn't he? Seems as if he can't do enough for you.'

'But *is* it enough, that's what I keep asking myself? Enough for me? Where's the excitement, the thrill? That's what I want to know.'

'Oh, grow up, Isobel love! I thought you were more mature than that. Falling for somebody doesn't have to mean being swept off your feet. Not at our age, not after the difficulties of the past few years. This is the peace we worked towards, remember. *Peace.* That stands for settling quietly, in a way that's going to lead to a calm life. Aye – and one that's right for bringing up children in. Excitement isn't meant for adults like us, not these days.'

Isobel wasn't entirely convinced, but she could hardly observe that some people could suppose Diana and the others were settling for young men they knew so well in order that they would feel *safe*!

When the time came she was feeling reassured that taking Daniel along to the church when Diana and Richard married needn't be construed as anything more significant. And she was demonstrating some independence, using the car she'd bought to replace her old Jeep.

Isobel enjoyed the wedding, and he appeared to enjoy it too. Among her friends and their future husbands, she felt quite glad to have Daniel at her side.

He *was* handsome, especially so when he wore a good suit with a shirt and tie. The resemblance to her great-grandfather seemed particularly strong, and made her smile to herself, if a little ruefully. Dared she discount all Daniel's ideas when Edward Johnson might have heartily approved them?

The concept of having the one-time owner of her beloved home endorse Daniel's qualities seemed to linger. Along with Diana's thoughts, it obliged Isobel to consider afresh Daniel's possibilities as her future partner. He was reliable, and he was affectionate, he also was undeniably attractive.

The attraction became evident when they danced together during the reception after Diana and Richard's church ceremony. Daniel held her very close, reminding her of that occasion all those month's ago at the American base. Isobel began to wonder if she might perhaps have been rather an idiot to persist in warding him off.

Afterwards in her car they kissed, fervently, and Daniel bemoaned the fact that she was the one driving them there, and she would be returning alone to Laneside House.

'I can't even run you home, or walk you there. There'll not even be a reason for a long cuddle on your doorstep!'

Isobel recalled something else Diana had said, about the strain girls might expect their men to endure. How long could she hope Daniel would be patient about all that she was putting him through? Need she hold him off forever? How would she feel – *really feel* – if perhaps she were to become engaged to him?

Isobel was aware that she had drunk quite an amount of wine at the reception, and she wasn't used to alcohol. She was having to take extra care with driving. This was not the situation in which she could make a balanced decision on such a vital matter. She promised herself, though, that she would think seriously about her future life.

Alone at Laneside House, Isobel soon felt that she was being bombarded with reminders of the decision to be reached. In the week after Diana and Richard's marriage, her invitation to Louise's wedding arrived. Again Daniel was included.

She caught herself looking forward to the event already, and not simply on account of enjoying an old friend's wedding. Because they loved dancing, each of the new brides had confided that there would be a few waltzes and quick-steps during their reception. And whatever her misgivings regarding Daniel, the way he danced did excite her. It was beginning to seem sad if she now was compelled to seek such an occasion as the only opportunity for being held close.

Isobel was well aware that if being in Daniel's arms happened all too infrequently, the fault was her own. He'd never blinded himself to her reaction on the rare occasions when he'd wished to deepen their relationship: Isobel often sensed that he was containing his own feelings lest he receive another rebuff.

These days, even away from him, she experienced a worrying longing that threatened to destroy her fondness for the home she was creating in Laneside House. There was more than loneliness behind her need, although being lonely there did nothing to distract her from its source. Isobel didn't wish to remain single for ever.

By the time they were going together to witness Louise marrying her Bill, Isobel felt ready to talk to Daniel again about his proposal. She wouldn't agree to marry in the near future, but she would be happy to become engaged.

After broaching this with Daniel in the car, Isobel was surprised when he insisted that she draw in to the side of the road, and then he hugged her. Kissing her feverishly, he seemed too thrilled to speak coherently.

'Lord, that's marvellous! Oh, that – that you – that we –! You make me so happy, Isobel – I – I'm ecstatic. I – I will be a good husband, to you, and just as soon as, well – you know . . . But it won't matter if you need to wait a while – I mean, just the promise that we have an understanding – Wonderful! Wonderful!'

'Glad you're pleased,' said Isobel, not without a certain amount of humour.

They would need to talk, but she had no wish to dampen his delight, and she herself could not avoid feeling glad that she had pleased Daniel so greatly. She was fond of him, after all, more so perhaps than she'd realised previously.

Watching the marriage ceremony and attending the reception afterwards, Isobel felt quite different, acutely aware of all that was happening. She began to wonder how she would feel when Daniel was the bridegroom and she herself the bride. The idea seemed totally unreal. Isobel was thankful to recollect that such a wedding would understandably be delayed until at least a year after her mother's death.

The prospect of committing herself to no more than an engagement enabled her to push the more distant future to the back of her subconscious and enjoy the day. The dancing proved just as lovely as she had anticipated, Daniel was a skilled partner, and she certainly did relish the sensation of being held close in his arms.

'You know I shall want to hold you like this at other times, don't you?' he whispered into her hair while they danced the last waltz.

'I'll be surprised if you don't!' Isobel exclaimed with a smile. She might have added that she also would be disappointed. She'd always been honest with herself about the needs which at that moment were reminding her of their presence.

Holding each other in the confines of her car, they kissed and kissed repeatedly before Isobel said that she really would have to be getting home.

'You could stay the night with me,' Daniel suggested. 'And I don't necessarily mean in the same bed, I do have a settee too, remember.'

'I don't think that's a good idea, not tonight,' she told him gently. 'We do need to talk, there's a great deal to discuss, and we'd probably sit up all night talking.'

'Tomorrow then, I am coming for Sunday dinner, aren't I?'

Arriving at Laneside House, Isobel discovered that she felt entirely differently about her home also. She strolled from room to room, relishing the effect of any colour schemes she'd completed, loving the well-tended furniture, now it was all destined to fulfil its true purpose as a setting for bringing up a family.

Too full of thoughts to sleep properly, she was glad to get up early on the Sunday, and began preparing their meal enthusiastically, taking particular care over each item that she planned to serve. Living here companionably with Daniel, she would love all this, and meant to show him from the start how good their life could be.

Daniel himself was still elated when he drew up in the van, and came running to the kitchen door, carrying a bottle of wine. Had he kept it for a special occasion since before the war?

'This is to celebrate our engagement,' he exclaimed after kissing her searchingly on the mouth. 'And you've got to tell me today how soon you're coming with me to choose a ring.'

171

Isobel hadn't even thought as far as having his ring. 'It's up to you to make the time, you're the one with a business to run.'

'Will next Saturday be soon enough? I thought we might go over to Manchester, the shops there could have more to offer than the ones in Halifax.'

'Isn't that a bit rash? I don't want you spending out on something extravagant.'

Daniel laughed. 'Isobel love, I'm that pleased I can't do enough for you!'

He opened the wine while she was serving their main course, they drank a solemn toast to each other, to their future together.

As they started eating, Isobel gazed all around the living-room. 'It will be grand to have you here all the time, you know.'

'But – we haven't discussed where we'll be living yet. I thought – well, my place is more fully furnished, isn't it? And I run the business from there, as you know, and being nearer the town is much more convenient.'

Isobel frowned. *Was* his place nearer to the town? 'That wasn't what you said though, was it – you talked about how this was a good family home. That's what we were going to make it.'

'Did I? Yes, I suppose I did say something of the sort. But we do have to consider the practical side though.'

'You haven't changed your mind already? Don't you want to live here?'

'I – I well, you know me. Whatever you say will do, I guess. The main thing is us being together.'

'I suppose,' Daniel said. 'Any road, don't let's have that spoil today. Of course, I'll come round to doing what you want. And what we need to sort out now is the more imperative stuff, like putting an announcement of our engagement in the paper, and when shall we have the party?'

'Do we really want it in the paper? We shall be telling friends, and so on. And – actually, I'm not so keen on a party, unless you're desperate to have one?'

'Not desperate, no. I just – oh, Isobel, I only want to please you. Is it too soon, is that the trouble, after – after what happened with your mother?'

'It is rather, if you don't mind.'

'No. No, I'm not too bothered. So – what else is there to be decided?'

They discussed a great deal during that day and subsequently, when they drove into Manchester to select an engagement ring. Daniel was taking charge of everything, insisting that if he was to run the business from Laneside House they must have a telephone installed.

'Won't that be difficult, isn't there a waiting list?' she asked.

'There'll be a way around that.' He'd been doing a bit of carpentry as a favour for one of the bosses who allocated telephones; ought to get one pretty quickly.

Although she hadn't thought very much previously about having a ring, Isobel was thrilled with the one Daniel bought for her. A solitaire diamond on a platinum band, it glinted in the light that evening when they returned to Laneside House. She couldn't stop gazing at her left hand.

Isobel soon realised that she liked being engaged. From the day when she and Daniel went together to her old church and told her friends their news she began to look forward to having someone always there for her. Daniel was so good!

Getting that telephone put in made her feel secure when he couldn't be at Laneside House, and he helped willingly with household chores whenever he came there. When springtime turned to summer he also proved to be interested in improving the garden. Taking the matter seriously, he encouraged Isobel to contribute her ideas while he sketched out a plan for the ground that went all around the property.

One suitably fine Sunday he arrived early in the morning and they started to dig out most of the neglected flowers and shrubs and all of the mass of weeds. Tackling the site energetically, they both worked throughout the day, pausing only to eat a hasty snack at lunchtime, intending to have a substantial meal in the early evening.

Weary, but exhilarated by their progress, they stopped work around four o'clock, and made a pot of tea which they drank sitting out on the garden wall. As they came indoors Isobel laughed over how muddy they'd both become, and said she must have a bath.

'You as well,' she told Daniel. 'I've bought some lovely big towels to go with the bathroom.' She had recently painted the walls in there a delicate blue and liked the effect of the colour against the white porcelain. It was so different from the shades she had used around the rest of the house.

Isobel wasn't sure afterwards if Daniel might have misinterpreted her intention, but initially she was astonished when he came into the bathroom as soon as she stepped into the bath. He turned it into a joke, starting to splash her as she sat in the water, but then he dropped the towel he was carrying, and she saw he was wearing nothing.

Never in her life had Isobel seen a naked man before, only the statues she had seen in the People's Park had given an indication of how he might appear. Daniel, however, was not allowing her more than a momentary glimpse. He slung one leg over the side of the bath, and there he was with her.

She had been soaping herself, he took the soap from her. From her fingertips upwards, he began on her arms, his hand warmer than the water, the bubbles creating a delicious sensation as he methodically covered every inch of her skin. Mesmerised, intoxicated by his touch, Isobel could not have prevented him, had she found a tactful way to do so.

'And now your turn,' she heard herself murmur, and took the soap from him.

The bath was large, but not large enough to accommodate their inexperienced lovemaking when the inevitable kisses grew demanding. Smiling, somewhat bemused, Daniel helped her to get out. He drew her against him, enfolding her in one of the towels, and recommenced his kisses, urgent caressing.

The other towel received them on the floor, warm to her back while his body increased her heat. She thought of all that her friend Diana had said, and knew that she had no wish to create discomfort for Daniel. And none for herself.

He was gentle at first, despite his urgency, her gasp at the moment of pain made him pause, but only to be certain he did not hurt her. Isobel was his, giving of herself, sating that long-existing need to belong this closely to one person.

They lay entwined, made love again, then kissed and drew apart. Isobel turned to empty the neglected bath.

A loud rapping on the front door startled them both.

'Who on earth can that be?' Isobel exclaimed. No one ever visited Laneside House uninvited.

'Don't answer it,' said Daniel, a hand reaching out to grasp her wrist.

'I can't ignore it. Happen somebody's lost on the moor. Or had an accident in a car . . .'

As his fingers slid away she seized her dressing-gown, thrust in her arms, and tied it at the waist. Bare-footed, she hastened to open the door.

'Gustav . . .' His name emerged in one long gasp.

He smiled, his sea-green eyes amused as he indicated her gown. 'Hello. I seem to have a knack of arriving when you are not quite dressed. You remember that first time . . . ?'

Isobel swallowed. 'You'd better come in.'

Gustav closed the outer door and followed her; he was walking slowly, admiring all the details of her newly enhanced hallway.

'You have made your house to look beautiful, have made so many changes,' he began. And he saw Daniel emerging from the bathroom clad only in the towel draped around his waist. 'Changes,' Gustav echoed dismally.

'This is Daniel Armstrong,' said Isobel. 'My fiancé,' she added, aware that she had to say something.

'But yes,' rasped Gustav.

'And you are . . . ?' Daniel demanded.

'Gustav's an old friend of Great-aunt Hannah's,' Isobel announced, and wished with all her heart that her aunt's friend was all he ever had been to her.

Gustav extended a hand for Daniel to shake. Daniel did not move to take it.

'I – I must go and get dressed,' said Isobel.

'No need on my account, I shall remain only a moment,' snapped Gustav.

Miserably, Isobel sought his gaze. 'I thought you had gone home.'

'I explained to you that I would not. I surrendered myself to the authorities, needed to set everything straight.'

'Over here, you mean?'

'Indeed, yes. They have been extremely generous in their – *judgement*. And now I am embarked in my career once more, with aircraft. Soon I shall again by flying.'

'Where's that then – somewhere in Europe?'

Gustav shook his head, could scarcely bring himself to tell her. 'Initially, they wanted me to work in America, only—' His voice faltered, he shook his head again. 'No matter.' He swung around, turned his back on them, and strode towards the door.

He should have taken the American job. The irony of having hung on, insisting that he preferred to live in England, made him fumble opening the door.

Isobel called his name. He ignored her, snatched again at the door handle and walked away down the path.

Clambering into the vehicle he had parked in the road, Gustav realised he had failed to return the key that he had made his excuse for visiting her.

Twelve

'Who did you say that was?' Although less perturbed than Isobel herself, Daniel was more than curious about their visitor.

'Didn't I tell you – a friend of Great-aunt Hannah's?' Isobel was too distressed to recall any word that she had said throughout Gustav's reappearance.

'A friend of hers? I don't understand. He's years younger than she was, and sounds foreign. Where's he from?'

'Germany, actually, or a part of it. He's a pilot, didn't he say he would be flying again?' That fact, at least, had penetrated her confusion.

'Bully for him. What was he doing over here?' Daniel had been in no state for solving conundrums when the fellow arrived, had no intention of taxing his brain now.

'He crashed his plane, just before the end of the war.'

'That's his story! Are you sure he's not a spy?'

'Now you're just being melodramatic.' Isobel ran a hand through her hair, was surprised to discover it was still wet. 'He's left, anyway, hasn't he? And it really is high time I emptied that bath.'

She was desperate to get away somewhere on her own, to experience privately all the turmoil aroused by seeing Gustav again. In that first moment on the doorstep she could have hugged him, and gone on hugging. He had come back to her, after all these months and months of waiting, of wondering.

Isobel was leaning over the bath when Daniel came in. She felt his breath on her neck, and his arms sliding around her. He was pressing close, nibbling at the lobe of her ear, one hand moved to cup her breast.

177

'One more time, eh?' he murmured. 'Upstairs, if you prefer.'

The suggestion shook Isobel, hauled her completely out of all thoughts of Gustav Kassel, and into the grave realisation of all that she was committed to with Daniel.

She quelled a sigh, tried to steady her voice. 'Later perhaps, eh? Still a bit sore.' And this heart of hers felt it would remain sore, always, because of what she had done with this man who was not really the person she loved.

'Has that bloke troubled you – by turning up here, I mean?' Daniel asked eventually.

He had dressed, and so had she, hastily, in order to avoid further encouragement to make love. She would need to take care now, bear in mind the situations which might lead Daniel to expect her to respond to him.

Isobel swallowed, hoped her voice would emerge with some degree of normality. 'It was a surprise, of course, opening the door to find him there.'

'Especially while we were too preoccupied with each other to receive visitors?' Daniel laughed. 'God, but it's no wonder that you were shaken! Must admit you'd surprised me earlier. Don't take this the wrong way, darling, but I didn't believe you were so entirely passionate.'

'I'm not—' Isobel began, and corrected herself hurriedly. She had experienced desire before, a desire haunting her for ages. 'I – I didn't think I'd ever give in to anybody, if you must know, not before we were married.'

'Fair comment. I must count myself lucky – I do already, of course. And the marriage bit doesn't have to wait, remember. You've only got to say.'

They were eating their greatly delayed meal when Daniel insisted he would stay the night. Isobel gave him a look, could find nothing to say. If she prevented that he might try to investigate her state of mind.

He reached across the table, grasped her hand and raised the glittering diamond to his lips. 'I can't rely on this to protect you. I won't have an easy minute wondering just how safe you are here. Not when folk can turn up out of the blue like that.'

Isobel didn't try to argue. With Daniel there all night she might be prevented from dwelling too much on Gustav's presence in the area. And where had he said he had been offered work – in America? Perhaps that would be a good thing, she'd certainly ruined whatever might have happened between them by destroying every second of Gustav's visit to Laneside House. It was over, finally at an end, and until that day she had not had any idea of the true extent of her love for him.

Before at last falling into a troubled sleep, Isobel reminded herself that Gustav, whatever his reaction that day, did have one consolation. He was to fly once more. She could be happy for him.

He drove through the day and into the night, thinking only to reach Farnborough and the work awaiting him. The irony that it was Farnborough, and not some place beyond the Atlantic, was too fierce to ignore. He must simply discipline himself to devote his mind to the task ahead, and leave no room for sentimental musings.

The Yanks would have paid him more, but that was of little consequence, as it had been from the start. Gustav's deepest regret was for the efforts he had sustained in insisting he must remain in England: to remain close to her.

He must concentrate on being thankful that he was needed at the Royal Aircraft Establishment, his introduction to life there had convinced him of that. He enjoyed serving them and, as a pilot with experience of the Luftwaffe planes captured by the British during the war, he possessed an ability rare in this country.

There had even been a certain wry amusement, on his part as well as his superiors', when, on his first visit to the RAE, he'd been re-introduced to the remains of his old Heinkel 162.

'Not much there, is there,' he had remarked. And from that day they expected him to complete their knowledge with his understanding of that particular aircraft.

There could be no going back, but Gustav had entertained

no thoughts of turning away since that day in the POW camp when this version of his airborne life had been offered to him. *Out of the blue* was the phrase learned in England. And into the skies was once more to be his destiny.

He might even, with time, come to believe that this cruel removal of all distractions by today's events would be good for singleness of purpose.

There was nothing to distract her now. With Daniel's departure for work on the Monday morning, Isobel felt the withdrawal of the only thing that had prevented her brooding constantly about Gustav. During those intervening hours she had forced herself to concentrate on whatever Daniel might be saying; and there had been enough words to occupy her. They had slept together that night, and Isobel had made no secret of their *sleeping* in the same bed being the aspect that mattered to her.

Perhaps she should have anticipated that Daniel would use her reservations regarding their lovemaking to urge that they marry in the very near future. Isobel was afraid that mention of her mother's death would not serve to withstand his suggestions for very much longer. And the absence of Amy Conquest was no longer her sole reason for experiencing so much grief.

Alone at last, she was bereft by losing Gustav. She could be sure that he would never even contemplate returning. Washing dishes, and later beginning to wash her clothes and a few belonging to Daniel, Isobel heard a keening sound. And was shaken to recognise her own voice.

She couldn't go on like this, could not, and *must not*. She could blame no one but herself. Isobel Johnson was the one who'd lacked the courage to be forthright with Gustav originally, had been too scared to even hint at the immediate attraction she felt towards him. Worse than that was her more recent lack of spirit. She had entrapped herself in this relationship with a man she liked rather than loved.

Daniel didn't deserve this, didn't deserve her; but nor did he deserve to have life shattered by an engagement broken before it had begun to trundle towards marriage. And yet –

perhaps making a break now could be kinder? Better than trying to free herself after a wedding day was fixed . . . ?

Isobel wished she could avoid thinking about weddings. Her three friends certainly had ensured that they were all tying the knot in rapid succession. The third couple were to marry on the very next Saturday. Daniel was talking about that last night, sounding elated for them – and, for himself, eager to anticipate the day when he might place that second ring on Isobel's finger.

He had even promised – if while ruefully wondering aloud how he might manage that – to abstain from lovemaking until he and Isobel were wed.

'You wouldn't keep me waiting for ever, would you?' he'd asked, quite jovially. And added that he suspected *she* might not wish to hinder their desire completely.

The telephone rang while her arms were immersed in soapsuds. Heeding her own, wild, fantasy that the caller was Gustav, Isobel dashed to answer.

'Darling,' said Daniel. 'Just to say that I am missing you already. You gave me such a wonderful weekend.' He paused, anxiously. 'You are still there? Isobel?'

'Of course, of course. Just – busy. Doing some washing.'

'Mine as well? I didn't mean you to do that. Still – practice for you, for later. But you do know that I shan't wish you to work too hard for us, don't you? I want to give you a better life, wish only to make you happy.'

Isobel cut him short, thanked him, but lied that the kettle was boiling and she must dash. 'I mustn't make a mess.'

But a mess was what she had made, of her own life and, potentially, of Daniel's.

That thought became fixed in her head, and remained there up to the next wedding they attended, and throughout the ceremony.

Yet again, Isobel drank more wine than she was used to at the reception. She realised what she was doing, but could find no acceptable alternative. And on this occasion she knew it surely was not through any wish to let her hair down. On their way from the church Daniel had raised the matter of their own marriage, and asked how they would arrange the ceremony in St Paul's church when neither of them lived in the parish. Their conversation in the car was still circulating around her head.

'That is where you'd like us to marry, isn't it?' he enquired gently. 'Where all your friends are, and you've known the vicar for years.'

'I hadn't really thought that far ahead,' Isobel admitted.

'There's the church near my cottage, of course.'

'Or the one just over the hill from Laneside House.' Providing alternatives might result in long discussions, prolong the wait . . . ?

'That should be the one,' Daniel confirmed. 'What could be more appropriate – your great-grandfather would be delighted. We'll see their vicar next Sunday, shall we? Or better still, tomorrow. Don't look so perturbed, we can fix a date some way ahead.'

Isobel had no relevant excuse, or none but the brutal truth that she had changed her mind about marrying him. She could not do that. Even while the wine was stimulating her brain, she could not summon the guts to wreck his future.

She had not been aware, not fully aware, of how deeply distressed Daniel would be if she were to reject him. Isobel had seen him afresh ever since their lovemaking, had witnessed an increase in his tenderness, a fresh relaxation that revealed his reliance upon their relationship.

There was no way out.

Returning that night to Laneside House Isobel had barely forced herself to face the picure of Edward Johnson. He would despise her for failing to acknowledge her true feelings, and think less still of her now that she meant to continue this deception. She must not depend upon wine to fortify her next day, and without its bolstering she was afraid she'd feel obliged to go ahead, increase her commitment, and marry Daniel.

The Rev Reginald Fieldhouse welcomed them into his vestry at the end of Evensong. He indicated chairs, invited them to sit, and asked how familiar they were with the service of Holy Matrimony.

Isobel could not be surprised, his job was to ensure that those he joined together were conscious of the gravity of what they were undertaking. What did take her by surprise was his early reference to marriage as an institution that should ensure that sexual relations took place as sanctioned between those benefiting from that sacrament. She felt hot colour raging up her neck and into her cheeks, saw Daniel shift uneasily on his chair.

'This is precisely the reason why we wish to marry as soon as may be arranged,' said Daniel. 'That plus our longing to start a family. The war years kept us apart for too long.'

The vicar smiled as he nodded. 'You seem to comprehend quite fully,' he told Daniel before turning to Isobel. 'And you, Miss Johnson – you also appreciate the sanctity of marriage, are ready to make such a commitment?'

'I take the Church very seriously, have attended for years near my home in Halifax. I think I understand the promises I'd be making.'

'We shall be touching on those, later on, when we run through the text of the service together. For the moment, we need to set a date that's agreeable to the pair of you and fits into our diary here. Did you have a Saturday in mind perhaps? Most couples seem to want to have their big day on one.'

'I'm not really certain . . .' Isobel began. If she and Daniel had discussed this, she'd no recollection of their deciding.

'You *are* sure you're ready to go ahead?' the Rev Fieldhouse asked anxiously.

'I've been longing to settle down for life, ever since I was a prisoner of war,' said Daniel fervently. 'I shall believe my dreams have materialised when Isobel and I are together at last.'

'Then we must do whatever we can to make that come true for you,' said the vicar.

Isobel tried to force herself to pay attention through the throbbing of her head. Daniel seemed to be reeling off possible dates for when their wedding should be fixed. She wanted to put a brake on that, couldn't think how. And then the vicar diverted to give an introductory explanation about the ceremony itself before pausing to ask if they knew

183

approximately how many people would be attending. As they saw, his church wasn't all that large.

'Not so many on my side, I'm afraid,' Isobel told him. 'A few of my friends and their husbands. We lost my mother and her husband in an accident a few months back, I haven't really got any close relations now.'

'I shall be inviting some friends too,' Daniel explained. 'A few I was with in the forces.' He turned to Isobel. 'Don't you want to trace some Land Army pals, so they can see you getting wed?'

'I suppose I might try to trace them,' she replied. But she really wished just to have the ceremony over. The prospect of filling the pews with a mass of witnesses felt quite alarming.

'You will need to decide who is to witness your signatures on the certificate,' they were reminded, echoing her thoughts. 'Someone representing each side, as it were, is customary. Though not obligatory,' he added. Miss Johnson was looking awkward, as if she would be unable to suggest anyone.

'Right then, fine,' said Isobel briskly, aware that she was expected to enthuse about this whole business. 'Is there anything else we need to discuss before we decide on a date?' At least, having attended three weddings this year had bestowed some idea of what was necessary.

The look Daniel gave her was strange. 'I thought you had nodded when I suggested the last Saturday in June.'

Isobel was appalled. She had been so distracted that she hadn't taken in their making a firm arrangement. Whatever was wrong with her? Hadn't she herself been leaning towards delaying until well into the following year?

The vicar noticed her frown. 'I believe this young lady believes that, after all, she will need rather longer in which to prepare. Am I right?'

'Well – well, yes, really. There'll be a frock to make,' she said swiftly. 'I shall want to do that myself – I design dresses, you see.'

'I shall expect you to produce something spectacular,' said Daniel, determined to please her. 'I know you'll make me very proud.'

'How about early October then?' she suggested. That seemed far enough into the future to be less perturbing.

'Mightn't it be a bit cold out here?' asked Daniel.

'I can bear that in mind when I'm designing my outfit, can't I?'

Leaving the church, it occurred to Isobel that there might yet be some other circumstance which could govern the features of her bridal outfit. She had been so incautious when making love, could not credit now that she'd been stupid enough to risk becoming pregnant.

For days Isobel worried in case she could be expecting. Would an October wedding be soon enough to disguise the fact? Ought she to have fallen in with Daniel's suggestion of marrying in a few weeks' time?

Worst of all, was living with the knowledge that she'd never disguise the truth from *herself*: she had let passion drive her to have sex that day.

Reassurance that she wasn't pregnant came as a massive relief, and Isobel permitted herself to enjoy shopping for the material for her gown. As soon as she found a fabric that delighted her, she set to work eagerly to draft possible styles. She could picture the effect that she wished to create. Both Louise and Betty had gone for very pretty dresses that were quite fancy, possibly a reaction to the Utility style of frocks available since the later years of the war. Isobel herself planned to have something plainer and more elegant. She had lost a bit of weight since her mother's death, and would rely on her streamlined figure to contribute to the svelt effect.

Beginning to cut out the cloth Isobel smiled, if rather ruefully. This was the one time that she would marry, and creating her outfit the one aspect of the entire business that she would enjoy.

Encouraged by her interest in the task, Isobel decided that she would write to one of her Land Army friends, Flora Bright, who was a fellow dress-designer and lived in London. She would love to see her again.

Isobel discovered that another good thing about designing and making her wedding dress was the reason the task supplied for seeing Daniel less frequently. And for discouraging him from staying the night at Laneside House. Following the weekend when they had made love he had taken to expecting Isobel to invite him to remain there overnight, and she was finding such an arrangement trying.

The difficulty was chiefly within herself. Daniel was an attractive man, and she was surprised to discover how frequently she experienced an eager response to simply having him around. Most times, they curtailed their kisses and caresses, but Isobel remained conscious that their situation was not ideal.

Daniel maintained that he was willing to bow to her decision, this only resulted in Isobel's fear that she was being unfair when she refused to make love completely. Somehow, she could not forget what Diana had said about the strain placed on a girl's fiancé. Despite her private reluctance to become Daniel's wife, there were occasions when she wished their wedding date were nearer.

On the other hand, Isobel also relished the times when she was alone in Laneside House, free to do exactly as she wished there. She was especially pleased with the way she had improved that kitchen, and loved using her new bathroom.

Even her bedroom, where she had done little more than decorate the walls and make new curtains and a bedcover, pleased her and provided a restful setting. Except for the one night, she had avoided sharing it with Daniel, insisting that he should use the spare bed whenever he chose to stay. Privately, she admitted that she didn't really wish him to become too comfortable in territory which she reserved for herself – at least until she could no longer justify excluding him.

They attended the church on the edge of the moors for the reading of their banns, and took the opportunity to ask the vicar what else would be required of them before the day itself. He explained that he would wish to have another chat with them nearer to the event, and asked them to arrange when they might be free to see him.

On the Sunday that they visited Daniel's church at Holywell Green, he insisted on preparing lunch for them, and Isobel was glad that his terraced cottage still looked just as lovely as it had on her original visit.

'I'm pleased to see you take care of this place still. That'll help it to sell quickly when you put it on the market, won't it?' And, she thought sensibly, the standard of care here indicated that she need have no qualms about his tidiness when they were together at Laneside House.

'I was brought up to look after stuff,' Daniel told her, gazing around them with a satisfied smile. 'And being in the building trade makes me aware of the benefit of having a place look smart.'

When Isobel's wedding dress was almost completed, she began to feel miserable. She had loved devoting all her skills and experience to creating the gown, and began to wish that there was some way of returning to a career in designing fashions. She also was missing Amy Conquest more than ever before. Getting ready for being married was something that her mother should have shared and Amy, who always encouraged her daughter's flair for style, would have loved to participate.

Isobel had no wish to reveal any details of the dress to Daniel ahead of the day, and concealed it in a locked wardrobe whenever he was visiting. Still needing to share it with someone, though, she invited Diana to come over one evening.

Isobel might have anticipated that Richard would bring Diana in the car, but she hadn't thought of that, and was somewhat disappointed to find them both at the door. Reflecting while she made a pot of tea for them, Isobel supposed that this was how it was for couples once they married, and she might expect that Daniel would accompany her when calling on friends. He might not feel happy if she often went out on her own.

That prospect didn't appeal, but perhaps after they themselves were married, she would feel more comfortable with it, especially if they made a habit of seeing her old friends. Since Daniel had sold his motorcycle he'd acquired the van, and she now had the car. They both drove, and would easily make trips back and forth to Halifax. And, of course, to see Daniel's friends – she'd no intention of being selfish.

Richard seemed happy that evening to catch up with the day's news on the wireless while Diana went upstairs to see Isobel's wedding dress,

The two women might have slipped back several years to the days when they had felt like sisters. Talking excitedly, the dress was acclaimed a huge success when Diana insisted her friend must try it on. By the time the couple were ready to leave Isobel was beginning to believe that she might, after all, start looking forward to her wedding. Even without her mother.

They had encountered a few difficulties though when arranging the ceremony. For Isobel, the most serious was not knowing a man who could give her away. As soon as she considered the necessity for finding someone, she'd become upset about her lack of family.

Isobel was mentioning this worry to Diana when they returned downstairs.

'Does it have to be a relative?' Richard enquired.

'Not really. I suppose that's only customary.'

'Well I if you've truly got no one else in mind, you may count on me. You did hang around with us all, at one time, didn't you? Folk could say that we're a part of your old life, the drama group, church, and so on.'

'And that's what it's about, isn't it?' his wife put in. 'Having someone mark the way in which you're moving on to a fresh existence.'

Isobel thanked Richard warmly and said how relieved she was to have the problem solved. 'Now Diana's approved my frock, I'm quite looking forward to this marriage.'

'You mean, you weren't before?' Diana was horrified.

'Happen it's because I'm getting on a bit for settling down. You don't get as excited at our age, do you?'

They both laughed. 'We're not exactly in our dotage, are we!' Diana exclaimed. 'You surprise me sometimes, Isobel, you really do. What sort of excitement are you expecting? You've had a job that was above the ordinary, fashion designing, then you had the interest of creating this lovely

188

home out of a wreck of a place. You've had this lovely looking man come into your life, and now he wants to wed you. What more could you ever wish to have . . . ?'

What indeed? thought Isobel afterwards. She suspected that something within herself was creating all the doubts she might have about marrying Daniel. She knew, as no one else ever would, that he was not the man she was madly in love with. Since the decision was made to go ahead with this wedding, she owed it to Daniel to become whole-hearted about her commitment. If she were not extremely careful to put her misgivings behind her, she might convey to him precisely how strong they were.

During the next few occasions that they were together, Isobel began to be afraid that she might already have passed on too much of her unease to her fiancé. He so often appeared preoccupied, and did not enthuse when she encouraged him to offer ideas of how they might decorate the other bedroom.

'This will be ours, remember,' she said when they were in the room one Sunday, looking at her sketches of the colour schemes she envisaged. She had emphasised already that she felt their new life together deserved a fresh beginning.

Daniel made a few suggestions regarding the shade of distemper for the walls, but he didn't make the expected offer to share the job of painting them. Isobel wasn't pleased. Admittedly, she had finished sewing her dress, but she'd since located material to make fresh curtains for this bedroom and a matching bedspread. With cloth still in short supply, Isobel thought she had done very well to obtain something suitable.

Sewing those items while Daniel was distempering the walls had seemed an ideal prospect to her, but without his assistance she didn't know how ever the room would be ready.

He does work hard, admittedly, she silently reminded herself. And Isobel herself hadn't looked for another job while busily sewing her wedding gown. She still felt torn between designing clothes and eventually setting up some sort of interior design company. She hoped that after they were married the necessary paints and wallpapers could be easier to obtain. If that should prove so, she wouldn't need much convincing that starting up in décor would be good.

Resisting the impulse to reproach Daniel for not offering to do more work there, Isobel began asking him again what he thought her chances were of making a success of a decorating business.

'You do like the finished result in the house here, don't you?' she added.

'I said so, didn't I? Ages ago. I can't keep on enthusing, it's not normal.'

And failing to enthuse about our future life together shouldn't be normal either, thought Isobel guiltily. She reckoned that she had infected Daniel with her own reluctance. She must cease trying to analyse every emotion and get on with the work that needed doing.

Isobel had covered the bedroom furniture with dust sheets, and was starting to distemper the walls on the day when Daniel arrived unexpectedly.

'I am working, no need to check up on me,' she teased when she saw his frown as she opened the front door to him. 'You'll have to come upstairs to talk, or the wall I'm doing will end up all patchy. If it's an eyesore, you'll notice it for the rest of your days!'

'We do need to talk, and I'd rather you set that aside for a few minutes. This is important.'

'So's this. Now come on up. I'll listen properly, I promise. It's only that I've got to put my best work into this house.' She had run upstairs and was picking up her brush again.

'In a way, that's what the trouble is,' David began, leaning against the doorframe, not watching her. 'You've got this house, and you've put your whole heart into it. I can see that, and I can't blame you for being that way. What you are disregarding, though, is my feelings about my own cottage. I gave just as much of my time, and energy as well, into making that as near-perfect as I could. Yet you won't even discuss the possibility of coming to live there.'

'But—' Shattered, Isobel paused, still holding the brush which she had just dipped into distemper. 'But you love Laneside House, you wanted it, even before I—'

Daniel interrupted. 'I've told you once, do I have to say it again – that was before I saw this place after the war, before I knew you'd inherited it. I haven't wanted to own it since then and, frankly, I don't really wish to live here.'

'Is that the reason you've seemed so – *different* recently? I wondered if you were just like me, wondering why it didn't feel exciting enough?'

Daniel seized on that. 'You're not excited then, about marrying me?'

'I said "excited *enough*", don't make it sound so awful. I reckoned it was just – well, that we're not that young any longer.'

'Okay. If we're as mature as all that, we ought to be able to work something out. Granted, there is a problem. One we've got to acknowledge. I really am afraid I can't live here, Isobel.'

'Won't, you mean – won't.' She was applying paint furiously, splashing all around her.

'I said *can't*. With good reason. Laneside House is too remote for running my business, and I'm not prepared to sacrifice that. Equally vitally, this house is *yours* – very much so now that you're completing everything to your taste.'

'You should understand that. It's precisely what you've done with your cottage.'

'Which is the reason I love it so much. Restoring my place became pledge when I returned from POW camp. It was, still is, a symbol of my new life.' He hesitated, forming the words of his next suggestion. 'All I wish is to share that with you, Isobel. Say you'll come and live with me.'

'Just like that – scrap all our plans. Alter everything?' She tossed her brush into the distemper. 'Stop all this, *desert* Laneside House? With all it means to me?'

'It's what you're expecting of me, with regard to my home.' His voice was ominously quiet.

'Daniel?' Isobel sighed, recognising precisely how determined he was. 'Would you really refuse to live here?'

'I'm afraid that is how it seems.'

'But what if I don't want to give up on Laneside House?'

'That is a decision only you can make. We both need to do some serious thinking. You know where I live,' Daniel added abruptly.

He turned away, went running down the stairs, then striding towards the door. He suddenly hadn't the least idea how he was to cope with any of this.

Thirteen

Isobel was too stunned to think of calling Daniel back. She watched him running towards his van, and felt a massive sadness overwhelming her. Sadness for him. Had she let him down? By failing to even discuss moving into his cottage, she had proved herself just as adamant as he appeared to be about where their future might lie.

Or their separate futures, Isobel reflected, and experienced the first hint of returning comfort. If they were not to marry, she need no longer be troubled by the necessity for concealing the limit of her love for him. She could cease pretending.

She was not in love with Daniel, she never had been, and attraction might have proved insufficient within a short time of ending the predictable honeymoon excesses. No one could wish to live on a relentless surfeit of sex, if there was no depth of emotion to support the relationship.

If it were destined not to last she, for one, would prefer that such a marriage should not even begin. A break now (and Isobel was afraid they did seem unable to avoid such a break) was upsetting enough, but separating afterwards would bring additional heartbreak.

Turning from the bedroom window, she retrieved her brush from the mess created by dropping it into the distemper. She wiped any surplus off the handle, and determinedly continued to paint the wall. It didn't look good, but Isobel was compelled to complete this one side of the room at least. No matter how plainly visible the areas where she had paused in applying the paint. Eventually, she would do what she could to restore its appearance with further coats.

The telephone rang before Isobel had finished, and she left it to ring. She was no longer going to have anyone come between her and her beloved home. When the phone rang a second time just as she was cleaning her brush afterwards, she decided she could not have it continue to disturb her at intervals for ever. Isobel wasn't surprised to find Daniel at the other end, but she was surprised by her own instant dread when she heard his words.

'I shouldn't have sprung all that on you, and I'm sorry, Isobel. I'll come over to see you again, and we will discuss this coolly. I can see now that I put you in a spot, which I shouldn't have done, not without warning.'

'It's all right, Daniel. And I'm glad there's no hard feelings between us,' she responded rapidly. He must not change his mind again! 'But I really don't want to sit down to talk this through, I don't believe there's any point.'

'No point? You can't mean that. We get on well enough, and you said you like my little home, have liked it from the start.'

'This isn't about houses,' said Isobel swiftly, fearing that Daniel supposed he could talk her round.

'Look – why don't we give ourselves a fair chance? We needn't sell either place immediately. I'd even give moving in with you a try – say, for a month.'

'I don't believe hints that any arrangement was temporary would do much to help us settle happily together, do you? I've waited a long time to be planning to marry, I don't intend that to be clouded by doubts.'

'We could possibly consider putting both houses on the market, and buying something fresh together.'

That offer was more than Isobel expected, and shook her resolution. How could she, without hurting him, say she was discovering she really was relieved to be handed a means of extracting herself? She did not wish to live anywhere with him.

'It isn't just about where we'd live,' she insisted quietly. 'That's just – brought things to a head.'

'Then what is wrong? Tell me, and we can sort it out.'

'It isn't something we could sort by talking, Daniel.'

'We're fond of each other, aren't we?'

'Ah. Yes, I think we are *fond* – I'm sorry, but that isn't sufficient.'

'You're breaking off our engagement?'

'*We are*, Daniel – we're doing this. I – frankly, I would have gone ahead if you hadn't begun to admit to problems. It's – unfortunate, but it's made me see I don't believe our relationship would work. It's never going to be the marriage we both need. I'll let you have the ring back.'

She had removed it, of course, before starting the distempering. Never putting it back on her finger seemed less of a problem than deciding when and where to return it to Daniel.

He wouldn't stop talking. He was saying she must keep the ring, that he had chosen it for *her*. But Isobel could believe that there would be more than enough reminders of him without that. Reminders of how guilty she must feel.

'I'll see you get it back,' she said, and replaced the receiver.

On that matter, at least, the discussion appeared to be closed. Daniel didn't call her again, and maintained his silence during most of the following day.

When she had eaten something that evening Isobel set out in the car. She had the ring in her handbag, and also made sure she carried an envelope, pen and paper. Timing her visit for evening when Daniel ought to be at home didn't guarantee that she would find him in, and she didn't intend mustering courage again to repeat this. Leaving a note might be a coward's trick, but she was prepared to admit to cowardice.

Her knock at the door was answered immediately, creating a tumult of emotions. Relief that the ordeal soon would be over, but also distress because their relationship was indeed ending. She couldn't dismiss how dejected Daniel looked.

Trying not to fumble, Isobel located the ring box in her bag and held it towards him. 'Please take this, Daniel, I don't want any fuss.'

Avoiding her gaze, he accepted the tiny box. 'As you wish.' He sighed. 'I shall keep it for you: in time you could change your mind.'

'That's up to you,' she said, unable to ram home the facts of how she felt about him and destroy the last glint of hope.

It was quite early in the evening, still daylight. Isobel

decided she should rid herself of another unpleasant task which was troubling her in prospect. When she neared the edge of the moors she turned off the familiar road and headed uphill. It seemed quite dark where the church was shadowed, and no lights were showing in the building, but there was one glow from a curtained window of the vicarage.

Isobel had visualised the encounter as being brief, conducted in the church where the air of formality might have aided her need to have her say, swiftly, and then depart. When the Rev Reginald Fieldhouse welcomed her with a smile at the vicarage door, she felt trapped by the warmth of his greeting.

'Come in, come in, my dear.' He faltered for a second, glancing beyond her. 'Is – is your fiancé not with you?'

He was taking the coat which she'd draped around her shoulders, hanging it behind the door, then ushering her through into the room she took to be his study.

'Daniel's not with me, and not likely to be, I'm afraid,' said Isobel, rapidly, in order to have the truth in the open. She was ignoring his invitation to sit. But the vicar seized a chair and set it immediately behind her. His fingers felt gentle as they pressed into her shoulders.

'No need to remain standing,' he asserted softly.

He seemed kinder than she'd anticipated, and Isobel was yearning for kindness. Even without deserving any. A tear splashed on to her hand, and then another. She scrabbled among the contents of her handbag to find a handkerchief.

'I feel such an idiot, I didn't mean to cry. I'm not that upset, not really. I only came here to tell you that Daniel and I won't be getting married. I thought if I cancelled straightaway you could let somebody else have that date.'

'That's very considerate. Is – does that mean the decision's quite recent?'

'Yesterday.'

That recent! thought Reginald, and admired Isobel's composure which she herself evidently didn't believe quite adequate. 'Do you wish to say any more?'

Waiting for a response, he offered her a drink, and poured the sherry which she requested.

Isobel shrugged away his question. The engagement might have expired, she hadn't anticipated holding an inquest. But this was yet another situation where she ought to have been turning to her mother. And she should not permit herself time to dwell on Amy's absence.

'Can I be completely honest with you?' she asked eventually, tears under control.

'I'll be perturbed if you feel you can't. Why don't you try me out? Parsons do acquire broad shoulders, you know, and broader minds than some folk suspect!'

His approach felt exactly right, Isobel found she was unable to withhold anything. 'I'm fond of Daniel still, but I'm not in love with him, otherwise none of the rest would have mattered so much.'

She explained how they had argued about where they would live, and how she had actually felt goaded to defend her right to remain at Laneside House.

'I know I'm not like that really, you see: with the right man I'd have gone anywhere, would have lived in a – in the proverbial shack because I was in love with him. With Daniel, nothing was quite right, even when we were trying to make it work.'

'And had you ceased trying?'

Isobel sighed. 'I didn't believe that I had stopped. I still wanted to give him a good home life, to make the house nice.'

'*Your* house.'

'There is that. Am I very wrong to love the place, because it's a family thing?'

'Roots do count for a lot; though where we put them down can be conditioned by situations. One cannot generalise.' He sipped his own drink, smiled towards her.

'Your great-aunt was fond of Laneside House, wasn't she? Until the roof began leaking so badly and it all was too much for her.'

'It was my great-grandfather's before that, and he loved it so much.'

'But never more than he loved his wife and family?'

'They were a part of it all.'

'Yet it couldn't work that way for you?'

'With Daniel, no. He didn't seem to quite fit my picture. I can't analyse why.'

'Too soon, I guess.' He considered for a moment. 'And you don't wish me to hold that date in reserve for you, just for a short while, just in case?'

'Definitely not. I'm sorry.'

'Don't be. I've seen worse things than broken engagements. Broken marriages, for instance.'

'Does it sound awful that I'm so sure we've done the right thing now that I'm not even dreading always living alone?'

'The solitary life might not be ideal, you know, but you may take it from me that it can prove – acceptable. You, however, are young enough to meet someone you will love greatly – someone who means so much that you would settle in that shack you mention.'

'I doubt that now.' She had met that man already, and now he was making a new life, in America. Turning his back on her, on her and Daniel.

'Sometimes,' said Reginald pensively, 'sometimes when one needs a second chance, that is granted.'

It was a second opportunity, yet in a way the first real opportunity he'd ever had to be himself entirely. In his old life, in the Luftwaffe, he'd been restricted by too many fears. By dread of antagonising the authorities, or by falling short of the demands of senior officers during training. Even gaining the ability to fly had not freed him of the need for circumspection.

Gustav smiled to himself, acknowledging that he'd finally escaped the limitations inhibiting him on account of being a Sudeten. There was no need now for backward glances, no dread that his being of a *different* German stock could invite trouble.

Here in Britain, he was accepted as he was – a former enemy perhaps, but beginning to win respect for his experience, and for his skills. This acceptance had taken a while, he had expected it might prove so, but the cameraderie surrounding him now was evidence that no one bore him any grudge.

The language pilots spoke, and engineers also, was their common bond. The strongest unifying force, though, was their understanding and love of aircraft. Gustav was fortunate here too, one of the senior men had lived and trained in Germany, and two of the technicians recently joining them were formerly from the Luftwaffe.

Both technicians had served in occupied Norway, and were glad to seek Gustav out during any free time as they hadn't yet acquired his fluent English. Their wartime histories, unfolding over a beer or three, sounded very different from his own.

It was the future, however, which preoccupied their working lives. The detailed examination of original planes and their many components was but a stage in the major aim, which was development. In his experience of one of the earliest jet-powered aircraft Gustav possessed a vital advantage.

To date, he hadn't flown since arriving at the Royal Aircraft Establishment in Farnborough, but his initial flight for them was scheduled later that week. In the meantime, refreshing his memory of that particular model of Heinkel was testing his intellect.

Gustav was surprised by the quantity of data the RAE had acquired, he knew how all German manufacturers had destroyed most records in the expectation that their planes might fall into the hands of the Allies. From what he recalled of work on the underground production lines, the specifications he'd seen there seemed less comprehensive than these available on site in England.

Studying in order to reconcile plans and specifications with the actual planes was tiring, a factor proving a disappointment to him, but hardly a surprise. Long months of tending crops or learning to grow vegetables wasn't exactly demanding mentally!

Gustav was glad to be stretched, though, to have his mind challenged again, and even despite the pressure under which they worked, those above him made time to approve his progress. By the day when he was allowed into the air again, he would feel that he was truly coming alive.

*   *   *

'How can you live like that, and live happily? Out there in the wilds on your own! Have you no regrets at all?' Diana was appalled by Isobel's news.

Isobel had anticipated that this would be her friend's reaction, and delayed for almost a month before calling on her to explain her broken engagement. She was obliged to tell them that she would no longer require Richard's helpful offer of giving her away.

Before she got as far as saying any of that, Richard heard his wife's exclamation and came hurrying through from the kitchen where he'd gone to fill the kettle.

'What's all this, Di? Why are you going on at Isobel? She hasn't been in the house five minutes.'

'Wait till you hear this, darling,' said Diana. 'Isobel's only gone and given Daniel his marching orders. Already!'

'That isn't quite the way it was,' her friend contradicted swiftly. 'All right – I have just said I've been to the vicar to cancel everything, but it was more – well, a mutual decision. And but for Daniel's ideas, we'd have still been going ahead.'

'Poor chap,' Richard put in. 'I somehow suspected he'd get the blame.'

Isobel shrugged. She might have anticipated Richard's reaction, if Diana had disappointed her. 'If he hadn't come out with not wanting to live at Laneside House, after all, I'd have let things take their course.'

Richard raised an eyebrow, and went back into the kitchen to make coffee.

'How's he taken it?' asked Diana, still unable to get her head round the concept of Daniel's being the one to topple the first brick. 'I thought he was dead set on settling down, anyway.'

'He's taken it like a man who's content to walk away. So long as that's towards his own cottage,' she added dourly, only privately admitting that was tailoring the truth to fit.

'Didn't you once tell me he'd made that place of his look really beautful?'

'Aye – he has. But it doesn't have the family history that Laneside House has.'

'And is that going to console you through those long winter nights on the edge of the moors? I don't think so.'

'I'm getting used to the idea again now, Diana. And I'm going back to work – designing.'

'What happened to the notion of starting your own business, decorating and that?' asked Richard, handing mugs of coffee around.

'To be honest, I'm not certain that ever would have worked out. The work I've done on Laneside House must leave a lot to be desired, or he'd not have been so against the place. Any road, it had been dependent for jobs on introductions that Daniel might put my way.'

'You've scuppered that then,' said Diana, and sighed. 'What are you like, Isobel? Can't you settle for a normal existence like the rest of us?'

'Happen I wasn't meant to.' She could hardly say that her expectations were too high, not when Diana and the others had married men they had known for so long that Isobel marvelled they weren't already bored with seeming over-familiar!

Richard was smiling at his wife. 'We are very fortunate, don't forget, Di. Not everyone suddenly notices that a person in their group is really rather special!'

'Okay, okay. Sorry, Isobel, sorry. You're right, of course, to be choosey – you're old enough, after all, to be aware of the future consequences.'

'Are you going to tell her our news?' Richard asked her, beaming.

'Not sure this is good timing.'

'You'll have to tell me now,' Isobel insisted. 'And you needn't fret – I'm not about to burst into tears.'

'Actually, I'm expecting,' Diana announced. 'We're both absolutely thrilled. And we're house-hunting in earnest. When Richard moved into this place with me, it was only to give us a bit of a start. We always planned to buy somewhere bigger.'

Isobel spent the remainder of the evening willing herself not to reveal her own sudden emotional turmoil, while she listened to every detail of how Diana had discovered her pregnancy, and how elated she and Richard were.

'We'd been trying for a baby from the start, but I was afraid that I was a bit on the old side for falling for one straight away. I can't tell you what a difference this is making to our lives already.'

'Having me turn into a model husband, for one thing,' Richard declared ruefully, bending to kiss Diana as he passed her chair.

'He really is, you know, Isobel,' she exclaimed. 'Tea in bed in a morning – when I can face it, that is. Can't every day. And you saw how he leapt to make the coffee just now when you arrived. Before all this, he wouldn't have got off his bottom!'

'You don't know that,' Richard argued, then laughed. 'No matter, anyway.'

Diana faced her friend again. 'Oh, you are a fool, Isobel, turning down the thought of marriage. I was so hoping that we'd be bringing up our families together. Betty isn't sure she wants children, although Louise seems to be coming round to the idea. But you and I are the ones who were special pals, I do wish we were sharing this excitement.'

Isobel refrained from pointing out that even if she were likely to be in a similar condition she lived too far away for very much of the sharing that Diana envisaged.

The thought of having a family remained with her, nevertheless, taunting her at Laneside House with reminders that her great-grandfather had centred his dreams on its being a home for his children. And this was one occasion when re-reading Edward Johnson's letters would provide the very opposite of consolation. Had she perhaps been very misguided to destroy the opportunity of creating a family with Daniel?

A proper family was something that felt so very basic to her needs, and would have provided a goal. Might that have proved sufficient if she'd only given it a chance . . . have given Daniel a chance?

Isobel could well never know, and must steel herself to relinquish such conjecturing. It was neither helpful nor productive. Hadn't she vowed that this must be the time for being practical? For the present she was awaiting the postman, hoping for the final answer on an interview that she'd attended which sounded promising.

The work would be in Manchester, for a fashion company that seemed larger than the one for which she had designed in Leeds. Meeting a new challenge among fresh people would be good for her, as would travelling in quite the opposite direction every day. Now that she had a car the journeys ought to be easy.

Isobel heard the letter box rattle, and the postman's footsteps hastening towards the bicycle he always left by her gate. And now she hesitated, torn between needing to learn the truth and dread of that truth disappointing her. She was in no mood for destruction of any more of her plans.

After hurrying to pick up the envelope, she hesitated again, feeling unable to face a gloomy letter. When she read the first couple of lines Isobel wished that she had delayed opening it. They regretted that, at this particular time, they were not offering the position to her. The assurance that they would keep a note of her name and her experience was no consolation to Isobel.

It was now that she needed the fresh stimulation of work, *now* that she was desperate for something to deflect her busy brain from repeatedly wondering how she ought to have avoided her current situation.

She was even beginning to dislike Laneside House, lovely though it looked, carefully though she had restored it. The walls she had painted, the bathroom she'd designed, the garden where she and Daniel had laboured, all conspired now to force her to contemplate this *real* future. The one in which she'd trapped herself.

Isobel did not enjoy living on her own there. No matter how frequently she had confirmed to Diana and other friends that she was aware of its shortcomings, she was only recently acknowledging that alone on the edge of bleak moorland was no longer the way that she wished to live!

Worst of all, the factor of its being intended as a *family* home (the very aspect first enhancing Laneside for her) was proving the source of her deepest distress. Never once had she believed that she wouldn't, one day, have children. Today it seemed she had tossed away that prospect along with any future with Daniel.

Noticing the second letter delivered that morning, Isobel slit the envelope, and discovered a reply from Flora Bright, her Land Army friend in London. Dismayed, she read that her invitation to the wedding was eagerly accepted.

She would have to tell Flora how everything had changed, and she didn't feel able to face sitting down to put that into words. Not permitting herself to delay, she went straight to the telephone. Embarrassing the conversation might prove, but it wouldn't last more than a minute or two.

Flora answered at once, and simply hearing her voice cheered Isobel immediately. Naturally, as soon as her friend learned the news she was extremely sympathetic. They talked for longer than Isobel had anticipated and Flora suggested that she should come to London for a long weekend, or even a week. For once in her life, Isobel was impulsive and snapped up the invitation.

The stay with Flora couldn't have occurred at a better time, forcing Isobel to pack hastily and go off to her train without a moment's reflection. And from the minute that the two women hugged each other at King's Cross Station, they both were too elated to allow time for misgivings about anything.

En route to the small house that Flora had bought, she pointed out the fashion house for whom she was designing, her enthusiasm reminding Isobel of the old days when *she* had dreamed only of working in the trade.

They sat up late that night, chatting, catching up on the years intervening since war-time. On the following day, Flora insisted on a short river trip just to give her friend a flavour of a few sights London had to offer. The instant the Tower of London came into view Isobel gasped.

'I couldn't be more pleased that you have brought me this way, Flora! Did I ever tell you that my great-grandfather served with the Grenadier Guards at the Tower? My paternal grandfather was christened there.'

'You'll want to see the place properly then – and I'm not certain it's been opened up to the public yet since they repaired all the war-damage. I could try to find out for you . . .'

Isobel was gazing and gazing towards the towers and battle-ments. 'That would be lovely, and one day I shall have to go and wander all around there. For today, though, this is such a tremendous thrill, I couldn't be happier.'

They didn't, in fact, manage to see the Tower again during that visit, but Isobel was inspired already by the glimpse that she had had. She would come here repeatedly throughout her life, this place was a part of her personal heritage, one that always would remain special.

Very briefly, in the train bearing her back to Yorkshire, Isobel wondered if seeing the Tower with Daniel might have mattered more because of his family connection. Somehow, though, she didn't feel that it would. So long as she herself valued its importance, and its reminder that she needed to learn more of the Tower's history, visiting the site would always be vital. An experience she might visualise as enhanced if she should ever take a special person there.

Although she had enjoyed the trip to London so thoroughly, Isobel experienced an all-too-familiar unease as soon as she unlocked the door of Laneside House. The evening was cool, which did not help, and even though the rain was holding off, the bitter wind was blasting its way across the moors.

Resolutely willing away all loneliness, she set down her suitcase and turned immediately to lighting the living-room fire. Filling the kettle, she set it on the stove and compelled herself to gaze about her, and admit that the complete effect of her kitchen décor was very likeable.

After two cups of tea Isobel's practical side resurfaced. Picking up her case, she headed for the stairs. In the doorway of the room which should have been the bridal bedroom, she looked around her. The wall she had been distempering on that dreadful day still appeared just as awful. Had she possessed a spirit less tired, she might have located the paint and brushes, and begun to try to improve its appearance.

Lacking the energy to accomplish that particular task, she settled instead for clearing out the wardrobe. Over the previous months this had become the receptacle for items moved out of the other rooms as she was putting those to rights. If nothing more, she needed to remind herself what was stored here, and how much of it she would be keeping. Probate on her mother's will and Marvin's had gone through remarkably swiftly, and Amy's furniture was available for collection from storage, along with some more personal belongings.

There was money also, through Marvin's will, in which he'd touched Isobel by remembering her along with his relatives in America. She was glad that she would afford to pay for any professional renovations of furniture.

A quantity of the possessions stored in the wardrobe were items she had brought with her from the flat but not yet put into daily use. No doubt she should be thankful that not being obliged to share allowed her more storage space.

At the back of the cupboard in a bottom corner, was an object that seemed just about one foot square and wrapped in a piece of curtaining. Trying to lift the item, Isobel discovered it was quite heavy, it also felt cold even through the enveloping cloth.

Kneeling on the floor, she stretched out her arms and drew the object towards her, then lowered it on to the floorboards at her side. The curtaining was only loosely wrapped and fell away to reveal a clock. The clock that she had forgotten.

Large and rather ugly, it looked to be covered in many years' grime, although its face was pleasant enough and the hands intact. Isobel opened the back searching for a key, and found none. Gently, she swung the brass pendulum, but of course it resulted in no motion at all. She examined the interior of the wardrobe again but no neglected key was lying there. She could not recall if there had been a key when she first discovered the clock. Or what she might have done with such a key.

Isobel carried the clock down to the kitchen, intending in a better light to be able to inspect it more thoroughly. Standing beside the sink, she noticed that words were engraved into the back of the clock below the tiny door providing access to its mechanism. The words which had thrilled her previously.

Presented to Captain Edward Johnson to mark his retire-ment from the Grenadier Guards.

Isobel couldn't hug a large, cold item, especially one that could be precious – was precious already *to her*. But she felt like hugging it to her. She must cherish this, clean it initially, and then—

Almost immediately, Isobel decided she would risk no possibly inferior materials on this clock. She had the money now, would take it to a reliable clockmaker, have him restore it, supply a replacement key, as she felt sure he could. The clock then would grace the sideboard which once had belonged to her mother.

She might be deprived of family of her own, but the clock and this house were inherited from Great-grandfather, further items once belonging to Amy Conquest would surround her. Isobel would envelope herself in all these reminders, and will her spirit never again to give in to loneliness.

Fourteen

Laneside House looked beautiful surrounded by snow, Isobel would never have dreamed that the old place could appear so picturesque yet still remain such a homely, *welcoming* house. And nor had she believed that she might feel so isolated there.

The sudden decision that she and Daniel wouldn't marry left her disturbed even all these months afterwards. So many of their plans had seemed rooted in this place, developing and being honed while she was completing its restoration to her satisfaction. Throughout their discussions and actual physical work, she had believed consistently that Daniel's original interest in the house would always ensure he was content to live there. Since they had split up, the whole miserable business was never far from her thoughts. Even wrapping her wedding gown carefully and tucking it away in the attic out of her sight failed to eliminate all those wretched memories.

With that unhappy vision hindsight, Isobel could see now how often he'd indicated that he possessed such enduring affection for his own cottage. Had she perhaps been content to blind herself to Daniel's misgivings? To herself, she now admitted freely that she had schooled her thoughts to live with any misgivings of her own.

It had felt like the ultimate stage in growing up – in her case, rather late in life – when she first resolved to accept that she would never know her ideal prospect of being with Gustav. That had been no more than a dream, and one that was based on just those few, insubstantial meetings. If she had thought of Daniel Armstrong as second best, though, she had compensated by her efforts to conceal that from him.

The fact that she had for so long proved convincing was little comfort now. Isobel felt embarrassed more than anything as she recalled Daniel's concern that love for his own home was the reason preventing their settling into a home together. Isobel could only remain thankful that not until he finally had challenged her, had she diminished his self-esteem by admitting her lack of love for him.

It was time to be practical. Leaving her shopping in the kitchen, she hurried through to the bathroom. The journey through snow had been long, and the chill inside that little Ford made her desperate for the lavatory. Despite her urgency, Isobel could not resist a swift glance around the bathroom and that, at last, encouraged a smile from her. The one room that was entirely *hers,* created from nothing, enhanced by her delicate blue colour scheme, and featuring that elegant bath.

Washing her hands, she reflected on how she had loved that bath, cherished it almost from the hour that she'd first seen it, freshly delivered. That day had meant such a lot, and all because it provided proof of Gustav's understanding of her, just as it demonstrated his tenderness . . .

Insatiable for memories of him, Isobel's mind strayed yet again, while her fingers moved without her realising to locate the contour of scarring on the wounded arm. She couldn't have known then that he would so swiftly walk out of her life, any more than she might have guessed that he would return – if only when it appeared so evident that she was fully committed to Daniel Armstrong.

There seemed a dreadful inevitability in the sequence of that particular encounter. No longer wishing to think, to visualise, Isobel hurried from the bathroom into the quiet of the house, closing the door, if unable to close her mind.

Remembering, her body announced its readiness for loving, replicating the awareness begun that other day after coming in from the garden. Had being alone there normally prevented her from bolting that door? Or had she subconsciously needed Daniel to follow her into the bath? Isobel continued to be plagued by thoughts that she might have avoided the sequence that culminated in those elements of farce.

The rapping on the door of her front porch had startled herself and Daniel, but she was more than startled after rushing to answer it. Gustav had looked so very different, yet the eyes seeking her own were warm with that well-remembered tenderness. He'd appeared so well, so happy that her own heart, in that first moment, had soared.

All too soon, his expression had changed. It was too late. Gustav needed no explanation from Daniel that marriage to Isobel was imminent. It had been anticipated.

Isobel sighed now, struggled to drag her mind into the present, and failed. Could she be surprised while everything felt dismal? The previous day had brought another letter, declining her offer to design for a new firm setting up not too far away in Rochdale. Thanks to her mother's legacy and Marvin's, she had cash sufficient to tide her over for weeks, but an occupation was what she sorely needed.

Diana had been right, as had her other old friends, living on her own out here was far from ideal. It was Diana also who had introduced the most recent disturbance to Isobel's peace of mind, but she must be forgiven for accelerating this yearning for children. Unfortunately, this additional longing felt harder to bear while Isobel could list in her weary mind so many reasons that were causing her to believe she had made a thorough mess of her life.

On one matter only did Isobel feel she was right: she could not picture the children she needed as being Daniel's. Knowing that was, of course, in no way useful, and did not console.

His name lingered in her mind when the knocking began at her door. Isobel cringed, sighed. Daniel had arrived there previously, three times during the weeks since their engagement had foundered. His last visit, the worst, was on the date when they should have married. If he had thought to influence her with its potent reminder, he'd certainly disturbed her. If nowhere near sufficiently to effect a change of heart.

Isobel had had nothing to say, as she could say nothing constructive during any previous occasion. This time, she would not invite him in.

The man on the step looked strange, darkly clad and

silhouetted against the surrounding snow, she couldn't immediately identify him.

And then he spoke, reminding her with his name. 'That clock of yours is coming on a treat. I'm looking forward to having it ready for you to collect in the week. It's ticking away nicely now, and cleaned up, I only need to make certain it's keeping good time for you.'

'Do you want to come inside? Sorry, I wasn't thinking . . . ?' Or had been thinking of Daniel, determined to keep him out.

He shook his head. 'Can't stop, and you don't want me trailing snow through your lovely home, any road. Only it's this—' He felt in a pocket and handed Isobel a sheet of paper that was tightly folded. 'In the bottom of the clock it was, tucked away like. I haven't read it, but it does look old. Might be important.'

Taking the note, Isobel thanked him. Bemused, she was wondering how she had failed to notice it inside the clock. But the man was turning to go back to his van, reminding her that he looked forward to her reaction when she saw her clock working.

The letter was barely legible, folded as it had been throughout generations, but she recognised her beloved great-grandfather's hand, and went to the nearest chair to read as much as she could decipher.

My dear Eleanor,
Forgive me please for the disquiet that I have passed on to you throughout these weeks. You are strong, I know, but should not be required to endure my misgivings regarding the new life that I have, indeed, chosen.

I have not felt able to expect that you might understand why I should fear that I have made our future to founder among the debris, after leaving my life with the army. But enough of that, I write this today in good heart, my spirits raised by the simple act of worshipping at our chapel of St Peter ad Vincula here.

The reminder of the baptism of our beloved child was sufficient to rouse me from a kind of stupor. I saw at once that sacrificing my career to savour our home life together is all worthwhile, no matter the price. You may be assured that peace has returned to my soul, and in quiet I anticipate the years that we shall spend in Laneside House.

Isobel hadn't yet read to the end when she was interrupted by further knocking on her door. Thinking the clockmaker must have remembered something else, she rushed to fling the door open.

'Daniel . . . ?'

'Let me come in, Isobel, please. I haven't known a moment's peace since you refused to talk when I came here before.'

Unsure what to say, she wordlessly led him through to the living-room and indicated the most comfortable chair. She herself took one with a straight back, and hoped he'd read that as a sign that she was not about to settle for a long conversation.

'I've put my cottage up for sale,' Daniel announced, and staggered her. 'I want you to know because this is how desperately I need to put things right between us. That little house became such a bone of contention, didn't it? Well, that's all over now. I'll live anywhere you wish, Isobel love, and if that should be here in Laneside House then I'd be delighted.'

'This isn't just about houses, Daniel,' she protested, and wondered how many times she'd told him that already.

'Okay, okay. But it's been a major stumbling-block, hasn't it? Now I'm proving how serious I am about giving us another go. I'd do anything to make you happy, to make you feel – *complete*.'

If she had been feeling less uncertain about her own contentment, Isobel would have reminded Daniel of all the things she'd already reiterated about his inability to do that for her. As things stood, however, all she could recall was her yearning to have a baby like the one Diana had shown off only one week ago. The baby she had held the other day, had felt nestling against her, warm in her arms.

Was she ready now perhaps to resign herself to a marriage that, however lacking in romance, could provide the family she longed for? And in this home to which she was so devoted . . .

Shaking her head dubiously, Isobel sighed yet again, still without knowing how to respond. She felt her gaze being drawn to Edward Johnson's portrait, from there to the man seated across the room from her. Was the likeness an indicator of how she ought to decide – had the time come for her to accept the relationship which she had struggled to resist? Daniel was prepared to sacrifice a very great deal, for her. He looked so anxious and concerned, while she possessed the ability to make him better.

'Is there nothing you can say?' Daniel asked, a shade sharply. 'Is there nothing I can do?'

Isobel managed a slight smile. 'Sometimes I believe I've said it all already. And then you spring something like this on me . . .'

'And make you think? Good.' He leapt to his feet. 'I'll allow you time to think further about my suggestion.'

'I wish you wouldn't keep popping up with more notions like this, it really is disturbing.'

'Oh, I shan't. Count on that. I really shan't be back. But you know where I live, you have the phone number.'

The decision to attend Communion the following morning was not readily reached, despite the restless night that Isobel had spent. The church over the hill was so unfamiliar that she felt nervous about attending. More nervous still, when she reflected on those wedding arrangements cancelled almost as swiftly as they had been made. To say nothing of her subsequent indecision which Daniel's latest visit evoked.

The Rev Reginald Fieldhouse must believe her idiotic for her age, an assessment close to her own; Isobel at twenty-eight had scant patience with her own faltering. Had she been honest from the first, she might have spared Daniel the hurt of a shattered engagement, and herself this wearisome embarrassment. An embarrassment which surely would remain even if she should eventually relent and marry the man.

Today the vicar alone would know about that cancelled

wedding, she reassured herself, and he'd been kindness personified. He would have no cause to publicise the matter, and would likely care far less than she herself supposed. And if she were to feel foolish, what of that? Isobel knew only too keenly the pain of creating a mess of her life. There would be nothing new in learning that afresh.

To take her mistakes, her confusion, her misery, and leave them in that church – wasn't that a sound intention? It ranked among her better ideas, for sure, and clamoured now that she must not ignore the impulse.

The snow was deeper on the crest of the hill. Struggling to trudge to the top left Isobel feeling that she'd achieved something. Restored memories of a childhood love of a snow-fall made her smile and, once she gained the summit, encouraged her to hasten.

The church was lit from within, its appearance a welcome feature on a morning when so-called daylight produced barely a shadow on the pristine icy surface.

Even with her last-minute haste, Isobel entered the church only as the bell tolled its final witness that a service was commencing. The weather seemed to be limiting the size of the congregation. Among several empty pews she noticed only one where, seated behind a stone pillar she might appear inconspicuous.

Kneeling in prayer brought the first hint of restoring quiet, familiar words, words learned from her mother, words structured to endure. Not quite everything was destroyed: no matter how great the muddle within her mind, some order still existed.

Words again carried her through, preparing her so that the strangeness of the aisle leading to the altar rail might have been that familiar aisle in Halifax. The folk kneeling to either side seemed no different from the friends surrounding her former life. The cup and the bread were received just as solemnly, and in Isobel were allowed to commence their healing.

After the final hymn, that last prayer of all, she felt a little of the old unease returning. Head down, hoping to escape ahead of the vicar's Sunday morning greeting, she seized her gloves and, neglecting to put them on, scurried towards the door only now opening.

The better humour remained, however, encouraging Isobel to smile at her own hurried departure, and strengthening her to battle against the wind as she climbed to the brow of the hill once more. She was looking forward to the first sight of her own home.

Laneside House did look lovely with snow covering the rooftops, she'd never seen it from this angle before in wintertime. Smoke emerging from its chimney made her hurry once more, eager to savour the warmth from her own hearth.

The vicar was looking for Isobel among the few parishioners who had braved the heavy snow to attend. He had been glad to note her arrival, and intended to have at least a few words and make her more comfortable with him.

Their previous encounter had surprised him so greatly that he had failed to give of his best. Isobel Johnson might not be the first woman to cancel her wedding, but she had seemed one of the few who struggled to hang on to some composure. He had not liked to think of her living quite alone in that house which, even in summer, appeared situated so bleakly! And now she evidently had scurried back there. Reginald blamed himself for providing so ineffective a welcome.

'You do not remember me. I think. But I am come here to offer a kind of apology, and an explanation.'

The man was rather familiar, tall, smartly dressed with neatly styled blond hair. Without his name, Reginald could not place him.

'I'm sorry,' he began; 'I don't quite . . .'

'Gustav Kassel,' said the German extending a hand, seagreen eyes smiling.

'But of course, forgive me. I was a little preoccupied.'

'And you have not seen me these many months since the day that I disappeared. That is the reason I would explain to you . . .'

'So you shall.' The vicar paused briefly to say a word to the final departing members of his congregation.

'We should be more comfortable at the vicarage, if you can spare the time?'

Transferred swiftly to a seat in Reginald's study with a pot of coffee between them, Gustav responded to the invitation to talk.

'You may not be able to stop me now! I am so elated by this new life. But first – to the reason why I needed to speak with you. It was rude of me, ungrateful to simply walk away after you had located some employment for me. But after we had talked that day, you made me to understand. I could do nothing worthwhile so long as I was living out a lie. I had to give myself up.'

The vicar frowned, wondering how this linked with the man's life here. 'I was never clear as to how you had crashed over the hill there, and why you hadn't returned to your homeland when peace came.'

'The latter was because my home no longer existed.' Gustav said, and told him briefly of the post-war situation regarding the Sudetenland. 'And I was compelled to conceal my original purpose, the aircraft I lost was a test plane.'

'Interesting. And, more recently . . . ?' he prompted.

'I surrendered myself to the police, as a preliminary stage.' Gustav went on to relate his life in the prison camp, and how he had been prepared to work afterwards in some kind of farming perhaps.

'From appearances, you're doing very well in your new life,' Reginald observed.

Gustav laughed. 'But not as a farmer at all. I have been so very fortunate. My name was remembered, you see, I was respected for my knowledge, certain skills. I am working now for your people – but in the job for which I was trained. My experience with jet-propulsion has won me that.'

'I'm very pleased to hear it. No man lives contentedly unless his skills are used. And I'm glad that you have chosen to tell me all this. So there is nothing I can do for you today?'

'There is one small thing, a question. Was I right to believe that I saw the lady from Laneside House here this morning?'

'Miss Johnson, yes.'

Gustav refrained from echoing 'Miss'. 'I knew her great-aunt, you may recall. The old lady was very kind to me. She also lent to me a key. I wonder perhaps if you would return it on my behalf to the present owner?'

'Why not do so yourself?'

Unable to speak of his dread, Gustav nodded. They talked for a while longer as he avoided asking further questions regarding Isobel. He had no desire to learn that she was co-habiting with Daniel Whoever-he-was.

When he prepared to leave the vicarage, he fingered the key in his pocket. He would push the thing through the letter-box, perhaps with a note. Finalise the business lest it continue to trouble him.

The only footprints through the snow to the brow of the hill were *hers*. It would be sentimental to believe they were showing him the direction he must take, yet he felt compelled to place his own feet in a few of them.

There Laneside House was, looking picturesque, homely, *welcoming*. He would be foolish, this time when he was prepared, to neglect to knock on her door. There would be no dreadful surprise in finding her with her fiancé. These days, his resurrected self-respect would bestow sufficient poise to facilitate the brief conversation necessary. And if – *if* his eyes had served him well inside that church, and Isobel no longer wore a ring – he might never forgive himself if he failed to speak with her.

The door he chose was the kitchen one so familiar from the old days when Hannah Johnson had been the owner. Gustav wished, fleetingly, that the easy-going old lady was the person he was about to meet once more. Hannah Johnson did not render him so vulnerable.

He knocked once, and the door was opened immediately. Isobel gazed at him, and gasped his name. And then she was hugging him, pressing her lips to his cheek, while he felt on contact the sudden rush of her tears.

'Oh, come in, come in,' she cried at last, and then she crushed him to her again as the door closed behind them. 'I can't believe you're here, Gustav! I never thought – never dared to believe . . . When did you come back from America?'

217

'America? I did not consider taking that job, how could I? I could not work somewhere that prevented me from seeing you.'

'But – but . . .' Laughing and still crying, Isobel shook her head as they drew apart slightly. 'Come and sit down, and tell me. Tell me everything . . .'

'In one moment. First though—'

And now he was the one to embrace her, holding her tightly against him while his lips found hers, his kiss deep and demanding.

Isobel took his coat, hung it up, then extended a hand for his, leading the way to the living-room where the newly stoked fire sent sparks high into the chimney.

Still holding hands, they went to the sofa. Only then she recalled that she hadn't even thought to offer a drink or anything.

'Sorry, you've surprised me so much I'm forgetting all my manners – I should have asked if I can make you some tea, or coffee.'

'You are giving me your company, Isobel. That is all I want, all I have wanted these many months.'

'Did you really turn down work in America?' she asked, and saw him looking at her ringless left hand.

'Certainly, I did. I could think of nothing worse than having the Atlantic Ocean separate me from you,' said Gustav, kissing her again. And yet there were questions he ought to be asking, he needed to know that she was no longer committed to another man.

'And this work you're doing?' asked Isobel, greedy to learn all that he had done. 'We must go back to the kitchen again, though, and I'll make us a hot drink. And then we must have something to eat. I was just beginning to get lunch going. I'll stretch it to make enough for two.'

Leaning against the sink, Gustav watched her preparations, teasing now and then about her efforts to provide sufficient food. But sharing seemed all that counted to Isobel, sharing with this very special human being.

While the food was cooking, he insisted that she must show him every room of the house, and they wandered through together, savouring the chance simply to be there. Gustav was delaying, he knew, delaying the time when he must be told whether he was a fool to come here.

When they finally sat down to eat, Isobel prompted him again to tell her about his work. Gustav began to smile.

'Is good, very good. Much of it experimental now, but utilising my previous experience of jet-propelled aircraft. I fly again, and also I learn and, occasionally explain, some of the technology.'

'I've made a mess of my life – the reason I was in church today. But you wouldn't know that—'

'But I do know you were there, I was present also. Isobel – there is one thing that I have to understand. You do not wear that ring . . .'

'Daniel was never the one I wanted, not really. The engagement should never have happened. It finally is over. I wasn't in love with him, how could I be?'

'How . . . ?' Gustav was puzzled. He had witnessed what clearly was evidence they had indulged in sex. But if it was only sex, he could dismiss the knowledge of it.

'When I love you, have loved you for ages,' Isobel answered his question.

'But then I left you.'

'In spite of that. Are you going to tell me?'

Gustav nodded. 'I went away because of you. Because of this love which grew so swiftly between us. I could not offer you anything while – while that I made no reparation for fighting against your country. World War Two was ended, but my war was not. I needed to face – face *whatever* for remaining here while I did not surrender myself. Your people were – *are* very kind; the police to whom I spoke initially, your military, those in charge at the camp. And so I paid my price, felt better immediately.' He paused, smiling. 'Until today, I believed myself rewarded beyond my dreams by being granted the opportunity to do my chosen work.'

'Until today? What has gone wrong now, Gustav?'

His laugh startled her. 'Nothing. Not anything, I hope. Today, I am come to you again, and my former happiness

219

on account of my work suddenly seems pale beside the earnest wish to spend my life with you.'

'You know that's what I want.'

'I do not know that, but I hope always, I dream so many dreams. Will you be my wife, Isobel? Make me complete . . . ?'

'Oh, yes. I will, I will. I'll go anywhere in the world with you.'

Gustav smiled, kissed her again, fervently. 'We shall discuss where we must live, I work now in Hampshire, shall work elsewhere in England. But this house, if you agree, should be our real home. The place we return to always.'

'I would have married you earlier, you know. Before you had this work.' But Isobel was glad that she hadn't. There was nothing she would have changed. Seeing Gustav fulfilled – the man she had sensed existed beyond his original simplicity – compensated for those many months of heartache.

He was looking at Edward Johnson's portrait. 'He is the father of your great-aunt, yes? I see the likeness, and she told to me, but only a little.'

'My great-grandfather, that's right. He was the one who bought Laneside House.'

'A soldier, and he fought in many wars perhaps?'

'I don't know that, not yet. But he served with the Grenadier Guards, at the Tower of London.'

Gustav smiled, sea-green eyes widening with increased interest. 'This is so unusual. You must tell to me all that you know about him.'

Isobel's smile was a little rueful. 'I haven't learned nearly enough, so far.'

'But we shall go there many times, together, search out his history, along with whatever we may discover about this, my new homeland.'